Sis Kirby,

When Push Came to Shove

Thx for the support.

When Push Came to Shove

LaQualla Tatum

Copyright © 2009 by LaQualla Tatum.

ISBN: Softcover   978-1-4415-9617-8

All rights reserved. No part of this book may be reproduced or transmitted in any form or by any means, electronic or mechanical, including photocopying, recording, or by any information storage and retrieval system, without permission in writing from the copyright owner.

This is a work of fiction. Names, characters, places and incidents either are the product of the author's imagination or are used fictitiously, and any resemblance to any actual persons, living or dead, events, or locales is entirely coincidental.

This book was printed in the United States of America.

To order additional copies of this book, contact:
Xlibris Corporation
1-888-795-4274
www.Xlibris.com
Orders@Xlibris.com

For: Dwan, and Judge Perkins whose readiness and willing bought life to the book and for Rodney, who never overpowered my dreams.
   To that one who ever felt like they had to choose between what they wanted, needed; was able to manage both with no regrets by never apologizing for anything that made them happy.

Introduction

Can you love one person and be in love with another? To Khylee, it was like having two best friends. One you can tell EVERYTHING and she still loves you anyway and the other you only share minor surface information, only the things that let her know that you aren't as saved as they say you are. JaVon and D'Kyra were those two best friends for Khylee. They both were married with children but JaVon and Khylee went 20 years with seriously deep history and do not live in the same state. She's a very successful recording artist.

D'Kyra, on the other hand, is in the same situation. Her husband treats her as though she is invisible as well. She bore three children for this man yet he ignores her. I don't know what's wrong with Stanley for treating her like that.

So, can you love two best friends the same way? That depends on the situation JaVon and D'Kyra would like each other because Khylee is comfortable with both of them. Now, can you love one man and be in love with another? Yes, the one man you want you can't have and the one you have don't want you.

*W*ell, I guess I need to start at the beginning. I may go a little fast but I really don't mean too, it's just that so many great things have been happening to me since my first book. I wasn't intending on writing another book this soon but God's plan for me was not my plan.

People have asked me, "Marie, how do you do it? How do you just sit down and just write a book? Do you write it all at once or is it in time frames? What?" To this day I still can fully give a satisfying answer because sometimes it takes days for me to complete one character, weeks for me to describe a house and months for me to my mind to quiet down so that I can continue in the real world. It's sort of peculiar really. I told my mother that successful authors are professionals that lie for a living. (I hope no one takes offense to that statement, you just have to know my mother to understand.)

Okay, where was I? Oh, yes. During Black History Month in 2006, my very first book signing was held at the new mall called Recreations at 2 p.m. It was a grand opening of the new bookstore, **Read All About It**. It was so profitable and people came from miles around because of the advertising. I heard it on the radio, some saw the commercials, it was even announced at black colleges within a 100 mile radius. It was so nice.

One woman in particular caught my eye. No, not like *that*. She looked like she felt that she was out of place. She looked confused and like she was looking for something, more like browsing. Sometimes you can tell a lot about a person by watching their body language. I didn't want to stare at her because I didn't want her to think that I was watching her like she was going to steal something. She looked to be a little over 5 ft tall and maybe 115lbs. The traces of gray in her light brown shoulder length hair were misleading. She looked 30-ish and had the figure that could wear anything. She wore a pair of military cargo pants with a pair of matching sneakers. Her double green and white tee matched her pants. She also had a matching bag as well; same fabric and everything.

She picked up one of my books from the display and flipped it over to read the back. She looked around and we locked eye for a moment. We exchanged smiles as she walked over to one of the chairs.

I lost sight of her for a few moments because there was a small group of women who bombarded the display. They didn't talk, they clucked. All of their voices were high pitched. It made me think that the dogs in the pet store down the block were going to crash this party. All of the women wore green hats and they all had pinched faces. One woman seemed to speak aloud for all ten of them. They huddled in order to make a decision. It was really something to see because they looked like they were very well to do. They all were very polite and I think they were even a little tipsy because a couple of them kept asking me what time service started. Another one asked where the pastor was and two of them wanted to know if "Antwon" was still the choir director. My publicist, Roni Taylor, was about to keep them from making a seen but I stopped her because I thought it was funny and I knew it was going to be useful someday, like now.

The "leader" announced, "Hello, we would like to purchase . . ." she turned around to count inaudibly each lady by pointing at them with her finger, "Ah 20 books. Do you mind autographing each one, Hun?"

"Sure" I smiled in agreement. While Roni was handling the cash, I was busy autographing each one personally. There was Margaret who smelled like peppermint and cocoa butter. I really do think they had been drinking because when Sarah hobbled up to me, she slapped both of her hands on table, batting only one eye, and whisper, "I'll have another Balm Mama. No, a Bah harbor Mama, I mean a . . . Oh, hell, just make it out to Sarah." Her breath was this horrific odor that reminded me of homeless people.

Gwen was very quiet when she came up to me. She was the only one that had her hat on backwards; you could see the tag and everything. Plus, her slip was hanging. Then, one of the coherent ones walked up to Gwen and said in a loud voice, "Miss Gwen, time to go." She turned around and pointed Gwen in the direction of a chair. The coherent one quickly turned back around to address me by saying, "I'm really sorry about all that." She said with her twisted face. She placed a sheet of paper in front of me with 20 names but only four were marked through. "They have been out celebrating and well, anyway, I would really appreciate it if you could write all of these names inside the book. By tomorrow they won't remember a thing but at least they will have these books. Oh, I'm Elaine."

"Nice to meet you, Elaine and sure, I'd be glad to." I answered, trying my best not to laugh when all of the sudden I heard a small but aggressive voice yell out, "Uh oh! Oh, Lawd have mercy!" Elaine snapped around and asked, "Miss Willie Mae, what's wrong?"

"I dun use the bathroom on myself." Miss Willie Mae said in a quiet, sad, shaky voice. "I told her she should have made water before we got to church." one elderly voice said.

"I told you." Elaine explained. "We're *not* at church. We've at the new mall."

"You all wanted to see that new author and get your books autographed?"

I guess it takes a special person to hang around older people all day long but apparently Elaine was equipped to do the job. Me, personally, I don't think I could do it. I would have dropped them off at the nearest nursing home.

Then the ladies wanted pictures. I thought that it would be one group picture but each lady wanted an individual picture. There was this one lady named Myrtle who kept looking at me rather than the camera. It was really awkward because I could feel her breath on my neck. I had to know, so I asked, "Is there anything I can do for you, Ms. Myrtle?"

"Y'all got any boil hen, baby?" she asked.

"Ah! No ma'am." I answered. "Look at the camera, Ms. Myrtle." She was the last one to have her picture taken with me. I looked to my left and there was another woman in a red hat that was unsteady on her feet. She was carrying a black purse that looked more like a black basket that the children made over at that blind school. The shoes she wore were not only run over but were on the wrong feet. One of the other ladies stopped her just before she reached me and said, "Hey, Helen? If you wear your shoes on the wrong feet, you'll go the wrong way." Helen stopped, reached into her basket purse and pulled out a silver flask, opened it and took a drink. She calmly put replaced the top, put it back in her purse and moved very close to her face and screamed, "Huh?" Everyone looked at her and shushed her while she walked up to me and asked, "Listen here, I got a question." She put her hand on my shoulder and looked at me but only one eye blinked. "If Pete and Repete was in a boat and Pete fell out? Who was saved?"

Okay, I fell for it and I said, "Repete" and the whole thing started all over again until she got thirsty.

One of the ladies even came to me and told me that they lost their husband. She approached me walking rather hesitantly with her pocketbook in her hands. She wore a blue polyester dress with a huge broach in the middle of her chest that read JESUS. The collar of her dress looked a lot like Queen Anne's lace. Her knees were wobbling like she was recovering from a hangover and I didn't want to stare but I swear she had a beard.

"I lost my husband last week," she said sadly in a raspy voice.

"Oh, honey, I am so sorry." I really felt bad about all those things that I had said about her, in my mind, that is, but she really did smell like bug spray and peppermint.

"Oh, hell. It's alright. It took him 3 days to find me. Do you know how hard it is to lose a husband in the grocery store?" she asked.

Okay, I was totally lost. Was she drunk? Was she delusional? Was she a joke?

"Hell, I tried to lose him," she continued. "But he keeps coming back just like a cat." She turned a walked away. I stood there with my mouth opened.

Finally, they left and the first thing Roni says to me is, "Sorry."

"Sorry for what?" I asked. "I actually thought they were rather funny. I know this is going to come in handy someday." I said as my eyes scanned the room for that mysterious lady. I was pretty sure she had left but then I saw her sitting with the book in her lap crying into a tissue. She wiped her eyes and pulled out a pen and paper to write. She then made her way over to me. She sat the book on the table and mustered up a smile. Her red, puffy eyes matched her red nose. When she looked at me, I could see that they were either hazel or chestnut and almond shaped. Her lashes were full and thick that complimented her arched brows. Her skin was a flawless glazed caramel color. As she ran her fingers through her thick hair to move it away from her face, she cleared her throat and said in a shy whisper, "Hi. How much?"

READ ALL ABOUT it was complete with a small café that served soup, salad, sandwiches, pastries and a variety of hot and cold drinks. It was also equipped with booths, tables and couches. You could buy a book, get something to each and relax will exploring your purchases. I even saw some people with their laptops plugged up.

You could hear the small tinkering of the spoons scooping soup from the bowls. There were sounds of laugher, conversations, and life inside that new store. The rhythm of the spoons clanging against the insides of the mugs was wonderful. People were enjoying their coffee and tea like it was no tomorrow. I wondered how soon the novelty of this store would wear off.

"Fifteen dollars, cash. Are you alright?" I asked. She nodded as she handed me a twenty with a piece of paper attached. I didn't read it right off because I was interrupted by Roni who leaned over and whispered in my ear and said, "Your group is here."

"Can you stall for a moment? I need to talk to this lady for a few minute." I asked her.

"What do you suggest I do?" Roni asked.

"Roni, we are in a coffee house / bookstore. Think of something. DUH!" I said as I cut my eyes over at her. Our relationship is more than just business; we have become close friends, like sisters.

"See, that ain't even funny. That ain't even in the same area code as funny." While, Roni walked over to the ladies to entertain them with coffee and muffins and what not, I took the "BE RIGHT BACK" sign and placed it on the table while I went over to talk to this mysterious lady.

The beginning of Khylee's journal starts:

Chapter 1

Recreations was the name of the new mall that just opened. It was a much needed added attraction. It had 50 stores but only 15 restaurants. It was great. There was a new bookstore inside called **Read All about It** and this caught my attention though I wasn't much of a reader. I couldn't help myself and it was like I was drawn to the store like a hypnotic trance. There was a small crowd gathering around the author's table and the rest of the people were strategically placed around the store in groups of 2 to 3 people all discussing the paperback that was in their hands. Some people were sitting in chairs a few feet across from where the author was sitting.

The book store was complete with a small soup, salad, sandwiches, pastries and a variety of drinks such as sodas, juices, waters and hot and cold coffees and teas. It was also equipped with deuces, booths, tables, couches and chaise lounges, you could buy a book, get something to eat and relax while discovering your book. I even saw some people with their laptops plugged up.

You could hear the tinkering of the spoons scooping soup from the bowls. There were sounds of laugher, conversations and life inside that new sore. The rhythm of the spoons clinking against the insides of the mugs was wonderful. People were enjoying their coffees and teas like there was no tomorrow. I wondered how soon the novelty of this store would wear off.

I looked around searching for any signs of what could answer any question before I asked. To the left was a poster with a woman's picture. It was only a quarter head shot but she was stunning. She had small round, friendly eyes. She was dressed in a red blouse and red lipstick.

The expression on her face was solemn. The poster read "*MEET MARIE WALTON, BEST SELLING AUTHOR of THE JOURNAL of KITTY LaRUE.*" The woman in the poster looked so happy. She looked very young and very content and this made me smile. I walked into the bookstore and marveled at the atmosphere. It made me curious. "What kind of book is this that made you wants to have a heated discussion at a book signing" I thought. I was mesmerized at how different the atmosphere was in this store. It was thick with questions and answers. I had never met an author before, much less been to a book signing. I went to the special display where her books were and picked up the paperback thumbing through it and read the back which made me decide to purchase it. I sat down and began to read. After a few minutes, tears welled up in my eyes. Someone offered me a tissue but I never cared to know who it was because I was engrossed in reading. In fact, I knew what I needed to do. I alternated between wiping my nose and fumbling for a piece of paper and a pen from inside my bag. As my dried her eyes, I began to write. I took the paper and folded it once and tucked it between the cover and the first page. When it was finally my turn to have my book autographed, I silently handed the book to her. Marie looked up at me and I asked as I cleared my throat, "How much?"

"$15.00 cash only please." Marie said. She also asked if I was okay. I pulled out a twenty and gave it to her. She pulled out $5.00 and handed it to me. I waved my hand indicating that I didn't want the change but would love to briefly talk to her afterward. She agreed. I walked over to the counter and ordered a tall white chocolate mocha coffee with hazelnut and a slice of banana nut Bread. I sat down at the corner table and started reading The Journal of Kitty LaRUE.

I was almost at the center of the book when Ms. Walton came over to the table. I quickly jumped up and asked if she needed something to drink.

"Sure, what are you having?" she asked

"Girl, my fav. It's a tall white chocolate mocha coffee with hazelnut." I said.

"Sounds good. Then I will have what you are having." she answered. I motioned over for the server to come over.

"Will you bring another one of these for her please?' I asked. The servers gladly agreed and walked away.

"Ms. Walton, I don't want to waste your time but I was wondering if you would assist me in writing my autobiography, sort of like the way you wrote Ms. LaRUE's? Money is not object."

"Well, do you have a journal or diary or something?" she asked.

"I have it right here." I said as I started rummaging through my bag and pulled out a flash drive.

"This contains all that you need. Would you prefer it to be in manuscript form?"

"No, this is fine. I can print it with no problem." Marie answered.

I pointed at the flash drive and said, "All the contact information is on the disk." We made plans and arrangements for her to come to my home for as long as she needed to see if my life was book worthy. Of course some minor legal details had to be worked out; namely confidentiality contract whether she prints me or not. So we got the ball rolling.

Mrs. Wilcox sent her driver to come pick me up and by 8 that night, I arrived at the mansion. It looked like something from a romance novel or a movie. It had red bricks on the outside with cobblestones in the circular driveway. There was a fountain in the middle of the driveway.

The driver parked right in the front of the house, there was a small, steep porch that had at least six steps to its entrance. The door was very tall and wide. I have never seen a front door that huge and wide before. It made me wonder if some plain looking, square pinched faced, monotoned butler would answer the door that creaked as it opened, needing a much needed oiling. At the top of the door was a small window and you could see a chandelier that hung and danced with sparkling rainbows. The reflections were so cool. There was a slight but pleasant breeze that welcomed me as I got out of the car. The driver held the door open and offered his hand for support. "Thank you." I said. He simply nodded and said, "Ma'am". The great door open, silently to my surprise, and I was greeted by two thin ladies. One only smiled while the other had a thick Spanish accent. They hurried down to meet me as the driver gathered my things from the trunk. I carried my laptop and my purse with me inside the limo and one of the two ladies politely rushed to me and grabbed my bag from my hand saying, "I take for you, please." Her eyes sparkled which let me know that she was true, genuine and loyal. The other lady that stayed on the porch gave me a coy smile and nodded, "Hola." I really didn't think she spoke much English if any at all.

Once inside, I was directed to the immediately left. The floor was a two-toned marble. The wood was dark, almost like a cherry wood. The only light was from the chandelier that seemed to be at least 20 feet above us but the further we walked the dim the light became. Soon, I was in a room that about 20 x 28 . . . maybe even 20 x 30. The room was all lavender décor and it smelled of fresh linen to mask the smell of paint. The first thing I saw was the bed. It was a full sized bed with lots of pillows. There were two small identical night stands on either side of the bed but only one table supported a telephone but you couldn't call out. I was an old French phone with no buttons. The bedding matched the curtain. The ceiling was vaulted adorned with a ceiling fan with stained glass lamp shades. The walls looked like they were made of cinderblocks. I could be wrong but I was tired so that my imagination ran on 90 nothing. I tried to visually as much as I could so that I could remember and I could write it as I am doing now. (This is so exciting.)

There was a flat screened TV mounted to the wall. There were also hard wood floors that were very shiny. I thought the floor was wet for a moment. The closet was a small walk in that lit and the adjacent bathroom was also decorated in the lavender array in French décor complete with a freestanding roll top vogue bath tub, Acajou dual vanity sinks and a Marion Bidet. It was all in an off white color and gold. It was beautiful.

The ladies sat my suitcases in the closet for me. "I hand for you?" Before I could agree or disagree, she opened the suitcases and started putting away the clothes in the closet while the other lady took a suitcase and put the clothes away in the drawer. Afterwards, one turned and pointed to herself with a huge smile and said, "I am Myra." She pointed at the other lady whose smile was equally as bright and said "Eva." She then pointed to the phone and said, "You call, we come ¿sí?"

"¿sí?" I laughed and said, "Gracias tú . . . ah, Myra and . . . Eva?"

"Sí" Myra and Eva said almost simultaneously.

"Maria." I said as I pointed to myself. I thought that the 'a' on the end of my name was easier that the 'e'.

"Oh, Myra. Cerciorarte de te para decirte que ella te llame para el servicio al cuarto y al mí si ella quiere comer y Travis si ella quiere ir dondequiera." said Ava. I didn't pick up anything she said but it sounded really cute.

"You call me for clean and you call Eva for food. Call Travis you want to go, Okay?" said Myra.

"Oh, Okay. I got you. Myra to clean, Eva for food and Travis to go, right?"

The next day, I opened the flash drive that Mrs. Wilcox gave me. They were many different folders, files and briefcases. One was called Temporary Inconvenience. When I opened it, it needed special attention. I have been given permission to open whatever was on that flash drive but the only catch; I was to print as is. Even if I thought that it was a typo or a misspelled word, I was to clear it with her first. So, I made notations on in red print on each page.

I printed everything out and sat down and began to read.

* * *

It's really hard trying to be a good wife when you feel like your husband is ignoring you. Food on the table, a roof over your head and clothes to wear does not a provider make. I have tried having my own life like writing for one thing. Sometimes it helps but other times; I just wanna run away from home and not come back until I totally get homesick. I have been married for over ten years and every once in a while he totally ignores me. We live in a $3,000,000 debt free, eight bedroom home with all the trimmings: two-car garage housing two debt free vehicles with in ground pool and other great things but a husband that works all the time. He spends more time running his three companies than being home with me. I heard on CNN just the other day that he was up to buy another company. It's like I am suppose to be grateful that I have all that I have and just sit back and keep my mouth shut. It doesn't work that way. Whenever I try to tell him how I am feeling, he accuses me of starting an argument and the first thing he says is that "I'm doing all this so that I won't have to work like our parents and so that we can retire in a couple of years." Well, it still doesn't make me feel better.

Sometimes I hate being anyone other than who I was but I never showed any of this to anyone because it was important to keep up appearances. I mean, after all, I had everything that I could ever ask for and all the things that I wanted . . . except his love. At least to others it looked like I had it all. Some would even go as far to say that people were jealous of us, as a couple, because it looked like we were the people that everyone wanted to be. We looked great together, sort of like the model couple. My husband's body is all chiseled with rock hard abs and his butt . . . WOW . . . . you can bounce a quarter off it. He started losing his hair about 5 years ago and now he keeps it bald . . . it's the perfect bald head. It's perfectly round, no bumps, lumps, dents or imprints . . . . just that perfect head. Giving a suggestion of underlying passion and sensuality, it always put a little tingle right where it counts.

His eyes were just as sultry with dark features. It's amazing how men don't worry about their lashes when we women do. I always teased him about his nose 'How do you breathe out of those two little holes in your face?' because it was so cute and small. His smile was like sunshine to me as his perfectly white straight teeth would gleam from behind his full lips.

When we first met he use to leave little notes all over the place with little love messages on them. He never let a day go by without saying that he loved me or how good I looked to him. He would always compliment me on my hair, dress, smell whatever it didn't matter. If I cried, he would hold me, if I worried; he would drop everything to make me better. One day, I woke up and it all changed and the sad thing about it, I didn't even see it coming.

My voice was heard internationally for cartoons, commercials and television and I was pretty good at it. I worked in the 7-story Ferguson Plaza building in the center of downtown and the floor that I worked on had so many people working there that it was like ants going in and out.

One day, there was a man who was working on one of the sound boards that was always making everyone's voice distorted like they were chipmunks or something. (The machine not the man.) At this particular time, he took what looked like a much needed break and was leaning against the wall talking on his cell phone. The soda machine was next to the sound room in the hallway and it was opened with a tool bag sitting in front of it. By this time, I saw this 'little person' come from around the corner and I wondered to myself how he could reach all the way to the top to fill the machine with sodas. I had heard the other girls talking about how cute the repairman was that worked for Blue Sky Repair, but I had never seen him. I was wondering if it was the 'short' white guy or the tall black guy.

This little guy's name was Leo. I wondered if it was short for Leonard. If it was, I could see why he went with Leo. You know, Leo the Lion. It made him look tough whereas Leonard made him look like a wimp. I wouldn't have even bothered to talk to him except for the fact that he started talking to me first.

"Hey" he barked. "Hand me that chair, will ya?" he asked. I looked around to see who he was talking to so rudely. I put my hand on my hip and said, "Excuse you?" to myself. I really wanted to hit him with that chair. Rather than be rude, I said nothing and walked away.

So, while the sound man was taking a personal call on company time and the little man was refilling the machine, I noticed that I seemed to be the only one there except for the repairmen. Just when I was about to call Jeff, he rushed through the door waving score sheets and muttering something about Amanda and her sister. I really don't think he knew I was there because he let out this horrific fart that seemed to vibrate the cymbals and the snare drum. I wanted to laugh but my eyes started watering. So I pretended to be busy with something else all while holding my breath.

I gave my attention to the sound room repairman. He looked young enough but his eye looked like a man who had an old soul and filled with challenges. His oval shaped face possessed his full lips perfectly which complimented his sexy bald head. This gorgeous man stood close to 6 feet and looked to be 215 lbs. of pure muscle. (when I say pure muscle, I mean he was ripped and gorgeous.) He always smelled of a mixture of that new car smell, dryer sheets and the inside of the Auto Store. I've always liked the way the auto store smelled. I use to go there and pretend that I was looking for something for my car and that I couldn't remember the name or what it was called. He wore his uniformed shirt without tucking it with only one button fastened over a simple white tank tee shirt as if it was only kept on a hanger in his work vehicle because of the heat being that it was the middle of May. He wore a pair of khaki shorts that were always neatly pressed that stopped short of his lower calf with ankle socks and blinding white K Swiss.

His conversation was a bit heated and his gesture on his right hand was like a choir director. I tried not to stare as I caught a glimpse of his biceps and triceps rippled in sequence. I tried not to listen but walking past him was the only way to get to where I was going. I wanted the table next to the television because it was time for my stories which was next to the soda machine. I caught him watching me walk away from the reflection in the window. I gave him a coy smile as I sat down at the table and started eating my lunch.

I dressed in beige slacks with a red and beige form fitting double tee. My shoes were a brown and beige wedge heel sling backs and since my hair had grown out, I wear a pony tail as often as I can. I wasn't trying to flirt; I just didn't want him to think that I was trying to listen to his conversation, so I turned the volume up.

My lunch that day was salad that I bought from home and a slice of cake from the restaurant on Sunday. As soon as I popped the lid on the Tupperware, I saw him walk up toward the table on my left side. Flashing that blinding smile, he announces, "Oh, I guess my conversation was a bit loud?" His accent was slight but obvious. It had a hint of Great Britain meets Trinidad meets Brooklyn, I couldn't quite catch it but it was so fascinating.

"No." I answered, between bites, "I just didn't want you to think that I was listening to your conversation." He kneels down and rummaged through his bag and asks without looking up, "So, how long have you been working here?"

"About six or seven months." I answered, still chewing.

"What do you do?" he asked.

"Have you ever seen the mall commercial where the lady talks about all the 'really cool places to shop 'til you drop' and the voice comes over and says 'You're born, you die but you haven't lived until you've shopped at our mall?'

"Oh yeah!" He said as he looked up."

"Well, that was my voice. I do voiceovers for commercials, cartoons . . . you know, stuff like that." I kept trying to catch a glimpse of his embroidered name on his shirt but all I could make out was 'C', 'H', something, something.

Standing up to pull open the back of the machine to unplug it, he looks at me and asks, "How do you get into something like that?"

"I answered an ad." I said slowly as I chewed the last of my salad.

His back was too me while he felt around the back of the machine and pulled out this silver looking square with all these colorful wires. I cut my eyes over to check out his butt and his legs. Pretty nice! I said to myself. I would really love to touch the hem of his garment.

Chapter 2

𝓘t would be another week before I would see this mysterious sound room repairman with no name. As our eyes met, I decided to play it cool, especially being married and not seeing a ring on his finger, I didn't want him to think anything after that but I'm a friendly person who will talk to anyone.

"Hey!" I announced with a smile.

"Hey!" he answered back with a smile. He wore his usual uniform, the shirt that still looked like it had been hanging on the hanger waiting to be put on at the last possible moment. He smelled like a new car and The Auto Store . . . it was a clean busy smell. I really liked it. It reminded me of outdoors late in the evening just as the sun goes down right when the breeze is just right. It made me smile.

"You eating today?" He asked as he flashed his beautiful, charming smile.

"Naw! I mean, I'm not hungry. I need to run some errands today. I just came down to get something to drink and here you are."

"Listen, I'm almost through here. What time do you get off?" he asked.

"My last taping is at 3. It should last about thirty minute. Why?"

"I know you're married. So am I. I just wanna talk. Is that okay? We can go somewhere wide open."

If only he knew what I was going through. Harvey wouldn't know if I was at home or dead and most likely wouldn't even care. This is the first man that paid any attention to me in a long time. It's nice to know that I can turn someone else's head other than the head I was married to.

"Why not! Sure. Can you text me?" I asked.

"Yeah." He took out his phone to store it in this cellular. His phone was just like mine . . . . what a surprise.

"Well?" he said

"Well, what?" I asked.

"Your number?"

"Oh." I felt stupid and stuttered out, "Ah . . . it's 555-0237."

"Well, I have to put a name by it. What's your name?" he asked.

"Oh, that's right. K-H-Y-L-E-E." I spelled it out on purpose just to see if he would try to pronounce it.

"How do you say this?" he asked.

"It's Khylee."

"Well, hello Khylee. My name is Chaz."

Sure enough, at 3:00 I got a text message from him: *R U STIL TAPE N?*

"JUZ FINISHD. WHERE R U?" I answered

"SIT N IN MY TRUCK N PARK N GARAGE. ROW E-9"

"IM ROW E-16. RED RAV4. TXT U WHEN N CAR."

It was Friday and as I said my goodbyes, we all wished each other a great weekend. I grabbed my bag to study over my Monday morning scripts. We all walked down the hall and got in the park garage elevator. As the elevator door open to the garage, you could smell the exhaust from the vehicles and your ears popped from the opened outside noises and the deafening silence. The echoes of the footsteps were just as loud as it was mixed with laughter from my coworkers. Amanda or Mandy as we called her was the producer of Over Our Heads. She's the master mind behind every rhyme and reason. Jeffrey was our producer and engineer who didn't talk much but know the business inside out. Lacie was really weird. She never came to work but they never fired her . . . . who does she sleep with. And then there was me.

As we all walked our separate ways, my cellular beeped. The text read: "DID ANYONE EVR TEL U THAT U HAV A SEXY WALK?"

As I closed my phone, I laughed. I looked around because I know that he was watching me. This man was watching me and I was flattered. My eyes searched for him, I needed to find him. My heart was pounding so hard and so fast that I thought it was going to jump through my mouth onto the concrete slab. Suddenly, to my far left, I saw headlights flicker . . . . two short, one long, two short. I guess this man thought I could read Morse code or something. It was all I could to keep from running to him . . . but wait, what if it wasn't him? I've seen too many Lifetime movies. What if this mysterious handsome man was a weirdo? No one knows we are together and no one saw me get into his vehicle. Just then in the middle of all my rationing, I got another text:

"DID U C THA LITES?"

I walked over to where the lights were. It was a Honda CRV, Candy Apple red with silver trimmings. The closer I got, the louder his music got, the more familiar the music was. It was my favorite song, MAXINE, playing. He got out of the truck, walked over to the passenger side and opened it for me. "Hey!!" He greeted.

'Hi, yourself." I answered.

He lightly but firmly touched my right elbow as to help me in the truck and closed the door behind me. He walked over in front of the vehicle and got in the driver side. As he sat there for a moment, he let out a deep sigh and asked if he could confide in me. As I nodded, he began to vent. He started telling me how he had walked in on his wife and this man in their 8 year old son's bed but somehow the man got away before he could see his face. As he talked, I could see how frustrated he was because he gripped the steering wheel and begin to discuss and describe to me what he saw and how he felt. I really felt sorry for this man and was ashamed at the same time. Here I was feeling suicidal and depressed because I felt my situation was grave but I really didn't have anything to compare. I wanted to reach out to him, touch him, console him but I didn't want to act inappropriately so I sat there. It was all I could do to keep from crying because it was so sad. He actually caught his wife in the bed with someone else, WOW! I'm surprise why I am not talking to him through six inches of glass because that would be enough to drive me over the edge. I mean, my husband probably is sleeping with someone else but I have tried to keep myself busy. I even asked him once "Since it's obvious that you can't stand to touch me after the incident, why do you still want to stay married to me?" He just looked at me all brand new and said, "Don't ask stupid questions. I promised to protect you. I failed so I have to make up for it. And don't worry, when I die, all this will be yours." I felt like the wife of a mobster.

I don't know how long we sat out there talking but the more he talked the more attractive he became to me. I am ashamed to admit that I stopped listening to the story about his wife and started wondering what he looked like naked. I know . . . I know . . . . it was a really insensitive thing to do but the way he licked his full lips as he talked all while lightly sucking on his bottom lip after every pause, the way his bottom lip curled when he would say any word ending with the 'e' sound, and the way his nose crinkled as he exhaled after talking a deep sigh. It was enough to put dew on your lily. "What the hell are you doing?" I screamed silently to myself. "This man trusts you with valuable information and you trying to picture him naked . . ." Suddenly, he changed the subject and asked, "Where do you wanna go? Let's get outta here, okay?"

As I nodded, I realized that I was about to leave my car behind in the parking garage and said, "Sure, but I don't wanna leave my car here.

As his face enlightened, he brainstormed and said, "Maybe I should trail you to your house and you can ride with me and I will bring you home?" For some reason I felt safe. I trusted him. I felt comfortable and without saying a word, I reached over with my right hand to open the door as I grabbed my belongings with the left hand. I slide down from the seat and reached around and closed the door. The echoes of my footsteps from my shoes on the concrete kept rhythm with my nervously pounding heart and I wanted to look back to see if he really did watch me walk. When I reached my car, I sat my materials on the roof of the car as to rummage for my keys. The beam from his headlights was just light I needed.

Sitting inside my car, I took a deep breath and insert the key in the ignition. As I strapped my seatbelt, I asked myself, "What are you doing? As much as I ache for the touch of a man, what the hell are you doing?"

It only took 17 minutes to drive to my house but it really seemed longer. Every few minutes, I looked in the rear mirror just to see if he was really there. So many things ran through my mind like 'AM I going to be in a movie of the week?' 'How much do I really know about this man?' Then I started thinking about how many times Harvey left me home alone claiming that he was working. All those times, he lay next to me not touching me, only snoring. It hurt . . . thinking about it now, it really hurt. When things go wrong in the company, he drops everything to fix it but when I ask him about us, he won't try to fix anything. I cried for 3 minutes.

The driveway to my house was like going into a prison. There were two huge columns that were connected by a steel French door gate. It always seemed to have a foggy or smoky look in front. As I approached the gate, I slowed to enter the code in the key pad. The gate was large, heavy and slow drawing; two or more vehicles could easily tailgate and that's what Chaz did. I drove to the left side of the house pulling the visor down to operate the garage door. I looked in the rear view mirror, Chaz still tailgated.

I didn't want to think because if I thought, I would come to my senses and right then, I didn't want to rationalize anything, I just wanted to be with Chaz. I turned off the ignition and reached underneath the left side of my seat to pop the hatch. Underneath the floor board, I always kept a small 'mad money case'. It was charcoal grey trimmed in black made of leather with a 4-digit combination lock command underneath the handle. Inside, there was a small green bag filled with Sugah Sweet toiletries including bubble bath, hair products and perfume oils. It also contained a thin gown with matching robe, two pair of undergarments and a simple change of clothing. Underneath the lining was a plastic Ziploc filled with cash. As I reached inside the floor boards to get it, I took a deep breath and look over my shoulder at Chaz. It was faint but from behind the glare of the headlights I could see his smile.

I slowly walked over toward his truck as I touched the lever to close and lock the garage, and didn't look back. I don't know where I was going or what was going to happen but I wanted to leave it all up to him. I wanted to run away, take a risk of something spontaneous. He jumped out of his truck, ran over to the passenger side and opened my door. This time, when he helped me in, he took my bag, and gently took a whiff of my hair.... I don't know if he noticed that I was watching him but I noticed. He smelled so good. It was like smelling warm, fresh bread early in the morning from your favorite bakery. The smell went through me like a piercing arrow but to my groin. I think I may have even jerking a little.

Once inside the truck, he asked if I was comfortable, I guess because the passenger seat was pushed back a little. Before I could answer, he looked at me and said, "Here! Let me get that for you." He reached his left hand over between the seat and the door to free the lever to release the reclined seat. His cheek lightly brushed my breasts which made me gasp. I looked down in time to see that he looked at me from the corner of his eye like it was an intentional brush. Who am I kidding? I loved the attention. I took a deep breath and smiled.

"When had the sunset?" I asked myself. I don't really know where we were going but I was enjoying the ride. I wanted to initiate conversation but what was I going to say? I was so nervous but I wanted . . . I needed the attention. He reached over to hold my hand which sparked a charge that caused me to feel a little nostalgic. I shifted our hands into an interlocking position and gloved a tightly fit squeeze.

"Are you okay?" He asked

"Yeah . . . . I am now."

"You hungry?"

"Not really, but I would like a little something."

"Wait!" He brainstormed, "I know the perfect place." He let go of my hand and made a U turn and I let of a chuckle as I held on to the dash board.

'What are you doing?" I laughed.

Saying nothing but only smiling, Chaz never told me where we were going. I know I should have been scared because I didn't even really know this man but I felt more comfortable with than with my own husband. He was fresh. He was exciting. He was new and he was interested in me.

He drove up to a restaurant called Luigi's which was inside this 5 star hotel. I don't remember the name of the hotel because I was paying attention to the fact that it had started to rain and I didn't have an umbrella. As he drove under the green awning, there was a narrow guy that raced out to open the car door for me but Chaz stopped him and said, "I got this, cat." He unfastened his seat belt and opened the door. As he walked around to my side from the front of the truck, it was almost in slow motion because our eyes met and never lost sight of each other. He handed the keys to the valet and opened the door for me. I felt like a princess.

There was a doorman standing there wearing a green uniform trimmed in gray. He looked more like toy soldiers. He was a short man that looked like he had a grudge against shaving. He wore a matching hat with metals on it. He greeted us with a heart filled, "How y'all doing? Step this way." he nodded in my direction and said," Hello, pretty lady . . . . my what a pretty little cupcake you are." His voice was thick, like he had been smoking all his life and his speech was rapid. Chaz and I laughed as we walked in, but my attention quickly turned to the chandelier that decorated the ceiling. There was marble on the floor and you could hear your footsteps echo as you walked. Directly under the chandelier was a beautiful flower arrangement atop a table. That was the first thing you see, normal but I noticed the chandelier. To the right of that was the front desk. There were three people holding down the fort there wearing the ugliest uniforms I had ever seen in my life and to the left of the table was the lobby where there were three different sets of leather sofa. In the middle was the restaurant, I heard a lady singing *Killing me Softly* with only a piano accompaniment. Chaz took my arm and we walked straight ahead to the restaurant and as I walked past the flower arrangement I took the time to smell the flowers, literally.

In the restaurant, we were greeted by a hostess who seemed friendly enough. She smiled and looked very well kept. She was a white girl who looked very young. She wore a simply black dress and her hair pulled back in a very neat bun.

"Good evening. Two?" She stated and asked at the same time.

"Yes." Chaz answered. "Something private, please." He added.

"Sure, sir." She said, "Right this way." She directed us to a small table for two in the corner next to a small baby grand. He pulled out the chair for me and made sure that I was comfortable and then took the seat next to me.

The whole place was beautiful. You could hear the murmuring of low toned conversation all over the dining room. The place was decorated around a waterfall which silently flowed and was connected from ceiling to floor. I stared at it because I wondered how it was done. The dining room was dimly lit which made it very romantic. I kept thinking to myself, why didn't my husband ever bring me here? Soon, a guy came over and asked if he could get us something to drink.

"Sweet tea, please." I announced.

"Sure, sweet tea sounds good." Chaz said.

"Ok. Here are your menus. My name is Kevin and I will be your server."

To be on the safe side, I decided to not turn my cell off but just put my Bluetooth in my purse. I asked him, "Have you ever eaten here before?"

"A few times, it's really good."

"What do you recommend?"

"Well" he started as he pulled his chair closer to mine and leaning over to look on my menu. His face was so close to me that I could feel his breath on my cheek. "I guess it depends on how hungry you are." he said.

"I'm hungry but not very hungry. Maybe an appetizer or just side items." I added

"Then," he said as he reversed the menu. "Try a side salad and a baked potato." Kevin hurried back to our table with pad and pen in hand and asked if we were ready to order. Chaz ordered the shrimp scampi with a baked potato and I ordered the salad and baked potato.

"Okay," Kevin said as he tapped his pad with the pen. "I'll be right back with your order." He scrambled to remove the menus from the table as if someone in the back as timing him. As he scurried off, Chaz reached over and touched my hand to hold it and asked, "Are you okay?" I jumped a little at the fact that he was actually touching my hand and nodded in agreement. My eyes scanned the room to find something funny to talk about just to break the ice a little . . . . even though on

Chaz' part, no ice needed to have been broken. Sure enough, I saw a woman sitting at a table to my far right whose dress was so tight that if a button popped off, it'll kill someone or at the least take an eye. To add insult to injury, her figure didn't concur with the outfit she tried to wear. In the mist of it all, her ankles were so ashy that it looked like she took at bath in flour and dried her feet with a foundation brick. I smiled to myself as I saw this woman try to push, pull and drag her body into this so called outfit. I guess the look on my face was rather bizarre because Chaz laughed and asked was I okay. I told him exactly what I was thinking about the woman. He snapped his head around, "Where? Where?"

It was all I could do to keep from laughing aloud, "You not suppose to look, not yet anyway. You are supposed to just glance and not be so obvious." He laughed along with me. I said, "I see I can't tell you nothing." Touching my hand, he looked me in the eye and said, "You can tell me anything." (Okay, so he did have a sense of humor. Good.)

When our food arrived, Kevin came with a huge tray of food in one hand and a make shift portable table in the other to stand the food on. The dishes were so hot, you could hear the sizzle from Chaz' plate of shrimp scampi. It also made me wish that I had ordered something other than what I had. You could smell the most inviting aroma from the garlic and butter with just a hint of lemon. The only thing you could smell from my salad was the vinegar from the dressing but it was delicious just the same. As Kevin proceeded to make sure that all our needs were met, Chaz reached over, gripped my hand for grace across the table. He released a long awaited sigh as he unraveled his napkin to free the utensils.

"I haven't eaten all day," he admitted.

Freeing my utensils, I said, "That really does look good."

"Here. Take a bite." he offered as he twirled the noodles with is fork and stabbed at the huge shrimp. He licked his lips seductively and flashed a mischief grin as he leaned forward to feed me from his fork. A little embarrassed and at the same time a little aroused, I ate from the fork like Adam biting forbidden fruit from Eve. I slowly pulled the morsel from the fork and raised my right eye brow.

"Mmm! That *is* good." I admitted as I chewed slowly. I reached over to attend to my salad and twirled a little on my folk to return to favor. Without saying a word, threw the hair back from my face and aimed the folk for his mouth with my right hand. He continued chewing in a taunting sort of way while the folk full of salad was at his lips. He then swallowed slowly, licked his lips and opened his mouth to receive. I snickered like a 12 year old.

"You so crazy." I said

"Ah huh." he agreed.

For the next few minutes, he talked about how he was supposed to go with his wife to Detroit for her sister's wedding. He talked about it like it was a sink filled with dirty dishes. They were driving this weekend and he really didn't want to go. For some reason my heart sank. I don't even know this man and I attached myself to him emotionally like a stray cat that was found on some old lady's porch and I didn't want to let on. Boy! Did I feel like an idiot.

"When are you leaving?" I asked as I reached for my glass of tea.

"She wants to leave this weekend?" He answered. Sitting the glass of tea down, I realized that I had to know. "Can I ask you a question?"

"Sure you can."

"Well, if you actually caught her in the act of cheating, why are you still with her?"

He sounded really sad when he answered. "I don't know."

Chaz leaves to go away for the weekend with his family. Harvey is gone on another one of his 'business trips'. My heart is so heavy that it feels like I have an elephant sitting on my chest. It's so hard to breathe. It feels like the next breathe will be my last.

Journal Entry: June 8

Dear Chaz,

Here me out, OK? I don't what happened. It wasn't supposed to be like this. We started talking about the crap that our spouses put us thru and all of the sudden it's like ... I don't know ... I can't believe I allowed myself to get so caught up into you like this. My very soul lights up when I get a text from you. It's like, you're just one person in this world and you mean the world to this one person. You have no idea how you have affected me, do you?

I'm feeling sad, hurt, angry and abandoned. I missed him so much but it was never about the sex. It was the way that he made me feel. I felt like I meant something to someone. I felt like I mattered and that he wasn't alone. I felt necessary.

I can't stop thinking about you. I'm afraid that I'm going to just well, just come back safe okay. Have a good time. Just come back.

On everything that I own and love,
Khylee

Chapter 3

Chaz Boomerang came to the states from Kingston, Jamaica in 1983 after his parents died. He came to live with his grandfather while in high school and since his grandmother's death this seemed to be the perfect time and it worked out great for everyone. His grandfather, who always called him Boomer, had a small local store front repair shop business that Chaz became fascinated but only for sport. When Chaz got suspended from school for setting a girl's braids on fire, he really started putting his grandfather through changes. He wasn't a bad kid just full of mischief that could quickly turn into a temper if pushed and she knew how to push everyone's buttons. She made fun of the way he talked. He felt like a loner and an outcast anyway and he had a bit of a chip on his shoulder.

The girl's name was Sheelah and she was a girl who looked like she didn't miss no meals. She didn't like nobody, not even herself. When she walked, it sounded like an old ringer type washing machine, especially when she wore those corduroy pants. Her thighs rubbed together something awful. You could hear her coming. As well as her voice because she sounded like a horse. She looked like one, too. (Sometimes she smelled like one.)

Chaz's complexion was clear but dark with full heart shaped lips. His hair was thick with waves but he always kept it low cut. His eyes were almond shaped chestnut with a light halo of turquoise indicating that someday they were once blue. His cheek bones were slightly high with gorgeous dimples that you could bathe in. His accent was thick but eventually thin and lightened as the years grew on him but in 1988 he was teased a lot. Some girls considered it sexy. Sheelah considered it a misfit and an opportunity to start in on him especially when she found out that this grandfather called him Boomer.

On this particular day, Chaz was fed up with Sheelah. She had her hair braided with those beads on them and she started in on Chaz as soon as he walked into the school cafeteria. "Boom, Boom Mon." Here comes Boom Mon." She would chant. She would make that African bush cry noises as well as Indian war hoots. This really showed how ignorant she was. She was bigger than any girl and most guys and looked to be about 170-180 lbs easily.

Chaz walked in with his tray of Mrs. McBride's dried out spaghetti; actually it seemed to be noodles and ketchup. He walked past the Hi C machine and she just appeared like a vampire, chanting . . . "Boom, Boom" He really wasn't in the mood that day. It was the anniversary of his parents' death.

Chaz pinched his face, bit his bottom lip, threw his tray down and grabbed Sheelah by her throat. With all the adrenaline flowing, he picked her up off her feet and slammed her across the empty table onto her back. She was screaming and squirming as best she could what with his hand gripping her throat. Her nails dug into her hand and arms as he tightened his grip. Students were screaming, some ran out but no one helped Sheelah—that bitch. She terrified everyone and no one liked her.

He took the cigarette lighter from his back pocket and twirled her around on the table onto her stomach. He fastened her onto the table with his knee pressing the small of her back. He grabbed a hand full of braids and it all happened so quickly ~~~ Whoosh!

Heart wrenching screams came from the depth of Sheelah. "I'm gon beat your ass, Motherfucker!" She barked out. As he pushed her off the table, she scrambled to get off the floor. It was a blessing that it wasn't worse than it was because her hair was synched and melted onto her head. Chaz threw the lighter at her and it hit her in the head. She sat there crying and cussing.

"What? No more singing, Mon?" Chaz mocked her taunting. "Sing, bitch! Boom-Boom Mon! He chanted as he danced and waved his hands. The police came along with the fire department. He served 16 months in a reformatory only because of his grandfather's status. Sheelah recovered but only 80% her hair follicle would participate.

After a few months, Chaz was returned to his grandfather's and he immediately put him to work. Being the rebellious and inquisitive person that he was, he would reroute things in his grandfather's house. Pop, as he called him, was torn between being upset and amazed. For an example, if you'd ring the door bell, the garage door would open. If you turned on the television with the remote, the lights would turn off, mischievous things like that.

Chaz once took the riding mower apart and left the parts on the garage floor. He did the same to an old motor cycle. Pop was furious, but then he brainstormed: "If Boomer can take them apart, could he repair and put things back together?" Thus, Blue Sky Repair.

Harvey announced that night that he's going to San Francisco first thing Saturday morning (it was Tuesday night) and he needed me to drop him off at the airport. This was really weird because he never asked me to drop him off before. Usually he takes a cab or gets someone to do it from the office like that secretary of his, Zoë, that bitch. It's like he knew I was about to be unfaithful.

The next day I got a text from Chaz as I walked into the building at work. The first night was premeditated. We made plans for the weekend which happened to be the weekend that he was taking his family to the Smokey Mountains. He said that they were going to be returning Sunday morning. There I was again feeling lonesome and blue. "You're the blue in my sky, Chaz.' I said to myself.

I wanted to keep my mind off him just in case he wasn't going to show up so I decided to go to the studio. After my first session, it was around 3 or 4 pm and that's when I got a text from Chaz:

"HEY. JZ THKN BOUT U. CNT W8 2 C U. DNT RESPOND."

I beamed. I was still in the sound room with her headsets on sitting on a bar stool with a small podium that housed my scripts. Ryan called out to me over the speaker, "Khy, let's take it from when Katy walks in with the birthday cake."

When I returned home, I dismissed all the help until Monday morning but only after everything was immaculate. I heard a familiar sound in the distance. It was the sound of a small bell. I looked behind me only to see Powder, my white terrier racing towards me. "There's Momma's baby. Hello!" I bend down to allow Powder to jump into my arms. Then I went upstairs to my bedroom where I sleep alone because Harvey's room was on the east wing of the mini mansion. I decided to draw a bath to prepare for the night. The tub operates either with a remote or manually. The 68" porcelain tub polished nickel and brass. I poured in my favorite fragrances. Since Chaz liked it, I liked it, too. It was called "Oh, My Gosh". It was a mixture of two of her favorite oils: Coconut Mango and Pineapple Crunch. When you smell it, your first reaction is "Oh My Gosh!"

I turned on my favorite jazz CD as I walked back through to the bedroom from the huge walk in closet. It was just a small CD player that only cost $60 but I liked it because it matched the décor perfectly in the walk in. I took her clothes off and put them in the hamper then rushed to slip into my favorite terry robe to check on the level of the bubbles in the water. I pressed the off button on the remote. I eased in to the tub then took the hair tie from the basket by the tub and pulled my hair up. I leaned my head back to relax for a few minutes on the terry bath pillow.

I must have fallen asleep because the next thing I remembered was the sound of my cell phone ringing an unfamiliar tone. The call went to voice mail before I could answer because it took too long to get out of the tub. I jumped up, let out the water and put the robe on that was on the floor. I picked up my cell and opened it to see that Chaz had left a message:

"Hey, it's me. Call me when you get this."

As I closed the phone, a warm feeling went through me that matched the warm smile on my face. I unplugged the cell from the charger, walked into the closet and sat on the chaise lounge dipping with suds underneath her robe. I caught a glimpse of myself in the full length mirror and realized how sixteen year old-ish I was acting. My hair was pulled up in a pony tail on the top of my head quite disheveled. My favorite song on that CD began and I immediately thought of him. How appropriate!

I keyed in '38' on my cell which was his speed dial number. It was easy to remember because of his age.

"Hello?" He answered.

"Hey! You 'bissy'?" I chucked.

"No!" He laughed as he noticed the fact that I was making fun of his accent. "It's funny, yeah? My accent?"

"No, quite the opposite. I think it's sexy." I explained.

"Oh! So, what are you doing?"

"I just got out of the tub. I'm sitting here deciding on what to wear. What are you doing?"

"Just got back in town. I told her that I had inventory."

"Do you, have inventory I mean?"

"No. I just wanted to get away to see you."

"So how was your trip?" I asked, changing the subject.

"It was fun but I couldn't help but think about and I couldn't wait to get back to see you."

"So, this inventory? What are you *really* doing?"

"Waiting on you.' He answered quickly. "Are you still coming?"

"I want to . . ."

"What's stopping you?"

"Nothing. I'm nervous." I admitted. I kept thinking about something that JaVon had told me. "Girl," JaVon said. "You can always tell if a man is packing by the way he walks." Chaz definitely had that walk.

"I'm not going to do anything that you don't want me to." He promised.

"Alright. Where do you want me to meet you?"

"I'm sitting in my truck in the parking lot of The Austin Suites. Do you know where it is?"

"Yes, I do." I said.

"I'll call you back with the room number, okay?"

Taking a deep breath, I whispered, "Okay."

After a moment of silence, Chaz asked, "You okay?"

"Ah huh! I just have to get dressed. Gimme a few minutes to do that."

I closed the flap on her phone and looked at myself in the mirror. I chose a red wrap dress that fit so tight, it looked as though it has static cling. I decided to wear black Patton leather sling backs sandals that complimented my freshly pedicure size 5 ½ feet. I pulled out of the closet the matching bag and filled it with things I was waiting to use with Harvey but to no avail: red lip gloss, black crotch less panties. (Oh how I love red.) I didn't wear a bra or panties but as soon as I reached for my ID, keys and cellular, it rang which made my jump. I wasn't nervous until the phone rang. "What if it was Harvey just pretending to be out of town?" I thought.

With a deep sigh, I answered the phone, "Hello."

"Hey, what's up?" Chaz asked calmly. His voice is always so sexy.

"I was about to walk out of the door. Where are you?" I asked

"In the room; room 211. You still coming?" he asked in a low sex voice.

"Of course!" I answered as reassuring as I could, while I took one last look at myself in the mirror as I ran my fingers through her hair once more. "I'm on my way okay?" I said in a breathy voice.

"Just come up; don't ask for me, okay? Hurry."

As I hung up, I walked down the steps and heard Powder's bell following me. I took another glance at myself one last time in the rear view mirror and said aloud "What the hell are you doing, Khy?" But in my mind, I answered. *It's been too long and I want to be loved even if it's just for one night.*

The Austin Suites were 2 exits away west of the mansion. The drive was so quiet that I put on a little Neo Soul for comfort sake. I guess I just didn't want to hear my conscience. When I pulled into the parking lot, I noticed how nice it was. I'd always seen The Austin from the interstate but never been inside. I parked my car on the side of the building and walked up and around the back to the front. Opening the door caused the guy behind the desk to take notice but I was uncomfortable with the attention but at the same time flattered. I looked down which caused my hair to fall in my face so that he couldn't see me at all, I didn't want to run but 'run fool' came to my mind. "Hold the elevator, please?!" I cried out. It was an older gentleman. He stuck his cane out as to keep the doors from closing. Old, feeble white and wrinkled hands rescued his cane and he chuckled a bit as he said, "Well, hello there, little miss!" His smile was so big that I thought that it would stretch the potential of thin skin from his cheeks until it snapped.

He wore a tweed tam (who worn tams) and a matching bow tie. A bow tie? C'mon! who wore these. The last person I saw wearing a bow tie was my biology teacher, Mr. McGee??

"Thank you, Hello! Two please." I said. The elevator ride was quick and quiet and once it finally got to the second floor and the doors open and on the wall was 201-219 that pointed to the right and 200-220 that pointed to the left. "211" rang in her brain as I walked left. The closer I walked to the room, the faster my heartbeat throbbed. Soon I was face to face with room 211. I stood there for a few seconds until I could feel my legs again. Then, suddenly, something happened. I felt myself knock as though someone or something else was controlling her arms.

"Clink! Clank! Click! Click up!" and then the door open. I took two steps and could see Chaz's face in the mirror standing their smiling behind the door.

"What? You skerd?" he teased.

"No." I said as I tried to keep my composer while walking through the door. The room smelled of roses. "Wow" I thought to myself. "He lit candles. How sweet."

"Click" as the door closed behind me, I jumped a little. I looked around for the candles but all I saw was actual rose petals and roses. There was bottle of Champaign chilling with a bowl of strawberries setting nearby. I stood there with my mouth opened and tears misting in my eyes. Chaz walked over to me, took my bag and looked me in the eyes and said, "I just wanna hold you tight all night long whether we make love or not."

"Alright." I whispered. Without even thinking, I moved closer and kissed his lips lightly. He accepted the kiss and them held my hands and stepped back and said, "DAAAAMMMMMM! You look so sexy and you smell so good, too." I smiled loving the attention but was sad that I didn't get that attention at home. I quickly returned to the here and now; the right here and the right now of me and Chaz were actually going to do this, that is if I didn't chicken out. He walked over to where the bottle of Champaign was and asked, "I thought that this would make it even more special. We don't have to, I mean I'm not trying to get you drunk or anything, I just wanted it special."

"Sure. It would be nice." I said as I pointed with my thumb, "I'm going to go to the bathroom." I turned and walked into the bathroom.

Pulling the toilet seat down, I sat with my bag between the toilet and the tub and pulled my shoes off and put them by the tub as well. I pulled out that red negligee and the crotchless panties and hung it on the hook behind the door. I unfastened the wrap dress and tossed it over the rod of the shower curtain. I took from the bag a small spray bottle of my favorite mist and sprayed the negligee. With a deep breath I realized that I was at the point of no return.

Meanwhile, Chaz was sitting on the bed and wondering if I was ever going to come out of that bathroom. "Maybe she is changing her mind. Did I come on too strong?" He picked up the remote control to the television and sat on the bed. Just as he got comfortable, I opened the bathroom door. He jumped and met me at the foot of the bed. I felt that I looked radiant because Chaz was beaming. He turned and got both glasses. He gave one to me, poured Champaign in the glasses and then plopped strawberries in the glasses. A tiny bit of the contents splashed on my neck. "Oh!" I gasped. Chaz, being the attentive gentleman that he is, leaned forward to set his glass down on the table, came toward me and gently kisses and sucks the Champaign splash from my neck. I giggled and pushed him away slightly only to lean toward the table to sit the glass down. I slowly look up and his lips met mine as he kissed me softly but firm. I was totally in rare form. I initiated everything.

From 7:47 pm to 2:13 am, it was like I was in another world. I know because I watched the clock. I wanted to remember the adjectives of every minute. I wanted to be very conscious of the time just in case Harvey really wasn't out of town. Hell! I even made him spell my name. He kept forgetting the 'H' so I made him start over. Oh, what fun it is to ride on a one horse open sleigh. HEY!!!! After about twenty-six minutes, I reached my climax every eight second in a ten minute period. By midnight, I was free. I felt loved and as Chaz entered me, I realized that I was talking out of my head in ecstasy. I was saying things in his ear that I only wished that I would say to Harvey. At that moment, I realized that our relationship was only out of sexual convenience.

At home the next morning, the buzz from my cell woke me. It was Chaz.

"G MORNING."

"G MORNING 2 U 2." I replied busting from the seams.

"CAN U TALK?"

"OH! YEAH. PLZ CALL ME."

I was anxious to hear from him but scared at the same time. I had never had any man to treat me the way Chaz had. He was someone that I could fall in love with but I was afraid that he was about to tell me that he had made a mistake. As the cellular rang, I saw his name.

"Hello?" I answered nervously.

"Hey. How are you doing this morning?" he asked. His voice was different. It sounded more relaxed.

"Perfect. I haven't had a good night sleep like that in years."

Chaz laughs a little. "Oh yeah?" he teased. "Why is that?"

"Anyway! What are you doing? I asked.

"On my way to check out a new studio building." Chaz oversees the installations of new equipment in new studios.

"Wow. Your business is really doing well."

"What about you? What are you doing today?' he asked. I had previously asked for that morning off for a hair appointment so I didn't have to be at the studio later that afternoon. I was still underneath the covers while on the phone with Boomer.

"I don't have to go in this morning." I said.

"Tell me something?" he asked. "Why do you work? I mean it's obvious that you don't need the money unless Harvey owes the mafia."

"No, it's not the money," I took a deep sigh as I pushed up from under the covers. "Harvey never pays any attention to me. He's always gone and I don't have any children so I decided to answer an advertisement for something I know I was good at—voiceovers. I only get paid $2,000.00 per session but its money that doesn't have to come from Harvey's account. It's money that I do whatever I want, shopping, trips, hobbies ~~ whatever."

"So why don't you come with me when I go to another appointment? It's in Birmingham." I knew that all this wasn't going to last forever. How could I pick between a marriage of loyalty and a relationship of convenient pleasure. I really thought about it.

"It's possible. I'll let you know."

The next time we got together, it just wasn't the same as last time. I don't know if Chaz was preoccupied or what but he mostly snored and I was looking for a way out and I think this is just the out I needed. Even though I wasn't getting the attention that I felt I deserved at home I knew I had a trusting husband.

The reoccurrences I had with Chaz was filled with excitement and I only did it just to see how long I could get away with it. I didn't want to get careless or in too deep so I felt that I had to stop seeing him or at least stop sleeping with him. You know, I kinda wanted to ease my way into dumping him or at least making him dump me. I didn't want to hurt him or make him angry because I didn't want a stalker on my hands but I missed him so much. It was never about the sex. It was the way that he made me feel. Part of me wanted to hold on so tight until my knuckles begin to swell and the other part of me wanted to just walk away clean and take advantage of the 'no strings attached' rule that we made in the very beginning. This is a prime example of why there is no such thing as a one night stand: someone gets hurt and there is no walking away free card. (**Do not pass go!**)

Chapter 4

One of Chaz's favorite restaurants was located in an up and coming part of town called Medon Park. TWIST OF FATE was owned by two best friends, Jackson and Jillian, who lived next door to each other all their lives and they did everything together. Jackson was born March 21, 1965 and Jillian's birthday was exactly one week later, March 28.

Even in school, Jackson played football and Jillian was a cheerleader. When Jackson was in the band, Jillian was a majorette. But they never dated each other because they were more like best friends. They always tried to have relationships with other people but it never lasted. Then something happened at the senior prom in 1983.

Ross Miller asked Jillian to the prom. Now, Ross was the type of guy who was the catch and even though Jillian and Jackson looked like a real live Barbie and Ken (complete with the golden tan, blue eyes and blonde hair) they never dated but always had each other's back. Just as Jackson was about to leave with his date in the limo, he noticed that Jillian hadn't left yet. He walked out of his front porch and down the steps to walk across the lawn to Jillian's. She was pacing back and forth in white lace gown trimmed in powder blue that matched her eyes. Her hair was modestly adorned with baby breathes. As he reached out to console her, Stacey yelled out from the limo, "Hey Jillian! Are you okay?"

Jillian said nothing whereas Jackson shaking his head said, "Ross hasn't shown up yet."

Stacey opened the car door and ran up to the porch and said, "Hey Jillian, I didn't know how to tell you this but Ross took Charlotte Forbes to the prom, yeah. She lives across the street from me and I knew it was him 'cause everyone was outside taking pictures of them. Girl, I am so sorry." As she leaned a little closer, Stacey added, "Girl, I'm Italian on my mother's side, right, and Latino on my Poppy side, huh. I know people. Wanna make him hurt, yeah? I got lots and lots cousins." Sometimes Stacey was a bit scary but she's the best friend you'd wanna have when you need someone to have your back.

They all piled in the limo and when they arrived at the Convention Center, sure enough, Ross was inside slow dancing with Charlotte. Jackson made a bee line to Ross and as he tapped him on the shoulder, Jackson said, "I think you forgot something." With Jackson's left hand, he tightly and quickly gripped Ross' collar and with his right, he punched him right in his nose so hard, Jackson came off the ground. Needless to say, the music stopped playing and people stopped dancing. Ross screamed like a 12 year old girl and gripped his nose with both hands and yelled out, "What the fuck did you do that for?"

"That is for standing up Jillian. I hope your nose is broken. Man, why you gotta be such a fuck up?" Jackson said as he tried shaking the sting from his fist. Just before Jackson walked off, Heather pushed through and said, "You lousy piece of shit, Ross. You did the same to me last year." And she kicked him in the ding ding.

Charlotte looked at Jillian's tear stained face and said, "I know, huh? I had no idea. I really didn't."

"I don't blame you." Jillian smiled and said. Stacey said, "Dam! Girl, I didn't know you and Jackson were like that. I gotta get me a friend like that him." Simply because it was what it was, no one told the adults and they were too busy getting the rest of the 'appropriate' music together to notice the Ross was bleeding.

At that moment, Jillian fell in love with Jackson and later, Jackson confessed that he had always been in love with Jillian. Best friends make the best lovers. Thus, TWIST OF FATE.

This one particular night, Jackson asked Chaz as he sat at the bar, "You waiting on someone, too."

"What? No. No. I'm just here for a ginger ale. I mean I am meeting someone but it's not until later."

Jackson leaned closer to Chaz and while drying shot glasses, he pointed out to Chaz the man that sat over in the corner to Chaz' left. Jackson, never taking his eyes off the glass, "Look. Don't look now, but there is a guy over in the corner just over your left shoulder that comes in here all the time waiting on a beautiful woman."

"So," Chaz said as he sipped his ginger ale.

"So? It ain't right."

"Man, how do you know?"

"Boomer, I've been in business for a long time and have seen many things go on in my own place more times than I can count. I could write a screen play and I'd call it *'That Ain't Right.'*" Sitting the glass on the counter, Jackson sharply says, "Now, look!" As they both turned, they noticed just at the right moment that this man took his wedding ring off and put it in his pocket. Chaz' head snapped back into play and thought about Khylee and said, "Ok. Now what?"

"Just saying that this ain't right that's all." Jackson added.

"Look." finishing his drink and laying money on the bar, "I gotta go."

"Aight. Take it easy, man." Jackson said. As Chaz walked out of the door, coming from the women's room was the mystery woman that this non-wedding ring wearing man was waiting on. He never saw who the woman was. How strange.

Chaz walks out to the parking lot and sits in his truck for a moment and sends a text message to me:

"CAN U CALL ME RITE NOW?"

Chaz sat the cell on the passenger seat and reached for his Bluetooth and put it in his ear. Starting the ignition, he put on his seat beat and looked at himself in the rear view mirror. He started thinking about his wife Annabelle and how she always traveled at the drop of a hat. She was in real estate and always made these trips out of town at the same time that Harvey was gone. Chaz and Khylee noticed that they were always free at the same time and really didn't pay much attention or notice a pattern. They just chalked it up to fate and that they didn't have to lie or make up excuses so they could see together. I mean, why look a gift horse in the mouth?

I was getting out of the car from the garage and on my way into the house when I got the text from Chaz. I sat in the car for a moment just in case and decided to call him. Chaz's tone was different. "Wouldn't it be funny if our spouses were seeing each other?" I, being ultimately confused, answered slowly, "Ok. What are you talking about Chaz?"

"Think for a moment, Khy." Chaz said. Silence took over the conversation for what seemed like days but only lasting for a few seconds. "Well, they do seem to be out of town at the same time, don't they."

"I never really thought about it but it does seem odd, right?"

"You know if I found out that she was messing around, I'd leave. I would take my clothes, Xbox, computer, my TV all my CD's and just leave." Chaz preached.

"Well, don't you think that's just a little hypocritical, Chaz? If it does turn out that Harvey is cheating, which I do believe that he is, I wouldn't say anything to him."

Chaz was in shock. "You mean to tell me . . . wait!" Chaz was adjusting the volume on the ear piece while turning the stereo off. "If he was with someone else, you wouldn't say anything?'

'No I wouldn't. Look at what we are doing. How am I gon just call him out on something that he's doing when I'm doing the exact same thing? It's like a parent using profanity in front of a 6 year old and when that same 6 year old starts cussing, the parent goes, "WHAT THE HELL I TELL YOU ABOUT ALL THAT GODDAMN CUSSING, SHIT. It's hypocritical." I replied.

"So,' Boomer's voice was much calmer. "You would just admit it to him?" He asked almost childlike.

"Naw. Oh Hell no. I ain't stupid just fair." I said.

"But would you *leave* him, Khylee?" Boomer asked directly. This is the first time he had every asked me this.

"Would I . . . ?" I stuttered. "Would I leave?" I sighed. 'Yes. Yes I would. I would most likely divorce him, too but I'd never make a big deal out of it because I am just as guilty as he is."

Chaz replied with no hesitation, "Well, if Bella did something like that, it would be just the welcome mat that I would need to open the door to freedom."

"Chaz," Khylee added almost sadly, "You're not gonna leave Bella. You still love her regardless to what she's done or what you think she is doing right now, you still love her. Think of the kids. What about them. Besides, Mr. Wolf Cookie, you ain't going nowhere anyway?" The conversation was getting rather heated when all of the sudden, Chaz interrupted and said, "Look, this don't need to get out of hand. You and my kids are all I care about and nothing more."

"But Chaz . . . ."

"No *buts*, Khy. I care about you a whole, whole, whole lot and I think about you all the time. I'm crazy about you."

"Then why are we arguing. You called me asking me all kinds of crazy questions about our spouses and then we start arguing? How did this happen? I need for you to hear me out." I asked almost in tears.

"Okay. Okay. What?

I took a deep breath and said, "Whatever you two had has to be more than what you don't have now. Do you kiss her the way you kiss me?

Do you hold her the way you hold me? When you two are intimate . . . ." I stopped short as I felt my words choke while fighting back the tears. " . . . do you make love to her the way you make love to me? I'd give anything for Harvey to treat me the way you treat me."

There was a short pause. Chaz thought for a moment and said, "You know, I tried all that. I really have but I'm tired of initiating and I get nothing from her."

"Then try again." I said quickly.

"Why is it so important to you that I do this?" he asked.

"Because you guys need to stay together. Find that common denominator. Plus . . . ." I couldn't fight the tears any longer. They cascaded down my cheek and fell hard onto my blouse. "I'd give ANYTHING . . . for Harvey to touch my soul the way you've touch mine. The way you look at me, it's like you really see me. He looks right thru me if he's ever looked at me at all. Don't give up. Go to her. Tell her that you love her. Tell her that you can't breathe without her. Hold her, kiss her, give her flowers . . . ." I stopped to wipe my nose. I really didn't want him know that I was crying but he wasn't a fool.

"Hey . . . . Hey . . . Wait. Are you crying?" He asked . . . there was silence and heavy breathing from me. "Oh, honey, please don't cry."

"I have to go." I said quickly.

"Okay, but are you okay?" Nothing but silence. I hung up and threw the cellular in my purse. I got out of the car, walked across the garage floor and opened the door and went into the house. On the counter next to the door was a box of tissues. I put my purse on the counter and put the entire box of tissues in my purse and went upstairs.

When I got upstairs, I threw my bag on the floor and pounce on the bed and screamed from frustration inside the pillows. Rage! Hurt! Loneliness! I wasn't sure; I just knew that I felt something that caused me to scream and cry. What an empty feeling when the one you're married to don't want you and the one you want, you can't have. When I looked up, Powder was sitting on the chaise staring at me tilting her head from side to side.

Chapter 5

*O*ur wedding was a fairy tale wedding. We were married in New Orleans in 1994 in a small castle like mansion during Mardi Gras season. The entire guest stayed at the mansion so it was perfect. The home was called La Mansion de Lisette, named after the daughter of a Frenchman, Phillip Pierre Boulanger, who settled there sometime during the late 1800's. Lisette was only 4 when she died after a cut on her foot became infected. She was their only child.

Anyway, this small mansion was built on only 40 acres and somehow Harvey had managed to rent the entire place for one week for the wedding. All activities were held there; from bachelor parties to rehearsal dinners, to the family's quarters. He made sure that they had everything that they needed. Nothing missing, nothing lacking and nothing broken.

The wedding ceremony itself lasted 47 minutes. I had 12 females standing up for me excluding the matron, maid of honor, bridesmaids and the flower girls. Harvey had just as many. They were freshly cut flowers, ice sculptures; musicians and even a day care on site. Harvey had thought of everything. It seemed that he loved me so much that he couldn't think straight and only wanted this day to be perfect. He pulled out all stops. They wedding cake was even baked on the premises. It was six feet high with cream and white icing with real lilies for decoration. There were doves flying around. There were also diamonds and gold beads sown in my wedding dress and the designer made a 10 inch replica of me and Harvey to put on the cake, right down to the details in our clothes. People marveled and were in awe at the creations Jo Walton, owner and operated of ***Sweets for the Sweet.*** It was amazing how things just came together. Harvey even sang to me at reception. I had no idea he could sing.

Afterwards, a carriage was waiting to whisk us away to the airport. It was only a 15 minute ride through the thick Mardi Gras traffic. With the police escort, it was simply cut and dry but Harvey didn't count on one thing. The weather was mixed with a slight breeze. You could hear the clop-clop of the horses accompanied by a few brays every now and again. You could also hear the people's voices combines with over the instruments of the parade. Women were screaming and men were yelling. Everyone seemed to be having a good time waving handkerchiefs in the air while dancing. The music was getting louder with each moment. The police escort could only take us so far. During some part of the parade, three men decided that the Mardi Gras was boring and wanted to start trouble. I didn't even see where they came from because the next thing I heard was this loud POP. I saw the driver slump over. Though I didn't know it at the time, he was dead. There was a gun pointed at the Harvey's head. One minute we were laughing and talking and the next we were screaming for our lives. With all the screams going on that night, they all sounded the same so no one helped us. They made Harvey watch as the other two had their fun with me.

I blocked out most of it or at least I told myself that. I vaguely remember the overnight stay in the hospital. Every time my mind wanted to remember, I felt shame and I wanted to die. Harvey just kept himself busy and paid the house staff extra to make sure that I wasn't left alone. Funny. Between the bad dreams, guilt trips and the shrink appointments, I wish I had developed amnesia sometimes or at least died in the process.

Even though there was a police report filed, Harvey's money and connections made it all go away except for the reoccurrences in my mind. Too bad he couldn't make that go away. I did, however, see a copy of the police report. (That's the only reason I knew one was filed because Harvey won't talk about it much.) Harvey told them everything and paid to keep names out of the papers and the media and away from everyone else. During the 'process of the attack' (which is what it was referred to) the driver of the carriage was shot point blank in the back of the head behind his ear. He died instantly. Harvey said that he tried to shield me from the splatter but it was too late. I never knew what happened to my dress. I never saw any of our wedding photos.

I never told anyone; not D'Kyra, not JaVon, not even Mom and Dad. Being an only child of a Pentecostal Pastor, they taught me to be honest and to be a good girl. I don't think I was spoiled but you tend to be stereotyped when you are a Preacher's Kid. I was well rounded. I was allowed to become a cheerleader and I was able to go out on dates but only when I turned16. I went to the prom and to sleepovers and I was also allowed to have slumber parties. They raised me to be a virgin and to save myself for marriage and that's what I did. I tried really hard and Harvey knew that and understood. He knew that I was determined to save myself for him and he took pride in that. Even though he confided in me by saying that he wasn't a virgin, it didn't matter to me because I loved him. At least he would know what to do on the honeymoon, but we never found out. That was stolen from me in a way that will never come back. I honestly believed that he loved me once but now, I just don't know what to think anymore. Sometimes, I think he still does in his own way. He's not nasty to me, we are civil to each other but it's just excruciatingly painful to watch him try to be loyal to me. He's never home and whenever he talks to me, he won't even make eye contact. He talks to the servants more than he talks to me.

Mom and Dad weren't rich but we were very comfortable. I had everything I could ever possibly need and most of the things I wanted growing up. Whereas with Harvey, was the only son of H.C. Wilcox Sr. and the 2nd generation of Wilcox Pharmaceutical Co. The Wilcox came from a long line of old money, mostly old blood money. Wilcox Sr. was from Chicago and was said to have worked with mobsters and that he is responsible for some to the money disappearing. After turning states evidence over to the Feds, he went into hiding and he became Wilcox of Wilcox Pharmaceuticals.

Someone once said that the best gift you can give someone is a chance. I wanted so much for that void to be filled in my life that I thought it was Chaz. When in all actuality, it was my own salvation that was dehydrated. It's almost like I wanted that two sides to everything lifestyle. I wanted someone to sweep me off my feet, someone to always love me without fail, tell me that I matter. I wanted, craved, for that fairy tale love affair with Harvey, who I loved but wanted to deeply be in love with him and for him to be in love with me as well.

What happens when you try to love someone and they don't return that love? I thought that if I tried to love Harvey hard enough that it wouldn't matter what his feelings were for me. If I tried to control the emotional environment and set the tone, things would be okay. I thought wrong. Things got worse. All that did was smother and push him further away. It made him want out of this marriage of convenience. We both knew the outcome. We lived through and survived the beginning; the middle of the present was blinding fog from day to painful day but the end? The final end was cold and very lonely. Love is a process that sneaks up on you. Love is also an absolute animal that happens when you are looking for something else. Love is so definite that if you love someone, you'll always love them. Right? Wrong. Broken hearts mend sort of like broken bones. There are different types of broken bones just like there are different types of broken hearts. After they both heal, you only acknowledge it in stormy weather. You can only see it if you look at it through X rays. You can only feel it when there's pressure thrust upon it. But what happens when you fall in love with forbidden fruit? What makes them forbidden fruit? If love is good and if every good and perfect gift comes from God, is there such thing as falling in love with the wrong person? Why are they the wrong person? Is it because they belong to someone else? This question goes back to Adam and Eve. The tree of the knowledge of good and evil. You can eat from any tree EXCEPT from that one.

Well, some people say that love is overrated. Some even say that it's complicated and that it's too much of a commitment. Those same "they" that say love is complicated, forbidden, or overrated say so only because they don't know the ground rules. You have to not only understand the ground rules but be willing to stick to them. These ground rules cannot be broken no matter what. Sure, I felt guilty after sleeping with Chaz but I knew that I couldn't stop myself from thinking of him. I will never be sorry for anything that made me smile and Chaz makes me smile. I wanted so much for someone to be with me because they loved me unconditionally, not out of obligation or a sense of duty.

Loving someone who only feels obligated to you is exhausting. You'll never know when that person will pull the rug out from under you. It's sort of like wearing that 18 hour bra and girdle set and realizing you only have 20 minutes left but have 2 more hours left before you can clock out and go home for the rest of the day. I realized that I was in love with Harvey once but over time, I wasn't *in* love anymore. I just loved him. I knew that Harvey provided for me abundantly and for that I will always be grateful but I know that there is more to life than this and I want to be happy. I deserve to be happy. I almost demand it.

The beeps from my cell woke me and put a smile on my face. I rolled over toward the night stand where the sun shone in my eyes and tilted the phone to see who it was, as if I didn't already know. Gripping it tightly, I cupped the phone in my hands and smiled. Stretching underneath the blue and white sheets, I let out the most satisfying sigh. I pulled the covers back, threw my legs along side of the bed and stood up. My red gown cascaded down my body as I walked toward the bathroom. I opened the flap and read the text:

"GMORNING!"

"GMORNIGN 2 U 2" I replied. I always wondered if he thought that I was sitting by the phone nursing and watching it waiting for him because most time I was. After relieving myself, I walked over to the sink and washed my hands but instead of drying them, I ran my fingers through my hair. I took the cap off the mouth wash, poured a little in the cap to rinse away the morning breath. As I took another few minutes to play with my hair, "AH, Snap!" I moved closer to the mirror with a frown on my brow and squinted as I parted my hair with my fingers. "Another gray hair." I said. I quickly rummaged through the vanity drawer behind me for a pair of tweezers. "MMmmMMmAAAAHHHH! OOOuch!" I cried out as I pulled the hair out. I woke up Powder who was sleeping at the foot of my bed. She came running and barking like she was getting ready to do something. I looked down at her and smiled as I replaced the tweezers. "I'm just not ready yet, Powder. That's why I pulled it out."

Turning on the shower, I got another text from Chaz, I mean, who else could it be? "GON B N MEETN ALL DAY. GR8 BIZNES OPP. THNKN OF U. MS U. TXT U LATR" After my shower, I watched TV all day.

Things seemed to be rather pleasant in the Wilcox Mansion. Harvey's business was doing well which made him happy and that made me content. He had even talked about taking some time off which didn't necessarily mean that it was going to be spent with me so I didn't get my hopes up. I always try to occupy my time with something that I liked to do. I was thinking of leaving Harvey but I wonder if Chaz wasn't in my life, would I even be considering leaving? There is no guarantee that Chaz will want me if I did leave. We told each other that there were no strings attached and that we didn't owe each other anything. He's always promising to leave Bella but always goes back or allows her to come back. Money wasn't the issue because of the years, I have been saving and setting some aside in my own personal account that Harvey can't touch. I wanted to live the rest of my life with Harvey. Getting attacked wasn't my plan or my fault. I know that now but I felt like a stray cat that was mauled by a huge dog and someone who don't particularly like cats, witnessed the attack, rescued me out of pity and felt obligated to take care of me. Guess who the cat is?

Harvey kissed me goodbye on the cheek at the door and drove off for the office. I went on with my regular routine. The cook laid my breakfast out on the balcony which over looked the lake. Myra sat the tray on the table as I sat down. She unveiled the food as if it was some sort of magic act: 2 turkey sausage patties, scrambled eggs, croissant with honey nut cream cheese and hot peach tea. There were 3 beeps from my cell phone sitting on the bed.

"Would you like for me to bring that over to you, Ma'am?" asked Myra.

"Sure." I said as I spread the cream cheese on the croissant. There were 3 more beeps as Myra walked the cell phone over and handed it to me. I sat the knife down and looked at the ID. As I silenced the volume, I said, "Thanks, Myra." She smiled and walked away while I opened the flap.

'GMORNING' I smiled. It's amazing how Chaz's text made me feel all warm and secure.

'GMORNING 2 U 2'. I texted back. I sat the phone down, wiggled my right leg in aspiration. I sipped on my tea and stared at my cell all while waiting for his reply.

"U BUSY?"
"NO. EAT N BKFAST ON BALCONY. WHATCHA DO N?"
"THNK OF U. WHEN CAN I C U?"
"D K. MAYB 2DAY. HOW'S LUNCH SOUND?"
"GR8! WHERE?"
"LUIGI. LOL"
"LOL LUIGI, HUH? REALLY?"
"U GOT ME HOOKED ON THE PLC. MEET ME @ 11:45."
"Y 11:45?"
"BCZ ITS 6:42. WILL GIV ME TIME 2 SHOP 4 NU OUTFIT."
"C U THEN."

I couldn't eat another bite because I had been boomeranged. I collected all the breakfast dishes and set them on the tray. I then picked up the tray and walked across the bedroom and out the door proceeding to take it downstairs to the kitchen. I heard an inaudible voices once I turned the corner and then they stopped. "Oh, señora Wilcox, por favor"

("Oh, Mrs. Wilcox, please.") Myra gasped and she put down the spoon that she was used to stir the contents of the pot. "Let me take for you. Why you no call me?"

"Don't be silly." I said as I sat the tray down on the counter. "It's okay." Myra took the tray from my hands and handed it to Eva. Eva then took the tray to clean and put the dishes in the sink preparing it for the dishwasher. I sat down at the breakfast bar on one of the bar stools. Myra prepared another cup of tea for me without even asking. Eva's English wasn't very good at all which caused me to want to use the little Spanish I knew at the time around her to show myself friendly to her. They were great ladies and very helpful. *"Ella parece tan hermosa, como una estrella brillante."* said Eva. *"¡Mirar! Ella está brillando intensamente."* (She looks do beautiful, like a shiny star. Look! She is glowing.") I fired back by trying to impress them and said: *"Gracias, Eva. ¿Cómo las señoras quisieras ir a hacer compras conmigo hoy? ¿Mi convite?"* (Thank you, Eva. How would you ladies like to go shopping with me today? My treat?")

They both gasped and laugh as they finished loaded the last of the dishes into the dishwasher. Eva and Myra beamed with excitement. "Gracias, señora Wilcox." I slapped the counter and announced, "Great. It's settled. We are leaving in 20 minutes and we're taking the limo." As I walked back upstairs, I could hear Myra translating it all to Eva.

They both cheered. I felt great.

By 8:22 a.m., we all were ready for ReCreations Mall that opened at 9. I called ahead to see if Shan was working and able to handle two makeovers. I also made arrangements for Graham's Boutique to be open for new outfits. I had to make sure that I was ready for Chaz just in case it happened to be more than lunch. While the girls were getting their hair done, I took the escalator to the next floor up to the lingerie department and picked out the sexiest black lace teddy I could find and paid cash for it.

After shopping, I had just enough time to make it to Luigi's so I had the car to drop me off and take Eva and Myra back to the mansion. "Just drop me off here. I have a meeting with someone and will get a ride back later." I said to the driver. It was 11:36. I went to the bathroom in the hotel lobby to freshen up and I got a call from Chaz.

"Hello?" I was afraid that he would cancel.

"Hey? Where are you?"

"In the hotel lobby bathroom by Luigi's?"

"Ok." He sounded preoccupied and I just had to ask.

"Why? What's wrong?"

"Nothing. I just need to see you. I'm sitting in the parking lot outside."

"Well, are you coming in?"

"Yeah. Gimme a minute."

"Well, should I get a table?"

"No. I want to get a room and we can have room service. We need to talk. Sit tight in the lobby and I will tell you what room to come up to, okay?"

"Ok. Are you okay?"

"I don't know." Then he hung up. I was really worried. I didn't know what to think. I walked from the bathroom and sat in the lobby and my mind rollercoastered. What if he says that he made a mistake by getting involved with me and wanted to call all this off in person? What if he contracted some STD and needed to tell me in person? What if his wife found out about us and she followed us?

"417" the text read.

I left the lobby and walked toward the elevator but then walked past it and decided to take the stairs to think some more.

There was a huge red 4 that marked the door in the stairwell that indicated I was at the 4th floor. Had the other numbers been that huge and red? The door handle was cold and heavy and made a creaking sound as it opened with a howling echo. It smelled of fresh paint. The sound of the door closing behind me caused a chilling in my spine. Room 417 was just down the hallway and I had no idea what Chaz wanted to talk to me about.

As I knocked on the door, I looked to my left and to my right to see if I saw anyone watching me. There was no one. I heard the door unlatch from the inside and it opened just a little. I pushed opened the door and walked in. Chaz stood behind the door to my right. He grabbed me with one hand and pushed the door closed with the other. He took my bag and sat it down on the bed and sat me down beside it. We didn't speak for a few minutes. He walked over to the chair and pushed it over in front of me.

"Ok, congratulations, Chaz. You're scaring me. Now tell me what's going on?"

He took a deep breath and leaned toward me and said, "Remember when I asked you what if it turned out that Harvey was cheating on you and I asked you what you would do?" Though I was definitely shaking my head from side to side, the word 'Yes' escaped from my lips. He said, "Well, remember my friends Jackson and Jillian who own that restaurant called Twist of Fate?"

"Yes."

"Jackson was telling me about a guy who would always come there who would meet a woman. He showed me the surveillances tapes."

"Okay?"

Chaz reached into his bag and pulled out a 5 x 7 manila folder. Inside this folder were 6 pictures in black and white. He said nothing as he turned the photos around to show them to me. They were shots from different angles. The first one I looked at was a face shot view of a very beautiful woman sitting in a deuce. The person she was sitting with could not be seen clearly because their back was to the camera and it was slightly distorted because of a plant. I looked up at Chaz. He sits back in the chair and looks at me with a frown on his face. "That's Bella." I didn't know what to say or what to do so I sat the photos on the bed next to my bag, leaned over to embrace him and said, "Oh, honey. I'm so sorry. So you know who the guy is?"

"Yeah. I think so." He broke the embrace, reached for the photos and shuffled them as to look for one particular one. "Look" he said as he handed me the photo. This view was of the same face shot of her but the person's head was a little more clearer because the plant wasn't in the way. It was something familiar about that person. "Remember when I told you that I caught Bella in the bed with this guy and I only saw the back of his head? I think this is the same guy." Chaz said.

"Well, do you have a clearer one?" I asked nervously. He said nothing as he handed me a side head shot view of both of them that was so clear that I started shaking. I stood to my feet gasping. Then I immediately sat down. I felt faint. My mind replayed all those messages from Harvey saying that he was going out of town for another meeting and I believed him. I felt the tears trying to form but I didn't want to give Harvey's photo the satisfaction.

"Khylee?" Chaz asked. "You okay? What is it?" Apparently Chaz didn't know who the male figure was but I did. "Khy, honey? What's wrong?" Chaz only knew it was the same guy that was at his house but didn't know who he was.

"It's Harvey." I tried to say but pain steals the words before they would come out. I couldn't breathe. I couldn't think. I thought I was going to faint.

"I can't hear you. What are you saying, Khy?" Chaz asked.

"H-H-Harvey. That's Harvey." I said. My chest hurt. Chaz stands up and snatches the photos from my hand and yells out, "WHAT THE FUCK . . ." He paces with the photos in his hands looking at them from every angle by the desk lamp. All those times he couldn't touch me because of the attack. It wasn't the attack at all; it was because he had someone else to go to. How could he lie to me like that? How long had this been going on? While I was trying to add up things in my mind to make sense, Chaz was punching pillows and cussing. Most was inaudible or maybe my thoughts were drowning him out.

"It's over." he said. "I'm going home and I'm packing my shit and leaving. I already got a place picked out; I just have to wait until the end of this month. Then I will get a key and give you one. You can come and go as you please. Okay?"

"Okay, just hold on a minute." I stood up and said, "You can't just go home and pass out ultimatums like they were candy. What are we doing? The only difference is that they got caught, on camera. We were careful."

"I told you that if I found out that she was messing around, I was leaving and I meant that."

"But why, Chaz? Why now?"

"What do you mean 'why now?'"

"You are so double standard. Why did you show these to me?" He sat down in the chair and said, "Because I knew she was and this is the proof."

"Are you going to show her these pictures, Chaz."

"Hell, yeah. Well, first I'm gon confront her. I'll give her a chance to tell me the truth. If she lies, then BAMMM. I'm pulling these puppies out. That's right."

"I don't think you should do this, Chaz."

"Look, Khy." He said as he grabbed my hands guiding me to the edge of the bed and gazing in my eyes. "Harvey lied to you and I know Bella has been doing this for at least three years and it's possible that my little baby girl ain't even mine. How long has he been doing this?"

"I don't know, Chaz but I just can't go and confront him. I just can't leave. I won't have *anything* if I divorce him. I just can't leave. Our situations are different."

"You don't have any children. You can come and stay with me so you won't have to worry about where you are going to stay. I will take care of you."

"Look, I gotta go. I gotta think about what I really need to do and you need to calm down and really think about what you are going to do about Bella. I have to deal with Harvey my own way." Chaz wouldn't let me go. He grabbed my arms and held me firmly but not smothering. His heart was beating fast and his breathing labored. He was really worrying me. I didn't know what to do.

"Stay." he said. "Stay here with me tonight."

"I can't." I replied

"Sure you can." he said as he pulled away and looked into my eyes. He was really making it hard to say no but I really had to go home to see exactly what I was feeling. I couldn't stay there with him knowing that my suspicions about Harvey were true. I had to go home and figure this out.

"Chaz, I really can't. We both need to go home and you need to figure this out with Bella. You don't wanna make any drastic decisions because after all, look at what we are doing. We can't be hypocritical." And what's more, I didn't want a pity fuck.

Chapter 6

D'Kyra de Silva is my newly best friend. She made partner 17 months ago at a brokerage firm. (MacAfee and Steele) She has the most astonishing personality that draws people. Her tactic is simple, sweet and short right down to her gown that evening. It was basic black with gathers down the sides. She wore a pearl choker with matching earrings, bracelet and purse. Her shoes were a pointed toe that fastened with a string of pearls around the ankles. Her hair was even adorned with them as it was pulled back with pearl studded mini claws. She was a knock out that night.

   Our husbands are in the same business and that's how we met. It was one of those Pharmaceutical Convention dinner party meeting thingies that was very boring and I do believe that the only reason Harvey even bothered to ask me was because he wanted a trophy on his arm. So I made sure that I look like a run way model on the red carpet. I did it for spite. I made sure that I would make up for all those empty stares and those times he didn't pay attention to me in one night. I made sure that I wore no underwear at all. My dress was the exact color of my skin, Bittersweet Bronze, and it fit like the skin on a grape. It was a sleeveless spaghetti strapped dress. The pearls were a present from Harvey when he went to New York. I got the sling back shoes online that matched perfectly and the handbag was bronze with pearls. My hair was pulled up with silver combs with coils. I had to go to the ladies room more than once to take it off and fan it dry because it hugged every crevice of my body. Hell, he should have paid attention to me. Now, every woman in that place hated me because every man's dick was hard from asking who I was. I felt like

I was getting all the attention from those men in one night that I was missing in all those years of Harvey ignoring me. It felt great and I won't be sorry for anything that made me smile.

Anyway, I met D'Kyra in the ladies room at that dinner and as I said before our husbands were equally inattentive to both of us. It's amazing how trials and tribulations form a tightly netted bond. Throughout all of our situations, we have been trying to get together for tea, lunch, dinner or something just to have some girl time. Our friendship is so deep that we shared everything, even our deepest, darkest secrets that make us cringe whenever we mention it. I am talking about things that I wouldn't even tell God if he didn't already know. (She knows about Chaz.)

Sometimes situations and circumstances happen that causes women to do things that they otherwise swore that they would never do. These are the things that other women would do we would do and talk about how stupid they were. I even had this discussion with D'Kyra who was torn with the decision that would ultimately change her life. We continued to share stories of loneliness and the feeling of unimportance. It's like the more we talked about our situations, the more our stories seemed identical. Alas! A kindred spirit.

"It's like he pays attention to everything that I wear, how I do my hair and everything." D'Kyra said she as she beamed while talking about her 'acquaintance'.

"Girl, I know what you mean. It's so easy to get lost in the moment, you know?" I added. "I'm so tired of being ignored that I don't know what to do."

"Have you tried talking to Harvey?"

"Girl." I chucked. "I have talked to Harvey so much that I am tired of trying because he's never home. And when I try calling his office or leave messages on his cell, he acts like I'm really bothering him. Once, I went up to work in pumps and a black London Fog."

"Ok . . . and? What did he say? What did he do?" D'Kyra asked while she moved her chair closer to mine.

"He took one look at me and told me to go home." She gasped without making a sound. I looked down toward my lap while trying to swallow that knot in my throat. I didn't realize how humiliating that was until I actually told the story to someone aloud. I mean, I replayed it over and over again in my mind but I wasn't ashamed of myself until I told someone. "Look," she tried to change the atmosphere a bit, "I don't know what's wrong with Pentecostal men. It's amazing how much Bible they know until it comes to the part where they have to 'love their wives as Christ loved the church.'"

"I just needed a man's point of view so I asked Chaz one day for his opinion." I said.

"I know, I wanted to ask Tony but I really tired not to talk to him but I knew he was watching me and I liked the attention."

"That sounds like Chaz. I mean. He's so attentive and he really pays attention to everything, too. It's getting advice from a man about another man. I don't wanna sound naïve but do you think he's being honest about me? I asked him if I had anything to worry about if your husband won't have sex with you."

"Oh my God, girl. What did he say?" asked D'Kyra.

"Well, at first he didn't say anything. He stayed silent on the other end so long, I thought we lost connection." I said as I chuckled. "And that's how it started. He listened and was easy to talk to. I kept telling myself that it was only conversation and that it wasn't going to go any further but . . . ."

"I know, girl. Tony is the same way. Stanley seems like everything else is more important than me and the kids and that I am suppose to just stay home and wait." D'Kyra seemed to stare over my head and talk from a distance at me rather than to me because her eyes squinted a little and she bit her lip a little. "I'm tired of being ignore, Khy. I hate Stan sometimes, you know? He really makes me feel like shit sometimes but not anymore. I think I wanna met with Tony."

"**Are you sure**?" I asked as I realized by that far away look in her eyes, I wasn't going to be able to talk her out of it, but I was going to try. "Look, even though I did, make sure that this is something that you really want to do, because once you do, you won't be able to undo what you did."

"Well what about you?" she asked as her face twisted.

I took a deep breath and sighed. I really didn't have an answer for her except to say almost in tears, "You know, D'Kyra, if I had you to talk to before I slept with Chaz, I wouldn't have in the first place. I mean, part of me wanted to and most of my brain was telling me that it was wrong. But if this is what you wanna do, I gotcha back, girl."

"Ok. He called not long ago and asked me to meet him but I wasn't sure until I talked to you." She said as she looked at me for nonverbal approval.

"Well, how about meeting me afterwards. Where and when is he going to meet you?"

"At Austin Suites on Friday."

"This Friday? What time? No wait, just tell me what time you need me to meet you and I will be there. Consider my schedule cleared, okay."

That Friday, we decided to meet for dinner. I stayed home until I got a call from her so that she could let me know what time to meet her. I sat on the chaise in the bedroom watching television flipping through the channels until I got a call from her.

"Hello?"

"Hey. Where are you?" It was D'Kyra and she sounded like she had been running.

"Still at home waiting on you to give me the word. Are you okay?"

"Yeah. I'm with you, okay."

"Okay. I gotcha back and I'm leaving now heading to the restaurant, okay?"

"Okay." As I hung up, I jumped up and down clapping and cheering 'YOU GO, GIRL!' I was so proud of her. Truth be told, I was a little ashamed of myself. It was like I was teaching a teenager how to lose her virginity and not get caught. I was also feeling glad that I wasn't the only one fucking someone else's husband. I guess this was saying to me that if we share this, we will be best friends for the rest of our lives and I have always wanted a best friend to share deep secrets. I really need to talk to someone about my wedding night incident other than writing this all in this journal. If we have this secret and it doesn't destroy us then maybe I can tell her but not until.

I decided on wearing a pair of red strapped pumps with a pair of jeans. My long sleeved collared shirt covered a red tank tee. I pulled my hair back into a ponytail with a part on the far right held back by a black thin band with a red barrette controlling my bangs. I only carried my license, ER cash, lip gloss, pen and paper and cell phone inside my red bag.

I arrived first and there was 45 minute wait so I decide to walk over to the bar to see if I could sit there and wait. I smiled because the bar reminded me of that television sitcom where everyone knows your name. It looked historic and it smelled of cedar and a very flattering apple tobacco. It reminded me of my mom's uncle. There were only four set of deuces on either side of the bar. The bar was decorated with stain glass at the top of the bar where the glass hung. The bartender looked very common; I mean there was nothing remarkably noticeable about him. There weren't any distinguishing marks, nothing unusual about his hair, nothing odd about his clothes. He was just a very common looking man. I walked toward the end of the bar with my back to the wall so that I could see D'Kyra when she came in. The bartender came over asked if he could get me anything.

"Sure, how about an Apple Martini." He nodded as he took a few steps back before turning the opposite direction. I checked my cell to see if I had any calls or texts. Nothing! Not even from Dee. I began to worry. I didn't want to call Chaz and I really didn't want to kill Dee's buzz if she was having the time of her life right now, so I checked my email while waiting on my drink. I really didn't want to talk to anyone and I really didn't want to check my email so I just pretended to be texting someone so that I wouldn't have to look up and make eye contact.

My drink appeared alone with two coasters: one was under my drink and the other was wearing a phone number. (I pretended not to see the number.) I only looked in two directions: my cell and my drink. I never had an Apple Martini before. This is something that D'Kyra ordered once and I wanted to see what all the fuss was about. As I reached for the drink, I knew I was being watched so I gave them something to look at. I licked my lips seductively and lightly licked the glass where I was about to place my lips so that my lipstick wouldn't stick to the glass. (I read that somewhere.) My first sip was filled with green apple but the next one was filled with the martini. It was interesting and I must tell D'Kyra how much I enjoyed this. Just as I was about to put my cell in my purse, it vibrated. It was Dee. I sat my drink down and answered, "Hello?"

"Hey? Where are you?"

"I'm sitting at the bar of the restaurant being gawked at. Where are you?" I said without looking up, only looking at my drink.

"Getting ready to walk through the door." she said as she literally walked through the door. Our eyes met and it was all I could do to keep from running up to here saying, "Oh my God! Tell me EVERYTHING." Instead, I took out my pen and wrote on the coaster, NO THX. I left the bartender a five and took my drink and slowly walked out of the bar while the hostess called out 'Wilcox, party of 2? Wilcox, party of 2.'

I couldn't wait to give her that Oh My God hug. I was about to bust. We followed the server to our booth and I asked her for another martini while she ordered the same.

"Ok, like, Hi. My name is Kirsten and I will be your server. Like, I'll be right back with your drinks, okay?" said the Blonde Barbie Bombshell of a waitress. She was pretty and she really did look like a windup toy. I couldn't wait for her to walk away.

"So . . . ????" I was about to burst.

D'Kyra slapped the table, threw her head back, took a deep breath and said, "Girl, when that negro parted my thighs and went downtown . . . OH, MY GOD. Girl, I thought I was gon break a lamp."

For some reason, that caused me to cheer but I didn't want her to think that I was rejoicing in the fact that she committed adultery because I wasn't. To be honest, I really don't know why I cheered. I just wanted my girl happy and she wasn't until Tony.

Right after we finished dinner, we sat there for a while finishing our drinks trying to decide whether we should go to the movies or go shopping. I was a little buzzed, seeing that I am not much of a drinker. I got a call from Chaz.

"Hello."

"Hey." His voice sounded rushed as if he was preoccupied. "You still out with your girl?"

"Yeah, what's up?" I pointed to the phone indicating to Dee that I was talking to Chaz.

"Man, me and Bella got in an argument and I really need to talk to you about it." His voice was lowly and almost childlike. I gave Dee a look as though to say, 'Girl, you hear this?' While the server bought the check to us, I asked Chaz, "Can you hold on a minute and let me call you back?" We made sure we left the appropriate tip and scurried out of the restaurant. Once outside, I told her what was going on and we discussed our next move. We decided on the mall. She trailed me to the mall and while driving, I called Chaz and asked what was going on.

"I'm in the ER."

"OH my God, what happened?"

"She shot me."

"She did WHAT?" I wasn't sure if I had heard him correctly or if I was hearing him with Apple Martini ears. "You heard me, she shot me. **That bitch shot me**."

"Well, where are you? So I need to come? I got my girl with me, we can ride by."

"No. I'm going to my grandpa's from here. I gotta go. I will call you later, okay. Are you gone be out for a while?"

"I guess, I don't know. I am worried about you."

Chapter 7

The story with Chaz and Bella goes like this: He went home and confronted Bella about those pictures. He asked her if she was seeing someone. When she lied about it, he showed her all the photos and when Chaz asked who the man was that she was 'swapping spit with' she gave a false name. This only made the situation worse and Chaz became hotter than fish grease. Bella started screaming and saying that he didn't trust her and he told her that this was the reason why he didn't trust her. He also told her about the time he walked in on her having sex in their son's bedroom. Bella stood there with her mouth opened because she really didn't know what to say because she was busted.

"Yeah, that's right. You are busted and this is the same cat that is in this picture, isn't it?" Chaz said as he slapped the photos in his hands. "You have been lying to me all this time, Bella and if this is what you want, then you can get the fuck out right now."

Bella charged toward Chaz like a raging bull waving her arms wildly and stopped short of his face and screamed, "Me leave? If you want somebody to go somewhere then you should leave 'cause I'm not going anywhere."

Threats were made and names were called and it got totally out of hand but what I don't understand is that why she's not in jail for attempted murder if things happened the way he said it did. "You know what?" Chaz announced, "I think I will leave. I can't do this no more." He took the photos and tossed them in the air. As they fanned and cascaded down, one of the photos fell on Bella's face. This is all she needed to burst into a ball of explosives. The atmosphere became very hostile and dense. Chaz was unaware that the photos grazed her face and tried to walk past her toward the bedroom to pack. Suddenly and without warning, Chaz felt an ice wrenching chill of a pain coarse through his skull. He gasped as he turned around toward Bella. She struck him in the head with the base of a brass lamp that was sitting in the hall way. As he turned around, his reflects took on a mind of its own and ordered his hands to take her by the throat with one hand and with his other, he grabbed the wrist of the hand that housed the lamp. Chaz struggled with her to retrieve the lamp but once she released her grip from it, she pounced on him and landed her opened hand across his face. He quickly grabbed that armed by the wrist and penned her against the wall and barked, "You don't wanna make that mistake again." Both were breathing rather heavily as she tried to free from his vice grip. "Now, Bella, I'm going in the bedroom and packing a bag." He wanted to take a minute to make sure that once he released her, he didn't get sucker punched again.

Releasing her, he walked away toward the bedroom to pack his bag. "You son of a bitch!" she roared as she pounced again with another candle but this time landing on the top of his head. Chaz staggered forward falling short of hitting his head on the corner of the door frame. He was dazed as he reached around to hold the rapidly forming bulge on his head. He moaned as he tried to comfort his wound and gasped as he peered at his hand and saw the blood. "That's right, motherfucker! Now what?" She cheered as Chaz quickly tried to struggle to his feet, he could hear Bella behind him in the hall closet making screaming threats. He staggered to the bathroom to see that it was blood that was in his face not sweat. He was shocked to see that his vision was blurred as well. He opened the draw where the towels were kept, wet it with cold water and applied it to his head first then wiped his face. He never spoke. He was in awe he literally tasted blood forming in the roof of his mouth. He also took a couple of aspirin from the cabinet and cupped his hand under the water faucet to swallow the pills before turned the water off.

He grabbed a few changes of clothing and got a few personal items and shoved them in his bag. He heard Bella racing toward him from down the hall way. What happened next can only be described as a miracle. According to Chaz, it seemed to have happened in slow motion. Bella rounded the corner to enter the bedroom screaming and charging toward Chaz. He turned just in time to see her waving a gun and managed to move toward his right to fall between the wall and the bed as the gun went off. She dropped the gun and ran from the room without even checking to see if he was alright. Chaz was hit in left shoulder. He managed to get up and grab a shirt to put on the wound and took his bag and staggered out the door.

Once at the ER, he told them that he was cleaning his gun and it went off accidentally. And this is when he called me but he said that he didn't want to leave the kids without a mother so he was going to tell the hospital that it was an accident while **she** was cleaning the gun. (Mind you, he told hospital that **he** was cleaning the gun.) Well, whatever! Hell, she shot him and I really don't understand what was going on. I have always said that he didn't owe me an explanation for anything and I will always stick to that but I don't appreciate lying in any form. I have never lied to him I just haven't told him everything about me. Anyway, when he called back later that night, he said that he was staying with his mother for a while until he found an apartment.

Thankfully there was no need for surgery other than stitches because the bullet went straight through and landed inside the wall. I figured that if he lied to the police and the people at the hospital, then he's lying to me and this just ain't worth it. He is too exhausting. I can't exactly announce that I think he should leave Bella but if he goes back to her after this then either he was lying to me all alone or she's got him by the balls. I can't believe I even slept with this man in the first place. Maybe he was lying to me but I don't wanna stick around to find out. I can't call him anymore because I can't trust him and I know I won't be sleeping with him anymore. I don't know what I was thinking because the big dick just ain't worth it.

A few weeks had passed by and I really let my work slack at the studio. I didn't answer any of my emails or anything. One day I was on my way home from work and I got a text from D'Kyra:

"CNT TALK. NEED 2 C U. WHERE R U?"
"N THE CAR ON MY WAY HM. U OK?"
"NO. WANT ME 2 COME GET U"
"YEAH. @ DR. OFC ON HANCOCK."

I had the driver pick up D'Kyra. When we got there, she was sitting in the garden beside the hospital on the bench. It more like a sitting area with beautiful landscaping but in the middle of that beautiful garden was a beautiful lady who was sad. I immediately got out of the limo and ran over toward her. Our eyes met and I could see that she had been crying.

She ran to meet me and she broke down and nearly collapsed in my arms. Travis came from the driver's side to help her in the car. She was sobbing uncontrollably and I couldn't understand what she was saying. I took the throw from the seat and place it in my lap as a cushion for her head. She cried the whole 27 minutes to my home. I didn't interrupt her; I only rubbed her back and reassured her that I had her.

I reached in my bag and called Myra and asked if she would prepare something light for us and that we will be arriving shortly. When I place the phone back in my bag, I nervously rocked back and forth in the seat and noticed that D'Kyra's breathing was stable. I couldn't tell if she was sleeping or not and I didn't know what to say to her because she hadn't told me what the matter was and I didn't know how to fix it.

When we pulled up to the mansion, Travis opened the door on her side and asked if we needed anything else. "No. I don't think so." I answered as I looked at D'Kyra for approval. She shook her head with coyness. I put my arm around her and walked her in the front door. Myra met us and took our purses and put them upstairs saying, "Please, eat," pointing toward the kitchen. I smiled at her and mouthed "thank you."

Our slowly moving steps echo on the cold marble floor that made a rhythm as we walked toward the kitchen. I could smell the sweet aroma of the oil burners. She never spoke therefore I never asked until she was ready to tell me her story. I pulled her chair out and as she sat, she almost looked catatonic with tears streaming down. She clutched her stomach as she rocked back and forth sobbing silently. I walked over to the counter to pour two glasses of wine. I turned to walk back to the table and when I sat her glass down in front of her, she grabbed my hand and said, "I went to the doctor today."

Fearing the worst like cancer, I swallowed and nervously asked, "What's wrong?" My body either fainted or melted into the chair because I could no longer feel anything except empathy for D'Kyra. "Well" she said as she cleared her throat. She reached for the glass of wine

It shocked my head in disbelief as the "TONY" and "pregnant" part of her sentence left me dumbfounded. "Wait, Tony? How, I mean, what are you talking about? What about Stanley?" I asked. She took a couple of sips from her glass and said, "Girl, I can't tell Tony because even thought it was just that one time, I feel like I was just a booty call to him because he won't call me or answer any of my calls. Well, he did answer my call a few times but he always acts like he's too busy or he makes excuses as to why he can't talk.

"Dee, you know he's married. Maybe it's innocent. Maybe he's trying to make sure that his wife is taken care of you know, to throw her off. Maybe she got suspicious and he's trying to smooth things over. I don't think you were just a booty call. Not if he *went down* the first night." I reached over and got her wine and poured it into my glass, got up and gave her an apple juice. Without missing a beat, she announced, "Stanley hadn't touched me in **3 months**." I didn't have an answer for that one. "I don't know what to do." she added.

"Well, you'd better get Stanley drunk or something and get on top 'cause you done messed up. Why didn't you make Tony use protection, anyway?" I asked with a raised voice.

"Oh, I don't know and stop yelling at me. I feel bad enough." she cried out.

"Okay, I'm sorry." I said as I stood up and embraced her. Pulling back and cupping her face in my hands, I looked her square in the eyes and said, "Stanley not gon turn down no pussy. Men never do. Just get him to fuck you."

"How the hell and I suppose to do that, **he won't touch me**?" she cried. "All we do is argue. If I could get him to fuck me **then** I wouldn't have been with Tony in the **first** place."

"Ok. What's his favorite drink?" I asked.

Throwing her hands up, she asked, "What does that have to do with it anything, Khy?"

"Tell me, Dee. What's his favorite drink?"

"Sweet tea." she said quietly.

Getting up from my chair, I walked over to the medicine cabinet in the hall bathroom. "Come with me." I said.

She let out a hard heavy sigh and I could hear her following me. I opened the cabinet and reached for the sleeping pills. I popped the top and shook out three pills and handed them to D'Kyra then fastened the top. She stood there with a brand new look on her face staring at me while alternating her eyes between me and the pills in her hand. As I returned the bottle to the cabinet, I explained, "Take these 3 pills, crunch them up into a powder and put it in his drink. As soon as he gets drowsy, sweeten up to him. I know a few inches of him that won't fight."

"Have you done this to Harvey?"

Chuckling, I said, "Hell naw. You don't seem to understand something; HE AIN'T NEVER HOME FOR ME TO DO ANYTHING TO. Look, how about if I get Travis to take you home?"

"Sure."

"Call me when you get home. I really wanna know how things turn out. Is Stanley home now?"

Looking at her watch, "He probably will be when I get home."

"Then you know what to do."

Chapter 8

I had a dream:
I was in some sort of building that was submarine battleship gray. It may have been a ship because I had to step up and over something every time I went from one room to the other. Anyway, I wasn't alone. There were other women all around me and we all were dressed in the same house coat, night gown, slippers, everything. We all had just given birth within an hour's time frame. All the babies looked identical; all the boys were in blue and girls were in pink. They wore the identical outfit, hat, long sleeved onesies and socks.

My baby girl, only hours old, mind you and was able to sit up, nod and shake her head when I would talk to her. I had to leave her but was afraid to because all the other babies either were stillborn, died right after birth or were stolen and missing. I hadn't' named her yet so I told her to sit still and not move and that I would be back for her. She nodded, closed her eyes pretending to be asleep and I covered her.

While looking for whatever it was I was looking for, I found an infant boy. I took him with me. He kept trying to nurse but I refused him.

When I got back, there was a woman there in the room frantically searching for something that I couldn't quite figure out yet. I was afraid that she would find my baby so I decided that I needed to give her the baby boy that I had and yelled, 'STOP!' "What are you looking for?" She never answered me. Soon, she was looking at the spot where my baby girl was and I yelled out to distract her. "Here!" I handed the baby boy. She jerked to a halt and looked at me with angry eyes. I opened the draws looking for anything to give her. The first drawer I open had baby bags inside. I took one out and unzipped it and slammed it on top of the counter. I took a quick glance over to where my baby was hidden. "Oh, please! God, don't let her find my baby." I prayed to myself. The next drawer had cloth and disposable diapers. Then I grabbed the bag and walked past her and I opened the drawer beside her. There were two dead babies inside. I pretended not to notice as I pushed the drawer shut and opened the drawer underneath it. I grabbed a pacifier, tee shirts, blankets and socks. I rammed all those things inside the bag and quickly moved to the next station where my baby was hidden. I swallowed so hard that my chest burned. I opened the drawer and took out bottles and formula, shoved it in the bag and as I twisted around to present the bag to her, she snatched it out of my hands and walked out with the baby boy I gave her with not so much as a thank you. Then I woke up.

It was on a Thursday morning when D'Kyra called and told me that the plan worked. I was still in the bed watching TV and it was a little chilly so I turned the blanket up. "Just in case," he said, "It didn't work with the tea, I mixed it with the small container of sugar that I sat to the side. I not only put it in his tea but I sprinkled it in the sweet potatoes. I fixed Salisbury steak, green beans with cornbread and you know I love cornbread with sugar. The kids wanted pizza which was even better so I ordered one for them."

"How did it go?" I asked

"Well, right at the table he started yawning? How potent were they anyway?"

"Umm, 800 m. each. It's good you put it in the sugar, right."

"I know huh?" We both laughed. "I started on top then after he reached his climax; he rolled over and got on top of me. Girl, I have 2 multiples."

"How far along are you anyway?"

"Only a few weeks." she said.

"Hell, his ass will not know the difference." I said.

"I know. Thanks so much for all your help."

"You my girl. You know I told you I had your back.

"But Dee, how are you going to fix this? What are you going to tell Stanley about being pregnant?"

"I figure I'll tell him in a few days but first I need to get him to have sex with me again."

"Good idea. What are you doing today? Wanna go shopping? I'm done with my sessions and I think I'll take a few days off. Let's go somewhere."

"Okay, I'll call you later on." Hanging up, I realize that I haven't heard from Chaz so I decided to call him; after a late breakfast. D'Kyra's news caused me to build up an appetite so I called downstairs and asked Eva for 2 pecan pancakes with extra butter with warmed syrup, 2 scrambled, hash browns and turkey sausage, hot peach tea and water.

I sank back into the 4 pillows and hid playfully underneath the heated blanket and the bright green comforter. Someone truly named this right because it comforted me completely. The night before I didn't even tie my hair up so it needed brushing. I ripped out of bed long enough to brush my hair while using the bathroom. Then I grabbed the mouthwash and rinsed my mouth out and ran back to the bed. I kept baby wipes by the bed on the night stand and got one to wash my face and threw it in the trash when done. I wore my pink pajamas and an uncontrollable grin of satisfaction on my face because I helped my girl and she was ultimately happy. I just wasn't ready to get up from the comfort of my comfortable comforter just yet. I needed to but I wanted breakfast in bed. I rather enjoy the basking.

I must have dozed off because the next thing I knew; there was a knock at the door. I don't know who long the knocker knocked but I only heard 2 separate knocks. Clearing my throat with a stiff sigh, I scrambled to the top of the blankets and yelled out. "Come in." The door opened slowly. Myra and Eva usually opens with a polite barge but this time she was taking her time. I shifted my leg under the covers which caused the remote to fall off the bed. When I leaned over to pick it up, I said without looking up, "I think I'll have my breakfast in bed today."

I felt a presence over me which was neither Myra nor Eva and when I looked up, I was shocked to see that it was Harvey. The first thing I thought of was him in those pictures with Bella, but I was happy to see him. Harvey was standing with my breakfast on a cherry wood tray accompanied with a rose and a gift box. He looked so handsome with his black pinstriped suit and I had forgotten how bright his smile was. For a split second, I lost myself in his eyes. "Good morning, Khylee." He said as he sat the breakfast on the bed across my lap. His voice was so gentle, so sultry that I'm thinking and wondering what his angle was. I was extremely baffled what with the roses and gift. I wanted to act surprisingly shocked and not suspicious. "Hey, Harvey. When did you get home?" Sitting on the bed next to me, he said, "I just got here. I wanted to surprise you so I asked Trey to bring me home and told the house to keep it a secret."

"Well, I am surprised." I tapped his leg and said, "Get comfortable. How long will you be home this time?"

"I was thinking about a few weeks." Harvey said as he stood up to take off his jacket and he loosened his tie while walking toward the walk in closet. Why would he go in my closet? We've never shared a bathroom much less a bedroom. There's nothing in there for him to get comfortable in. When I told him to get comfortable, I meant for him to go to his room so that I could call Chaz, but now I can't. I really wanted to see how his wound was doing. If he calls me, I can't talk to him, especially if he is in my room. DAM! When I want him to be here, he finds excuses and things more important. Now, he's in my arm pit.

I took a sip of tea then reached for the gift box. I shook it. It rattled. "Diamond, no wait, pearls." I opened the box and pushed away the tissue inside. It was both, a diamond and pearl tennis bracelet. The clasp was in the shape of a butterfly. It was a beautiful. It also must have being a guilty gift. What was his angle? Harvey went out of the room and down the hall and returned with his overnight duffle bag. "Oh, Hell naw." I said to myself. I would have given anything for this to happen a while ago but now? Why now? He went in the bathroom and showered. I almost lost my appetite but what the hell. It was a quick shower. He returned and playfully sat next to me. Since the breakfast was kept warm with a hotplate. Harvey reminded me to be careful. I noticed that he only wore a tee shirt and pajamas bottoms. I slide over while he decided to get under the covers next to me. "The bracelet is so pretty. I love it. Thank you. "I said. I'm not use to Harvey being this close to me or even in the same bed for that matter; after all, he is having an affair with Bella. He had no idea I knew and since he doesn't know about Chaz, I really needed to play this cool.

His gentleness disturbed me. Should I be alarmed? Should I shun him? Should I play along? Maybe Bella told him about the argument and the attempted murder she had with Chaz. Maybe, since I haven't heard from Chaz, he talked to Harvey. I can't call him so I will never know at least not with Harvey's in my ass.

Harvey wanted to feed me breakfast. I let him, as nervous as I am. What if he was trying to poison me? "Why don't you help me eat it?" I asked. For moment he hesitated but them he took the knife. He picked up one of the two forks and cut the pancakes and licked his lips and opened his mouth. As he places the fork in his mouth, he closed his eyes and moaned as if it was the best thing he had ever tasted. I must admit, it was turning me on but I had to wonder: did he do the same to Bella? Why was he trying to be so nice now? I figured that I needed to leave well enough alone. I didn't know what to say to him. I had questions but I just didn't know what to say to him.

As we finished our late breakfast and Harvey sat the tray on the floor beside the bed. It's amazing how things work out. When you pray for something for so long and it doesn't happen, you tend to stop believing. But when it happens, when your prayers are finally answered, you don't know whether to believe it or if it's a dream or if it's a trick of the enemy. All I have ever wanted was for Harvey to love me and for us to be in love like I've seen in the movies. I wanted the attention and affection of Chaz to be in Harvey. Now that he invited himself in my bed, I didn't want to push him away but I couldn't help but wonder: will be we a family now?

I reached for the remote and surfed through the channels. Harvey adjusted himself in the bed and laid his head on my chest and put his arm around me. We laid there for a while in silence. The next thing I remember, it was late afternoon and the phone rang. Harvey was asleep and I reached over to get my cell phone from the night stand. It was D'Kyra.

"Hey, girl". I answered.

"You still wanna go shopping?" she asked.

"Yeah." I answered and I gently moved Harvey's arm and sat on the side of the bed. "Can you go?"

"Yeah. I got the kids taken care of. They're with the nanny. Can't wait to see you, I have so much to tell you."

"Okay, as soon as I get dressed, I'll have Travis to take us." As I closed the flap on the phone, I got up and walked to the bathroom to turn on the shower. Then I went back to the tray to get the gift box. I pretended Harvey wasn't even there. I needed to get out of there because I really wanted to know what was going on with Chaz. He hadn't called or texted. I wondered if he was still alive.

When we got to D'Kyra's house, it started to rain. Travis drove up the cobblestone driveway and parked beside the stone pillars next to her wrap porch. Her mansion was beautiful. The landscape was so immaculate that it looked like a page from a magazine. She had a fountain in the middle of the circled driveway. It was shaped like an old house with all the trimmings. There were two fireplaces and each porch had a wrap porch and two balconies. It was very beautiful.

Travis got out of the car with an umbrella and walked over to my side of the car. He opened the car door and offered his hand to escort me out of the car. "Thanks. Do you mind sitting until she's ready?"

"No. I'll be right here." Travis is very loyal. He doesn't have any family to speak of. He only had us. He didn't bother to tell, I didn't bother to ask. Travis wasn't a tall man, as a matter of fact; I was a bit taller than he with my heels. I'm not even sure what his nationality is because for a while I thought he was biracial but now I'm not so sure. But regardless, it doesn't matter because I consider him family. He's part of the family that doesn't speak much and whenever he does, his voice is quiet but deep and he's very mild mannered. Travis's eyes are big, around hazel eyes with long dark thick lashes that I envied. His hair is very dark, thick and wavy and he keeps it in a pony tail. He's always clean shaven with a mustache trimmed thin to outline his full top lips. He was quite handsome.

Travis walked me to the door and he handed me the umbrella as I ran the bell. I could hear the click of the door being unlocked rather worn and tattered. Ms Connie was at the door. She was a rather dark older black woman that looked hunched. She announced me as she waved us in while walking backward.

"Hey, Miss Connie. How are you?" I asked. Travis turned to walk away. She called out to him in her familiar raspy voice as I walked inside, "Mr. Travis, would you like to come in for some coffee on this rainy afternoon?"

"No, ma'am. Thank you." he said quietly and turned and walked away. As Miss Connie closed the door behind us, she put her hands up to her mouth and snickered saying, "I do believe that's a record."

"What's that, Miss Connie?" I asked.

"He actually said 5 words to me." she said as she nonverbally asked for my coat by taking it off for me. She took both the coat and the umbrella and put them in the closet next to the door. "Miss Connie, you're so funny." I said.

I heard D'Kyra's call from the intercom saying, "Miss Connie?" She scurried to the nearest intercom, "Yes ma'am?" Miss Connie answered.

"Is that Mrs. Wilcox?" D'Kyra asked. I tipped over to Miss Connie and put my index finger over my lips indicating for her not to make a sound. I pushed the call button and answered in an old ladies voice, "Yeah 'sum. She right here. Look a bit po'lee though. Reckon she need some nourishment?" It was all Miss Connie could do to keep from laughing aloud.

"Very funny, Khy." D'Kyra said as she turned off the intercom. "Go on up." Miss Connie said.

* * *

When you first enter her home, the first thing you would see was marble on the floor. The staircase is in the middle of the house with tan carpet in the steps. At the base of the staircase on either side are trees that are planted inside the marble and are as tall as the building itself. My eyes immediately traveled up to the top landing of the stairs. There facing me was a rather large family photograph of the MacAfees. When I got to the top of the steps, I called out, "Dee?" I looked at the photo again. It wasn't a photo at all but a painting. It was a stunning oil painting that was so lifelike that the eyes seemed to follow you. I saw no one but heard children playing. I followed the sound. It was coming from the left. I heard toddler feet that appear to grow in sound. A beautiful little girl came running past me giggling completely nude except for the fact that her right foot was adorned with a blue sock with ruffles. Gaining behind her was the nanny. She was a little person, literally, who Dee says work miracles with the children even though the children thought that Faye was a little girl because of her height. Faye paused in front of me long enough to curtsy and muttered a greeting being careful not to lose sight of Zuaenette.

"Zuaenette! You betta do what Faye tells you, you hear me, girl?" Dee calls out. I followed the voice while Zuaenette answered, "Okay, Mommy Lady!!" It caused me to turn around and clinched my chest. "Oh! She sounds so sweet!" I told Dee. I really wish I could have children. "*Hey, Mommy Lady*!" I mocked as I walked into her suite. It was gorgeous. It really did look like something from a magazine. The ceiling fan was the first thing that caught my attention. She had a vaulted ceiling and the walls were a soft bluish green with painted designs around the top edges. The décor in the bedroom was purple and gold and everything matched perfectly. The floor was chestnut brown mahogany. I've seen that color in a magazine and thought it to be so remarkable that it left such an impression on me. There was a chaise lounge in the southeast corner of the bedroom and next to it was a purple and gold vanity that looked like it belonged in the movies because of the lights. It was very nice. Her walk in closet seemed to have a mind of its own. It was very similar to mine except for the color. The floor in the bathroom heated, just like mine and her tub was a Jacuzzi just like mine, too.

D'Kyra came from the closet with only a robe on with her hair pulled back. "Whew! Girl, Zuae is three and I have been trying to keep her from calling me this Mommy Lady person but she thinks it's funny," she said as she walked over to greet me with a friendly hug. "I think it's cute." I added as I laughed. 'So, what are you wearing?

"I was thinking about this." Dee said as she walked over the hanger that was on the back of the closet floor. It was a pair of wide legged jeans and a blue sweater. She looked at what I was wearing and we always tried to coordinate. We both wore jeans but instead of blue sweater, I wore a red one. Our shoes and purses matched our tops.

"Girl, check this out." I announced as I extended my right arm. She walked slowly towards me with her mouth open, "Shut Up! That is gorgeous. You betta wear the stink out that bracelet, too." D'Kyra screamed. "Please tell me it's from Harvey and not Chaz."

"It's from Harvey alright and get this: he came in this morning. Trey picked him up from the airport. I didn't know he was coming home. He brought me a late breakfast in bed." I said with a frown.

"Okay, you must have got some." D'Kyra said, pulling her sweater over her head.

"No, I pretended he wasn't there. He fed me, though."

"Oh, so an invisible man fed you breakfast in bed."

"Girl, what was I suppose to do." I followed her to her vanity and sat next to her on the chaise while she applied lip gloss and finished her hair. "Nothing happened anyway, I am still mad about those pictures. He didn't know I know about Bella. I wanted to beat the brakes off him but that would have been hypocritical. So, he put his head on my chest and went to sleep while I surf the channels until you called me a few hours ago."

"What do you think he's up to?" D'Kyra asked, walking over to put her shoes on.

Shaking my head, "I don't know. He was still sleep in *my* bed when I left, like he Goldilocks or somebody."

"You didn't leave anything incriminating behind, did you?"

"No. I ain't stupid enough to get caught like he is."

Just as we were ready to go, Simone' walked up to D'Kyra. "Please make sure that you take the list off the refrigerator and go to the market. Go to the one where you have to put the quarter in the basket because you can get better fruit there. Oh and don't forget to make Deuce check under his bed and he needs to clean out his closet. Don't baby him."

(*"Veuillez s'assurer que vous prenez la liste outre du réfrigérateur et aller au marché. Aller à celui où vous devez mettre le quart dans le panier parce que vous pouvez y arriver un meilleur fruit. Oh et n'oublient pas de faire le contrôle de deux sous son lit et il doit nettoyer son cabinet. Ne font pas le bébé il.")*

"Oui Mme MacAfee." said Simone'. Simone' Syrai' walked like she was sneaking up on people. She looked to be in her mid fifties but looks can be deceiving, after all she was from Milan. She wore her brown hair in a short bob tapered around her ears. Her eyes were big and just as brown as her hair and her lips were full and pouting with the corners turning up on sides. There was a small cleft in her chin. Her nose was gracefully small and round. Simone' mannerism was humble and relaxed. She walked off down the hall and I followed D'Kyra downstairs.

"You really have this house running like a well oiled machine. How do you do this with children?" I was dumbfounded.

"Trust. I couldn't do it without the help. Simone' was recently widowed and she moved here just a few months ago after her husband Dennis died of cancer. They were married for a really long time." Miss Connie met us at the door with umbrellas and our raincoats. The rain had let up a little. Travis met us at the porch to take my umbrella to shield me from the rain. "Afternoon, Mrs. MacAfee." He greeted D'Kyra. "Hey. How're you doing?" she answered. We adjusted ourselves in the limo and as Travis opened the sliding window and asked, "Where to, ma'am?"

"Ah," looking at the clock inside the limo. It was 2:46 p. m. and looking at D'Kyra for approval, I said, "ReCreations?" She nodded. "Then Recreations it is, Ma'am." Travis answered.

I really wanted to finish our conversation about our house whole employees. "What about Faye? What's her story?" I asked.

"Oh, that is very interesting." she started. "Faye is from Great Britain. All of her children are grown and on their own and after her husband died, she always wanted to come to the U.S. so here she is. Her children are very successful. Her son, Barnard, is a Chef on that cooking show. You know the one, COOKING With BARNARD. Have you seen it?"

"No. I don't think so."

"Well, anyway, her daughter, Penny is very successful, too. She has her own design firm. She lives in L.A. with celebrity clientele like me." She said as she patted her chest and cocked her head to the side and flashed a huge smile. "So that leaves Pierre and Ms Connie. Pierre is very special to us. He's never been married and has no children of which he's certain. He's such a snappy dresser when he's not on duty. I know this because instead of him calling, he comes by on his days off to see if we need anything before he goes places. His shirts are rather tight, like spandex and the other day, I could have sworn I saw mascara on him. I think he's gay."

"Dee, why you say that?" I laughed.

"Cause. I ain't never seen him with a woman."

"So?"

"I know my gaydar. So, how about you. What's going on with your house?"

"Wait, first. Have you told Stanley you were pregnant?" I asked, reaching in the refrigerator for two waters. As I handed one to Dee, she shook her head and waved her hand with a frown, saying, "No thanks, and I did tell Stanley. He's excited."

"How are you going to do this?" I asked while returning the one bottle of water.

"Very carefully. Now, tell me about this Myra you keep talking about."

"Myra and Eva are sisters and they came from Cuba. I wasn't really crazy about the idea of hiring sisters or family for that matter thinking if one wanted off then the other would, too but they are live ins. They all live with me except for Travis. He said that he'd rather have his own place and it's in the apartments down the street."

"So, is handsome married?" D'Kyra asked as she pointed toward Travis.

"I don't think so. I really don't know too much about him. Don't worry; I did an extensive background check on everyone, especially if they are going to be living in my home. I hope you did, too. Especially since you got kids, you can't be too careful. You do have nanny cams, right?" I asked as I drank water.

"Oh, Hell yes. Those are my nine months. She better not hurt my kids. She's only 2 ft 2 and won't take much to bury her in the ground." I nearly spit water as I laughed at Dee. It was so wrong but it was funny but she didn't crack a smile. She only flashed those brown eyes.

"So what do you think I should do about Harvey?" I asked.

"I say ride it out. Have you talked to Chaz?"

"No. What about you, have you talked to Tony?"

"No."

"I really want to talk to him. I am really trying not to think about him but it's so hard. I am not in love with Harvey anymore and I can't get Chaz out of my system. Should I call him? I mean, part of me really wants to see him and the other part of me wants to break it off. I mean, we can't sneak around for the rest of our lives."

"Ok, when was the last time you talked to him?" she asked.

"I think it was around the time that he told me that Bella shot him."

"So that was about two weeks ago, right?"

"I think so. What the hell is wrong with me? Why can't I get this man out of my head? I just wanted Harvey to pay attention to me and treated me like he loves me. I've never told anyone else this, at least not the whole story but Harvey and I never consummated our marriage."

"How long have you two been married, Khy?"

"Thirteen years." She looks at me all why pointing and snapping her fingers toward the fridge. "I think I'll take that water now."

"Sure." I said. "You okay?" I asked. Reaching in the fridge, I got the bottled water for D'Kyra, opened it and handed it to her. She closed her eyes, took a deep breath and turned the bottle up to her mouth so that the bottom was literally up facing the roof of the car. She took three hard, loud gulps and as I handed her the top, she looked at me and asked, "You're kidding, right? Please tell me you're joking?!" I took a few sips of water from my own bottle and turned toward the window to look out to see where we were. Our exit was coming up and with a heavy sigh; I realized that it was a great mistake in telling her what was going on. If she freaked out on that little bit of information, what would she think if I had told her the truth, the whole truth, and nothing but the truth. I couldn't even look at her anymore. I felt really weird. I felt ashamed. I felt even guilty. I was a little angry with her because I felt that she was judging me. I wonder if she felt that I was judging her when she told me that she was pregnant by Tony.

The rain had stopped and the sun came out. It was a little cool outside so I decided to keep my coat on. Travis pulled up to the front of the mall and walked over my side and opened the door. I left my water in the beverage holder. D'Kyra left her water standing on the floor. "Travis, park the car somewhere and just hang out or do whatever it is that you do, okay?" He smiled at me and said, "Yes ma'am." As we walked in the entrance, I pulled out my cell and called Hannah to see if she could fit us in for a facial.

"Well, I just arrived at the mall. I came for a little shopping but also in hopes that you can fit me and my girl in for a facial and possibly lashes?" Hannah put me on hold for a short minute and then said that she would call me when she's ready so that I wouldn't have to wait especially since I will still be in the mall.

After hanging up from Hannah, D'Kyra says, "Look. I hope I didn't sound insensitive back there. I just can't believe that after thirteen years of marriage you and Harvey have never had sex. What happened?"

"I thought I was ready to talk about this but I can't. This has nothing to do with what happened in the limo. I just can't. I've never talked about it with anyone. I've never even talked to Harvey about it."

"Wait. OH MY GOD! You're a man?"

"D'Kyra MacAfee, You really have an over active vivid imagination. I was born a female, okay? I just can't tell you right now."

* * *

One of my favorite stores is Sugah's. Dee has never been there before and I thought it would be really cool to take her there. I've been there so many times; I should own stock in the company. Sugah's is a small boutique that has oils as far as the eye can see. Whatever oil you like, they can make it into a lotion, body butter, perfume, air freshener, linen spray, bubble bath, shower gel, you name it. They also have hair care products. I love this store. The people are so nice there that we are on first name bases and I tell everyone about them. My favorite fragrance is *Superior*. The scent is a fresh clean smell with a hint of musk. I introduced D'Kyra to Sugah's and she fell in love with the place. One other fragrance there I like is called *Dew on My Lily* which is a little more potent with a fruity smell. Time passed by rather quickly while inside that store. The atmosphere is so pleasant and the people are so friendly that I never mind waiting. Then we ventured to my favorite shoe store called **IF THE SHOE FITS**. I love this place because it's the only place where I can find shoes the fit like they were tailor made for me. Next, we went to the lingerie store called **THE PASSION FRUIT**. It was so much fun shopping together even though I would never get to wear it for Harvey and by D'Kyra being pregnant, her window of opportunity will be closing soon. I mostly purchased things like bras and panties or the gown with matching robe. Never anything else because I slept alone. D'Kyra on the other hand had a rather different situation. While walking out of the store, wouldn't you know it D'Kyra spotted someone? Her whole demeanor changed from playful and giggles to stutter and awkwardness. She saw him before he saw her so she pulled me into the bookstore, the same book store that I met Marie Walton.

"Honey, what's wrong with you." I asked.

"It's Tony." she said as she made sure that her back was to the door.

"Where????" I asked.

"SHHHHH! I don't want him to hear you." She said as she panicked. I took her by the shoulders and gave a short quick jerk and said, "You don't have anything to be ashamed of. If anybody needs to be ducking and diving it should be him. Don't let him reduce you to this. Now point him out to me."

D'Kyra took a deep breath and slowly turned and pointed out this beanie headed sawed off shotgun looking bastard to me. He was dark, bald and looked to be about 190-200 lbs. He was fit and trimmed but totally hugged up with this woman who looked like she didn't miss no meals. She had what could only be described as coochie fat. She looked like she needed a front end alignment.

"Dee, are you sure that's him? Are we looking at the same person? That man over there with that woman who looks like she ate Joanie Craig? The man over their picking up those blue shoes?" I asked in disbelief.

She looked up and frowned as she nodded. "Yeah. That's him." It's amazing how I can give other people advice and can help them take charge of their lives but couldn't do shit about my own.

"C'mon. He needs to see you see him." I took her by the hand and walked across the floor to the shoe store. I accidentally purposely bumped into him while seeing but not seeing him. He looked up and saw her face. I distracted his *whatever* she was to him and started talking about how much I loved her shirt (NOT!) and told her how much I thought it complimented her complexion (when in all actuality her face looked like a gravel road.) I was really beginning to get pissed at what he had done to Dee. I couldn't believe it. I talked to this person as long as I could until D'Kyra came up to me and said that she was ready to go. I didn't even say goodbye to this person, I just walked away behind D'Kyra and followed her. She soon sat down at the Food Court and just sat there for a moment without speaking. I had to say something to make her feel better. I can't let this son of a bitch take my girl through this and reduce her to sobbing flesh.

"You had at least 3 good minutes. Five tops for him to explain to you why he hadn't returned your calls. What did he say?" I asked.

"He said that his wife's mother is in the hospital and he said that all they could do was to make her comfortable. He said that she is an only child and feels that he really needed to be there for her right now."

"Did you at least tell him that you were pregnant?" I asked.

"Yes I did. Right before I told you that I was ready to go." She said slowly and softly. Just then I got a text from Hannah saying that she was ready for us.

"Fuck him. Let's go." I said.

"Where are we going now?"

"Let's get facials." We went upstairs to Hannah's and they sat us in chairs side by side. We got facials and lashes. It was really fun. They had juice and cookies for us as well. Every few minutes I would ask if she was okay. Soon she got tired of that.

I don't know what the big deal was about me not being able to tell her about my wedding night. I guess I didn't want to appear weak or like I was stupid for staying with a man who obviously treated me like I wasn't alive but willfully has affairs with ironically the wife of the man I'm sleeping with. Hell, you can't make this stuff up. I can't believe my life was so screwed up.

Afterwards, D'Kyra really needed to change the subject apparently because she only wanted to talk about me. I called Travis and asked if he would meet us at the Food Court and get our bags and put them the trunk.

We decided on Chinese and sat down to eat while waiting for Travis. "Tell me something?" she asked. "Tell me why you and Harvey never ever sleep together." I picked up the chop sticks, took them from the paper envelope and broke them apart. I twirled my noodles onto the chop sticks and ate them. I figured there was no way to be evasive. I took a few swallows of my soda and I had to tell someone. I couldn't keep it to myself any longer or I would go nuts. "I have to believe that Harvey really did love me once because I know I loved him." I started. "Our wedding was better than a fairy tale. He rented a mansion in Louisiana for a week that looked like a castle. Everyone stayed there, all our friends and families. It was beautiful. After the reception, Harvey had a carriage ride waiting for us. He'd thought of everything. It was so romantic. Anyway, I don't know where those guys came from. I think it was three of them. It was during Mardi Gras and people were dancing, screaming and their was music playing so loud that no one heard me scream because one of them shot the driver in the head point blank and two of them held Harvey at gun point and made him watch while they each took a turn with me. I was saving myself for my wedding night."

D'Kyra took a napkin to wipe away her tears. I thought that I would react differently but all I feel now is numbness. I'm not angry anymore for myself because it's too late but I can take that anger and channel it toward D'Kyra's Tony. I don't wanna hear advice about my life right now. But what I don't understand is why did God allow something like this to happen to a girl who was a virgin? I saved myself for my husband. My parents are Pentecostal ministers and I obeyed them by doing the right thing and this is how God rewards my good behavior? I wanted a healthy sexual relationship with my husband not this roommate relationship that we have now. Sometimes, I wish I had died that night.

Travis walked over and gathered the bags. "Are you ready to go?" I asked D'Kyra.

"Yeah, I need to get ready for church tomorrow. Are you going?" she asked.

"No, but I really had fun today, regardless."

Tony Watkins is married to Salome. She just happened to walk into MacAfee and Steel. Dee's saw a picture of Salome once from Tony's wallet. Salome was finishing up paperwork and Dee just happened to be the broker to process all the paperwork. Salome is an only child and her mom is terminally ill. Tony's excuse for not returning any of D'Kyra's calls was because of his mother-in-law. That may be true but I think he was using that as a crutch so he played on it. He also told D'Kyra that he was not having sex with Salome but when she walked into her office, Salome was either pregnant or she need a strong soda to pass gas. She looked very much pregnant.

Chapter 9

It was about 8 p.m. when I got D'Kyra home. It had been dark for a while and I asked Travis if he would drive the long way home. I just wanted to enjoy some down time. I was really worried about what I had told D'Kyra and also wondered what was happening to Chaz. I also wondered if Harvey was still in my bedroom. I reached down in my bag to retrieve my compact. I opened it with a deep sigh and looked at the expression on my face. "Ump! I don't have 'fool' written on my forehead. So why do I feel like one." I said. As I closed the compact and returned it to my bag and saw that my cell was flashing. It read "3 missed calls". I quickly took it out and opened the flap. I had 3 missed calls from Chaz. "Ah, snap." I said. I was hotter than fish grease. When did he call? Why didn't I hear the phone? I should have worn my Bluetooth but I didn't want to look insensitive to D'Kyra's company today. I tried to see when it was that he had called. It read: 5:56 p.m., 6:02 p.m. and 6:08 p.m., which was about the time I was sitting at the Food Court with Dee spilling my guts. I can't very well call him now because he's home with his family. See, that prime example: *the one you want you can't have and the one you got, don't want you.* I knew what I couldn't call him especially on a Saturday night because he was with his family and I didn't want to get him into trouble. Well, at least I knew that he called. I took out my cell once more to see if he had left a voice mail. He hadn't but he did, however, leave me a text message that read:

"JZ WANTED 2 LET U KNW M THKN OF U. MS U. GIMME HUG. DNT RESPOND"

I saved that message and locked it so that Harvey couldn't get it. I read it over and over again and each time made me want to cry more and more. I really hoped that I could see him but I know what was going on with him, I mean did he or didn't he leave Bella? Maybe this is why Harvey was acting so clingy towards me.

"Mrs. Wilcox?" Travis addressed me over the speaker.

"Yes?" I answered.

"We have another 4 or 5 blocks before we come to your street. Should I take another route?" He politely asked.

"No." I said softly. My eyes lifted to see if he was looking at me. BINGO! He was. I quickly snatched my head toward the window and waited to be dropped off like I was an unwanted puppy. I gathered my things together and waited for Travis to open the door. He pulled up to the front door and parked. Travis turned off the car, opened the trunk, unfastened his seat belt and opened his door. He walked over and opened my door and helped me out. As I walked over to the door, I looked over my shoulder to see if he was okay with my bags but he had already closed the trunk and was only steps behind me. "Travis, do you mind bringing all those packages upstairs for me and setting them in the closet for me?" I asked. "Yes ma'am." Eva met me at the door with a hysterical grin and a rehearsed broken English greeting, "How you do this night, Mrs. Well Cox?" She waved her arms like a game show model like she was mastering a great accomplishment. She straightened her hair several times and tidied her uniform as if she pretended that the palms of her hands were irons. "Thank you very much, Eva." I said to her. I was very impressed that she wanted to impress me enough by trying to learn as much English as possible. "Food ready please?" She asked as she pointed toward the dining room. "Yes, please, thank you." I answered. She walked away with her head held high and her shoulders back walking with pride. It was a bit funny to me but in a cute funny way.

Travis followed me upstairs with the bags from my shopping spree. As I walked through the bedroom door, I was scanning the room for the latest Harvey sightings but it looked like he was long gone. I walked over to the chaise and sat down. I pointed to the closet saying, "Just sit them on the floor in there. I'll get them later." I took my shoes off and flexed my feet and yarned. Travis walked over to the door to leave but before he walked out, he turned and gave me the most disturbing look as if waiting for me to give him permission to speak. "Travis, you okay?" I asked. "Well" he said as he walked toward me. "I know that this may not be my business but . . . ." He took a deep sigh saying, "Okay, look. I've seen the way Mr. Wilcox treats you and I don't like it is all. I just don't think it's right. There, I said it and I hope I still got a job in the next three seconds 'cause I sure do like working here but I just wanted to say that. It's not like the whole house don't see this." He walked a bit closer to me and lowered his voice, "If you don't mind me saying so, the whole mansion is talking about it. Even the ones who don't speak that much English know." He walked backward nodding until he reached the door. He then turned and walked away.

I sat there for a moment wondered if this is what the house was saying and thinking. I was enlightened and humiliated and upset all at the same time. I felt a bit unnerving knowing that the house was discussing me and Harvey.

* * *

Let's see, the highlights of my life thus far are: the reason my billionaire husband don't wanna touch me is because he couldn't protect me after the attack that happened on our wedding day and that's how I lose my virginity. MY HUSBAND is having an affair with the woman who is married to the man that I've been sleeping with and now my husband is being all up under my armpit. Oh, did I forget to mention that I cannot have children because of the attack? I also take antidepressants but double it at night so that I can sleep. WOW!!!!! Gee!!!! Anyway, I thank God for my friends.

Harvey had gone but I'm not quite sure where he went. He may very well be down the hall and I wouldn't even know it. I realized I had sat there on the chaise lounge for a while daydreaming. I think I may have even blacked out and lost track of time. I took a deep breath and stood up but my purse fell from my lap and overturned. Most of the items were right there but my lip gloss rolled under the bed. Aggravated, I threw my purse on the bed and kneeled down to look under the bed. The gloss had rolled very far under there and the second thing I saw was a medicine bottle. When I retrieved the bottle, there was nothing on it. It was in one of those tented pharmacy medicine bottles complete with the white child proof cap. I grabbed my gloss and reached up to put it in my purse. I sat on the bed, turned on the lamp from the night stand and held the bottle up to the light. They were round and medium size pills. I shook the bottle and squinted my eyes trying to see if I could read what was on them. I mean, I knew they weren't mine and the only other person that was in here was Harvey! I gasped. I froze. I opened the bottle of pills. I poured a few in my hand and I looked for something, anything on the pill to identify it. I took a pencil and pad from the drawer and wrote down as much of the information that was on it. *Zal 4* was printed on each pill in black. I then put the pills back in the bottle, fastened the cap and put them on the bed. I got my lap top and the bed table and sat on the bed trying to see what I could find.

I tried looking online for information on *Zal 4* and *Zalnoprotrexone* came up. The first few sites weren't very helpful and were a bit boring until I saw something about its use being for pain caused by AIDS/HIV and most cancers but that was on the Wilcox Pharmaceuticals website which means it may not be released to the public. It may still be in its experimental stage and that would explain the fact that it wasn't from any doctor. However, it wasn't used for pain. Zal 4 relieves constipation caused by pain medication. So not only is he in pain, he is constipated. My mind wondered. Okay, I had to wrap my head around this before I went any further because the more I read, the more afraid I became. Harvey was the only person in my room. It *had* to be his. He was the only person that it could belong to. Even thought the house keeper was in my room making the beds, cleaning and what not, in all the years they have been here, they never drop anything so important. It had to be Harvey.

My feelings roamed and I didn't know what to say. I didn't know what to think. This man as put me through so many changes that I don't know whether to hate him for not telling me that he was sick or hate him for being sick. Harvey! Are there anymore announcements?

I started to call Dee to see if she could shed some light on this for me but I didn't want to tell her anything until I knew the whole story, so I buried my face in the laptop. I researched everything I could about this experimental drug on www.wilcoxpharm.com but since it wasn't FDA approved yet not much information was given. Since I didn't have company access codes, I could only research so far. If Zal 4 is what he's talking for constipation, what is he taking for the pain that caused him to be locked up? I really didn't have anything to go on because the only way I found out about Zal 4 was the fact that it was underneath my bed. I wouldn't have gone there if I hadn't dropped my lip gloss. I was very confused.

The website said that it *Zalnoprotrexone* or *Zal 4* was very safe because it was all natural. If only I could find out the pain medicine he was taking and what he was taking it for. I thought about calling him but I don't really know what to say. I walked over to the fridge and pulled out a juice and popped it open. As I stood there drinking that juice, I kept looking over at my cell. I noticed that it was lit up indicating I had missed a call or text. I walked over to the phone and sat the juice on the night stand and opened the flap. I had two voice messages. One was Chaz and the other was from Harvey.

"Hey, it's me. I was wondering if I had left anything behind. Call me." This one was Harvey. I didn't listen to the one from Chaz yet because I really didn't want to hear anything he had to say.

I called Harvey's cell but I only got voice mail so I left a message:

"Hey, Harvey. It's me. Um, I got your message. I'm at home if you wanna call. I won't be going anywhere the rest of the night. And by the way, you did leave something behind. It rolled under the bed. Okay. Talk to you later. Bye-bye." I took a deep breath as I hung up. I felt a little nostalgic and I didn't really know why. I would have given anything for Harvey to show me even the slightest affection and now that he was, it's a little weird and I don't know how to except that.

The next morning, I got a call from Zoë, asking if she could come over and talk. She's never been to the estate (that I know of) and I didn't want to start now so I suggested that we go to Luigi's for early lunch. She agreed and I hung up the phone and sat on the bed. My mind was blank. I don't know exactly what I was feeling but whatever it was, it was really heavy and I couldn't stand it. I didn't want to see Zoë either but I knew that if I refused, it would somewhat make me look like the bitch so, I accepted.

I decided to text Dee for moral support and she asked if I needed her to come alone. I told her no and that this was something that I had to do alone even though I had no idea what was about to transpire. I had to look like I had the situation under control even though I was a raw nerve.

My stomach felt like someone had hit me with brass knuckles. I felt like I was going to vomit at any given moment. I wanted to die. I wanted to see God face to face and ask him what I did for him to allow all of this to be upon me. I felt like that wimpy, asthmatic pee-on that's on the play ground with bullies playing keep away with my inhaler while I'm struggling for every breath and no one is helping me. Or, it was like I was pushed in a pool and the pusher knew I couldn't swim. They only did it just to get a laugh. Still, no one helped me.

I was the one who didn't go off. I didn't lose my cool. I stayed polite when people hurt my feelings and I was the one who held my tongue and watched people who I knew were walking all over me. I was the one who they lied on and I got punished for that lie and everyone believed that lie. I was the one who did what my parents told me. I didn't try alcohol or drugs or cut school or skip class. I felt like I needed to be compensated for all that mental pain and anguish. I felt I need restitution. Well, where are my 40 acres and a mule? I wanted justice. I didn't understand. I couldn't understand. I wanted answers and I wanted them right then. I took two antidepressants with a bottle of apple juice just before I decided to get dress otherwise I wasn't going. I never made it to morning service.

    I took out a pair of black slacks with a green and white blouse. I matched my purse with my shoes. I pulled my hair back in a green ribbon with a few strands of hair down in the front so that I could pull it behind my ears. I took one last look in the full length mirror before I walked out of the bedroom as I always do and took a deep breath. Walking across the floor to the door was like I was about to go to a point where there is no light, no heat and no sound. I turn the knob slowly with my left hand and holding my purse in my right. Travis met me in the hallway and asked, "Where to, ma'am?" I walked up to him and put my flat palm on his chest and said, "I think I will drive today, Travis." "If you need me, call me." He said. I managed a smile and nodded in agreement as I walked past him headed downstairs. I wanted to cry. Those antidepressants better work a little faster because I don't think I can keep up this brave front and the strange thing is I don't know why I wanted to cry. I had to hold it together because I wanted to control my emotions. Just in case I was about to hear something from Zoë that I didn't want to hear, I would have ample time to teach myself to not cry. My mind was playing tricks on me.

    At Luigi's, there were many memories that were still alive in that place. For some reason, I expected Chaz to walk up or worse, what if the same waiter was there recognized me and ratted me out to Zoë? Okay, here's the deal: I would say that it was business for the studio. Yeah, that's it. It was business for the studio and since Harvey has all these *secrets* and has nothing to do with the studio, he would have no reason to doubt me. Yeah. That's it. The more I said it over and over in my head, the more I believed it. I can do this.

    I was seated across from the table that I shared with Chaz. It was eerie. A young girl walked over to me wearing black jeans and a white shirt with a black apron. "Hello. My name is Holland and will be your server. Can I get you anything or are you waiting for someone?" She was so friendly. Her smile was warm and her voice was squeaky.

"I would like to order the Champagne Brunch special for myself and I have a friend coming but she's running a little late. Can you please bring me a croissant for now?" I asked.

"Sure. I'll be right back." Holland said. She twirled and walked away with a bouncy walked. She was totally a redhead but with color to her. Most red heads are pale, but she wasn't. it made me think if that was a bottle redhead. She was quite stunning. Focusing my attention on Zoë, I realized that it had been a while since I last seen her and I wasn't quite sure what she looked like. Soon, I saw a full figured woman walking toward me with a glowing face. She had micro braids and gold hoop earrings. "Zoë?" I asked myself? I found myself smiling because she looked friendly and very happy to see me. She was taller than I was and though she was full figured, she looked remarkable. She looked like she was a model, I mean everything was in place; nothing was jiggling or wobbling. She really looked elegant and looked to be a size 24 but wore it well. I was so intrigued that I stood to welcome her to the table.

"Mrs. Wilcox. Hi, I'm Zoë. Do you remember me?" Her voice was very soft and almost childlike. Even her chuckling was childlike. I walked over to her and embraced her like she was a long lost family member. I wanted to say, "Please, call me Khylee." but I wanted to see how this meeting played out. "Good to see you, Ms. Emerson. How have you been?" I asked.

"Oh! Great and you?" she replied.

"Doing great. Please, sit down." I said as I pointed to the chair and motioned for the server to come over. As we sat down, the server came over with a menu and addressed Zoë by saying, "Mrs. Wilcox is having the Champaign Brunch. What would you like?"

"Ah. Sure that sounds great." agreed Zoë.

"Very well, Ma'am." she said as she bowed and took a sharp turn right.

Well, as awkward as it was, it was rather refreshing. I mean, she really wasn't the bitch I made him out to be. She was very articulate. I repented in my heart on that one. I may even tell her, who knows?

We sat there for a few minutes complimenting each other. Zoë was actually married once but it turned out that Addison, who was a pilot, had more than one wife at one time in four different parts of the states. Let's see, this is how it happened: there was Amanda in Fort Worth, Sharon in New York City, Desdemona in Sacramento and then there was Zoë in Chicago. Now, the way she found out was almost musical. I mean, if that magical moment where everything had hit the fan was put to musical, it would have been an opera.

He married Amanda first in January 1993 (they had 2 children: Staci and Ericka) and met Sharon while on vacation with Amanda in Cape Cod. Then in 1999, he decided marry Sharon (they had 3 children: Bret, Clark and Bryce). While in California, he met and married Desdemona in 2001 (they had triplets: Rhonda, Ronald and Randall) and he met Zoë in Chicago in 2003 and they had one child, Jewlah.

This is how he got caught: Addison contracted food poisoning when he was in Florida. The idiot had all, count them ALL of their names listed on his insurance and all of their other information (names, social security numbers, dates of birth, contact information, blood types, etc) listed in his wallets. He had different wallets for each family as well as different wedding bands for each wife. This man really thought that he had everything figured out but he just didn't plan on getting sick.

While in the hospital, Addison was very sick and had to stay a few days and someone had to be contacted. They called every Mrs. Addison Emerson that he married but the one that answered without them having to leave a message was Zoë. She got on the first plane to Florida and tried making arrangements for him to be flown back to Chicago once he was well enough to travel. But there was a small problem. All the other Mrs. Emerson wanted Addison "home" too. When Zoë got to the hospital, she was immediately transported to the family waiting room. Walking through the waiting room doors, she saw three other women with their children. All the children decided to play together and that's when the shit hit the fan. They thought it was peculiar that all the children had the same last name so the wives started talking and this is how Addison got busted. Instead of them getting mad, they got even. They did the smart thing by not holding grudges against each other because they were innocent by standers. Plus, the children were innocent as well. They got lawyers to see what their legal rights were. By law, the first Mrs. Emerson was the only one that had legal claims on anything but since the wives wanted their children taken care of and for them to continue to live in the manner of which they were accustomed, they were allowed to keep their homes, vehicles and the money was divided accordingly.

All of this happened in a manner of months between the time he was in the hospital and recuperating. By the time Addison was coherent, he was handcuffed to the bed, read his rights and was arrested for bigamy. He was stripped of all whatever it was he had because he was a lousy sack of shit to begin with. But Zoë looks great. I haven't met any of her other co-wives but Zoë looks great. She was a very dark woman with very clear skin and the whitest teeth you have ever seen. The only way I can even try to phantom what she was going through or how she made it was through the grace of God. It's like God worked for other people and his angels of protection were encamped around everyone else but me. My angel quit.

I can see it now. My angel: Let's call her . . . Sarah. Sarah goes to the Heavenly Unemployment Office because she quit being my angel of protection. Since Sarah quit and didn't get fired, she can't draw unemployment. What's an angel to do? While sitting in the lobby, she waits nervously for another human to protect. Soon, an elderly angel comes up to her with a blinding white smile and says, "Please, walk this way. Of course she already knew who she was, it's Heaven. DUH! So, Emma starts interviewing her. She already knows the answers but there's a process that angels have to go through, especially if you're in the first grade.

"Now" Emma starts. "Tell me about your last human."

"Well, let's see. Khylee wasn't the human for me. I had no idea she would be attacked. That wasn't in my job description and besides, she's a little hardheaded. She don't listen. She stopped praying since the incident anyway. I don't know if I can ever get through to her." Emma listened with a few nods, making sure she made eye contact between pushing the pencil.

"Sarah, how did that make you feel?"

"Unnecessary and unwanted. It also made me feel like I was wasting my time."

"So, you felt like she didn't heed your acknowledgements or acknowledged your presence?"

"I tried everything I could to let Khylee know that I was still there for her and that I was sent to protect her but she . . ."

"But she didn't notice, huh?"

"No. Can't you just gimme a dog? Or maybe even a gold fish to take care of and if I pass that test, then can I graduate to another human?"

"But animals have no soul, Sarah."

"But I think I'm getting lacohaloitis, see?" Sarah got up and walked toward Emma and held her head down toward her so that Emma could get a better view of her halo. It looked like a neon sign with a couple of bulbs loose.

"I see." Emma said as she wrote in her book.

"How does that make you feel?

"Like I don't know what I'm doing. I feel like I can't get through to her. I don't think she listens to me. You know, once, I kept her safe when that car accident was about to happen. My assignment was to keep her from getting hurt. Do you think she was thankful?"

"How do you think God feel?

Chapter 10

I found out why Harvey was so clingy to me. He had full blown AIDS and contracted it the night before we got married. He's been away on business 80% of the time but the other 20% he would undergo treatment. He set up visits with private nurses in hotels so that no one would be the wiser. He was in San Antonio, Sacramento, Boston, Atlanta and St. Louis. They flew him back home to the hospital and Zoë Emerson, the personal secretary at the Cooperate Headquarters, made all the legal arrangements with Harvey's permission; his will ~ all of which he left to me. I was to get everything when Harvey died. All the paper work is in order and has been for over a year but what I don't understand is why I had to find out about it now, like this? All this time, I thought that he was sleeping with Zoë but Trey swore that wasn't the case. I never even mentioned any of this to her. She only knew that he was preparing things just in case but never knew he was sick. No one knew Harvey was sick except for Trey, who was appointed temporary power of attorney because Trey and Harvey are best friends plus Trey is Deputy Attorney General or something until Harvey legally turned everything over to me.

There was a box delivered to the estate. Travis bought it upstairs to me and knocked on the bedroom door. It was one of those brown and white boxes that they use when you are given a pink slip. It was filled with many things that I didn't understand like the stock reports and the financial reports. There were also desk photos and many different types of office things. There was a letter from Harvey addressed to me:

Khylee,

On May 13, 1993, I met you and I started living but became whole on February 24, 1994. I have to let you know that I never blamed you for what happened. I felt guilty because I failed to protect you so I gave you every material thing you needed or I thought you needed so that you wouldn't have to want for anything. But I still messed up because I know that all you ever wanted was me.

You truly were every breath that I made and I am so sorry that I was never the husband that I should have been. I was afraid for your life that night. I knew that if I had intervened, you wouldn't be here today so I punked out. I paid them off to keep our names out of the media but not for you. I paid the legal system to make sure that those monsters went straight to jail without a trial and it was to save my face and my company. I didn't want the Wilcox name taken thought the mud. I am so sorry and I have regretted that every day of my natural life.

Why didn't I tell you this? Well, Khylee, you made me proud. You saved yourself for me and I, selfishly speaking, bragged about you at the bachelor party. I told Trey and the guys that you were pure ~straight from your Daddy's lap. I bragged that on our wedding night, your pussy would be the shape of my dick because no one else had touched you and I was going to make everything special.

The night before we got married, I was at Trey's with the rest of the guys: Bobby, Douglas, Ben, Danny, Josh and this dude we call 'Monk' because he looks like a gorilla and all of them. One of the guys knew of 2 girls they could call to come over. We paid them well that night because we all took turns having sex with them. Turns out, we paid for more than sex, I contracted HIV that night. I didn't use protection.

Here I was, so worried about you after the rape thinking that you had a STD, all while it was running through my veins. I swore Trey to secrecy.

One of the girls was Annabella who was infected that night as well and since refused to sleep with her husband because she didn't know how to tell him so we've been sleeping together since we found out we were sick. She contacted me right after we got *married that she was positive and that I needed to get tested. When I found out that I was positive, we swore to each other that we would never be with anyone else but stay married as long as we could. Having HIV is not like Salt Peter. I still got urges; I just pretended I was with you. I couldn't risk you finding out but Bella's husband found out, of which we were not prepared for. We were caught on tape and photos were printed from the surveillance cameras but what I don't understand is who gave him the photos?*

We've been going for experiment treatment which was being tested in the lab at the main building. We never meant to hurt you it was just easier this way. Now, I can't conceal this any longer. While the experimental drugs are working, it doesn't cure us. It only prolongs the inevitable. It preserves us only on the outside until the day our immune system shuts down appearing that we would die of cardiac arrest, respiratory failure or pneumonia, etc. This lets you know that the drugs are no longer working. Once the system becomes immune then it's all down him from there and just a matter of time. My system started shutting down five weeks ago.

Zoë took care of all the paperwork so all you need to do is call Trey when you are ready to sign. I'd understand if you never want to talk to me again but just in case, Trey has all the information you need. I am in Sacramento. The name of the Hospice is Redmond's on Blackberry Court. My family doesn't know and I don't want them to until after my death.

I only ask that you forgive me and at least try and understand why I did what I did.

H C Wilcox

I wasn't sure how to take this letter. I don't understand why he didn't come clean with the truth. I needed to hear all this from Harvey so I decided to go to Sacramento to get closure. I packed a few things and asked Travis if he could take me the airport. I also had to call Trey to let him know what I was about to do. I had so many unanswered questions that I literally had to write them down because once in Sacramento, I wasn't sure what I would find.

Chapter 11

*I*t was on a Monday when I called Trey. I sat on my bed and called him on his cell:

"Hello?" he answered.

Cleaning my throat, "Hey Trey, it's Khylee. How are you?"

"Oh, Khylee. I'm fine. How are you?" He sounded very surprised to hear from me but at the same time, I heard a hint of 'It's about time you called. What took so long?' in his voice. I heard papers rustling, the sound of a chair being moved across a wooden floor which indicated he may have still been at home. I could also hear him swallow which means that he may have been eating breakfast.

"I didn't disturb you, did I? I really need to talk to you." I asked.

"No, you're not bothering me. In fact, I am glad you called. What can I do for you? Are you okay?" His voice sounded calmer now.

"I need closure on Harvey." I said with a sigh. "I'm leaving for the airport today. I'm going to Sacramento." I paused for a moment, just to see if he would say anything but he didn't. "I really wish someone had told me what was going on."

"Well, Khylee, he told us not to. He swore us to secrecy but you don't have to worry about a thing. I have all the paper work ready to sign everything else over to you. I was temporarily in charge of everything until such a time as this." Trey really believed that he thought that he was doing the right thing; I could hear it in his voice.

"Trey, if one more person tells me that I don't have to worry about anything, I'm really gon hurt somebody. Understand?"

"Ok. What do you want me to do?" He asked

"Nothing. I don't know. I just need to go get closure." Travis knocked on the door that was slightly opened and looked at me while reaching for the bag as if he was nonverbally asking if it was okay to take the bags downstairs to the car. I nodded.

"Should I fly out with you?"

"No. I'm a big girl. I can do this alone. After all, I'm the last person to know anything anyway. I almost hate you, you know that? I almost hate you and Zoë for not telling me because what if I were you? Wouldn't you want to know?" I hung up and walked downstairs to the car and Travis helped me in the car.

It was a little over 30 minutes drive the airport. I wanted to call JaVon and D'Kyra to tell them what was going on but JaVon was away on tour and I knew that D'Kyra may have been at the office. I wasn't sure if she could talk or not. I needed to talk to both of them at the same time because I didn't want to repeat myself in telling the story so I waited until after so I could talk to both of them at the same time.

I saw over to my left that there was a thermos. I took the top off and took a sniff. Hazelnut coffee. Good ole Myra. It had just the right amount of sweetener and it was great. I poured a little in the cup and sipped on it for a while. Not finishing the thermos was a great possibility. I started thinking about Harvey and for the life of me, I couldn't picture his face. I could only see a silhouette of him but not his face. I couldn't remember his smell, his voice or anything. I soon realized that if my memory of him was growing faint now, what would happen once he was actually gone? It scared me. Even though we were not a traditional married couple, it still scared me.

People think that since you have every material thing imaginable at your fingertips that you don't yearn for anything else. I would have given all this up just so I could really have Harvey rather than a ghost of a man that shared the same address. Suddenly my cell indicated a text message. It was Chaz and I really wasn't in the mood to talk to him. I knew that I had to break this off but how could I do this without hurting him. I really cared about him because he really helped me just when I needed someone. Looking at the screen, it read: "GMORNING". Should I reply? I have grown tired of bored of him. Then another text came. I don't want him to think I was waiting by the phone for him. I waited for a while before I answered.

"U BUSY?"

"NO." I replied.

"CAN U TALK?" he asked. I really couldn't handle him right now so I told him no.

"WHATZ WRG? CALL ME PLZ."

"M GO N THRU SUMTHG RITE NOW. HAV 2 LEAVE TOWN 4 AWHILE." I was only going to be gone for a few days at the most but I didn't tell him that. I really wanted to stay focused on Harvey.

At the airport, Harvey's private jet was all ready to go. I took my bag, my purse and the thermos. There was only me, two attendants and the two pilots and I felt that it was good because I really didn't want to talk to anyone. Stepping on the plane felt a bit numbing because I didn't know what to expect. I used the laptop that was on board to surf the net just to take my mind off things but it really didn't help. I tired watching a movie and that didn't help either. I was certain to think about this until it was over.

* * *

The three story hospital looked like it was brand new. It makes me wonder if the people who worked there knew what they were doing. There were two sets of double doors that opened automatically. Once the second set opened, you were hit with the smell of antiseptic and rubbing alcohol. I took a deep breath and to this day, I don't know why. Maybe it reminded me of that stuff my grandmother use to put on me when I skinned my knees when I fell off my bike in her graveled drive way. I only remember the container and the smell. I don't remember what it was called. You know how black women like to put some old experimental concoction on you that they inherited from slavery time.

As I exhaled, the tears came. There was a white lady standing there at the registration desk. She came over to me and put her arm around me and asked if I was okay.

"My husband is here. His name is Harvey Wilcox. Can you point me in the right direction?" I asked. I really tired not to cry.

"Sit here. I will find out his room number and take you to him." She said. While sitting there, I tried to wrap my brain around what was actually about to take place. I didn't know what condition he was in and since he didn't know that I was coming, I don't even know if he wanted to see me.

I heard footsteps coming over. It was the nurse. "Ma'am, do you have a photo ID with you?" She asked. Her badge read Teri. Her photo looked like a glamour shot

"Ah, yes." I rummaged around in my bag and pulled out my wallet. My hands were shaking. Teri kneeled beside my chair and without speaking; she took the wallet from my hands and only glanced at my driver's license. She closed it and pushed it back into my bag. She stood up and grabbed me by my arm and said, "Okay, Mrs. Wilcox, come with me if you don't mind." As I walked along beside her, she didn't talk. It was about 4:47 p.m. and his room was 3049. Before I could enter the room, I was stopped short of the door and asked to dress in a gown, a mask and gloves. "This was really happening." I said to myself. I was at the point of no return. I was praying that he looked the same and not distorted in any way because I really didn't think that I could take that. It was like I was moving in slow motion. The room smelled of bandages and latex gloves. My chest pounded and every time I tried to take a deep breath, I got light headed.

"Are you okay, Mrs. Wilcox?" Teri asked.

I only nodded. "We don't have to go in right this minute. Take all the time that you need." I took a deep breath once more and said, "I'm okay. I can do this."

Two nurses and a lab tech made their way out of the room so that me and Teri could fit comfortably in the room. For a minute, I couldn't look at him. I looked around the room. The television was showing CNN. I thought that it was typical of Harvey. The view of the garden was tranquil and the fountain that stands in the middle of the park was peaceful. It seemed to fit the moment. I kept looking at the clock. It was 5:12 p.m.

"If you need anything, Mrs. Wilcox, please let me know." Teri said. I nodded as I walked toward her. "Teri, should I expect anything like a miracle or some tremendous break through? I can't believe it's gone this far." She shook her head and rubbed my shoulder.

"We have a Chaplain on duty. Would you like to talk to him?"

"No."

"Well, we'll be checking back with you from time to time. Stay as long as you need. There's food set up for the Wilcox family and close friends directly across the hall from this room. Help yourself." Teri pointed as she walked out of the room and closed the door behind her. I stood there for a moment looking at the wood on the door. I could hear Harvey's labored breathing behind me. I slowly turned around and I saw the tan thermal blanket with his hands draped across. When I finally mustered up the nerve to look at his face, he was staring right at me with a smile on his face. He was attached to oxygen and there was an IV in his right hand to keep him from being dehydrated. He also had a fresh shave like he was expecting me. I walked over to his bedside and he reached his hand out to me.

"My beautiful Khylee. You're the best looking thing I don seen all day." He said with a slight smile. "I'm so sorry about all of this. I really thought I was doing the right thing at the time." he said. I was stunned and I didn't know how to respond to that. I sat on the bed next to him. He reached over and put his left hand on my thigh.

"Are you in any pain, Harvey?" I asked.

"No." He answered and dozed off again. I watched him sleep for a moment. It's been a long time since I saw him sleep. I had forgotten just how full and heart shaped his lips were. Wow! Had that mole on his eyelid been there all this time?

There was a knock at the door as it slowly opened. It was a very young looking Asian man. "Mrs. Wilcox, My name is Dr. Chad Nhavilay." he said as he extended his hand out to me. He walked over to Harvey and checked the oxygen, his IV, the catheter and all the other little things that were attached to him. "Is there anything I can get for you? Do you have any questions about anything?" His olive skin indicated to me that he had to have been biracial.

"No! Not that I can think of." I answered softly.

"Well, if you need anything, ask for Dr. Chad, okay?" then he walked out and closed the door behind him. I jumped up and ran out after him unfastening the gown and taking off my gloves and mask.

"Dr. Chad?"

"Yes?" He said as he turned around. "Do I have to wear these?"

"No. It's more so to protect his immune system, not yours."

"How long does he have?" I asked. His piercing eyes were calming.

"Not long. When his breathing starts to labor, it's only a matter of time. All we can do now is make him comfortable. But I will say this, whatever this Zal 4 is that he was experimented with, it really helped. Have you noticed how healthy he looks? That was all due to Zal 4."

"Can you give him the Zal 4 now?"

"No, because it's something that Wilcox Pharmaceuticals was working on and it's not released yet to the public and I can't use something that is not approved by the FDA. We can only make him comfortable. I'm sorry. There's nothing more that we can do." I turned and walked back into Harvey's room. He was sleeping. Good! This will give me time to think for a minute.

I have all the papers with me that I need to sign so I sat down and looked in my bag and got the folder with all the paper work. After I signed the last set, I called Trey and told him everything was all done.

I moved my chair closer to Harvey's bed side and changed the channel on the television. He's breathing was beginning to become more labored now. His heart shaped lip parted slightly. Harvey's left hand twitched a little and his eyes where shifting from side to side underneath closed eyelids as if he was dreaming. I didn't even bother with all the questions I had written down.

I felt like there was something I was supposed to be saying to Harvey but I didn't know what. This could be it. He could very well take his last breath and all the "what if's" will be gone. I don't know what I am supposed to be doing right now. How am I supposed to be acting towards a man who only stayed married to be out of convenience? I don't know what to do.

It was 7:08 pm when Teri came back. They checked Harvey to make sure his morphine drip was okay and work like it was suppose to be working. After she left, I took off my shoes to lie in the bed next to Harvey. I got as close to him as I could without disturbing any of the tubing. He reached over with his left hand and put it on my arm.

"I read the letter you wrote, Harvey." I whispered to him, "I can't pretend I understand but at least the explanation was relevant." Harvey nodded.

"I forgive you." I whisper as I pressed my lips to his ear. Tears rolled down the side of his face and trickled on the side of his face. I was careful not to ingest any bodily fluids so I reached over and grabbed some of the tissues and stuffed them between us.

"I left you everything. Did you sign the papers?" he asked slowly.

"Yes, I talked to Zoë and Trey but why didn't you trust me with this information, Harvey? I *am* your wife."

"Believe it or not, I wanted to protect you." Harvey said with a few moments of pausing then he asked, "Do regret marrying me?"

"No. I just wish things had been different. I wish we could have had a normal marriage. I appreciate you telling me the truth about everything. I always felt that you were with someone but I couldn't prove it so I never confronted you. I thought that after the rape, you looked at me with disgust and that you didn't want me."

"You were never supposed to find out through a letter. That morning in your bedroom, I wanted to tell you then but I didn't know how. You forgave me and now I can go peacefully."

"Harvey," I really wanted to tell him about Chaz but I figure why put salt in an open wound? Here's my chance to come clean. "I love you" came out instead.

"I love you, too. Bella was just sex. We went in telling each other that it was only sex. She knew that I was never going to leave you for her. You were the air I breathe. You were every good thing that happened to me. I love you more deeply, completely." he said. Those were the last words he spoke to me. I think that was the moment that I knew I really did love him. Harvey was the first man that I every truly loved and I never got a chance to consummate or marriage so that means my first (was a gang rape) and my only was Chaz Boomerang. Chaz, *people*! This man whose big dick just wasn't worth it; this same man who didn't belong to me and who I care for deeply. He was the worst mistake I ever made in my life. A mistake that I decided to keep away from Harvey seemed to make me feel that I somehow won and got one over on him before he would die. It made me feel powerful when I felt so much like a pee-on during our marriage. I felt taller, in a sick sort of way. I know that I shouldn't find this kind of refuge during what could possibly be the last few moments of my husband's life but I don't know what else to feel. Harvey did love me. I mean, he left EVERYTHNG to me without question.

Understand this, readers, this is why I am so screwed up. I am lying here on my husband's death bed thinking of another man. How sick am I? But at least I realize that somewhere the Devil is cracking his side laughing at me right about now. I didn't care. What mattered is that me and Harvey made peace with everything but I will have to take my affair with Chaz to my grave. I don't think I was better for knowing about the *situation* of Harvey and Bella. I do appreciate the fact that he didn't want to infect me but I still wish he had told me. Would it have made a difference? I think not but I would have been in the know. Think about it? Would you have wanted your spouse's best friend and coworker know that they were HIV before you? Would you have wanted to find that out by a letter? I must admit that knowing I just inherited a multibillion dollar company with all the bells and whistles softens to blow but still . . . I'm just saying.

This was his death bed and he has the right to go peacefully. Then it happened. Harvey's chest stopped moving. I wasn't sure so I tried to lie as still as I could. I even held my breath to see if he was breathing . . . but he wasn't. One minute he was inhaling short shallow breathes and exhaling which sounded more like sighing. The next minute there was nothing except the Darth Vader sounding breathing apparatus and the humming from the

IV. Harvey's last words to me were that he loved me. That was magical. I didn't cry. I didn't even whimper. I just laid there next to him for a few minutes trying to pretend that he was just sleeping but that was cut short when Teri came in. She stood at the foot of Harvey's bed and as we made eye contact, she touched my foot and softly said, "I'm so sorry, Mrs. Wilcox. We need to clean him up, okay?" I mouthed the words, 'No'.

"Okay, stay as long as you need. We'll be back later, okay?" As Teri turned to walk away, she smiled but her eyes looked like Powder's when she threw up on the carpet. She closed the door behind her. CNN just announced that WilPharm was up another 28 points. How about that? He's body not even cold yet and he's still making money.

Harvey's body was still warm. For a brief moment, I could have sworn I saw his chest move but I know it couldn't have. The little breathing apparatus what once sounded like Darth Vader had stopped in the middle of his inhaling.

I reached down and touched his well manicured hands and the warmth was beginning to leave his body. Had I been lying here that long or does a body grow cold sooner than I thought?

Then it happened. Teri came back in the room but this time she came with Dr. Chad. Teri walked over to me and touched my shoulder and said, "I'm sorry, Mrs. Wilcox, but we have to clean him up now. C'mon, let me get you something to eat, okay?" I wanted to stay but I wasn't allowed so I had to get up and leave the room.

I pulled out my cellular and tried to call Trey but all I got was voice mail. I didn't want to leave something like this on his voice mail so I just told him to call me as soon as possible. Then I called D'Kyra but I only got her voice mail too so I just told her to call me back. I never felt so alone in my life.

When I was allowed to go back into his room, it was like entering into a walk in freezer. Harvey looked like he was sleeping. I never really saw the life literally leave from someone before. Somehow, I feel that I may need therapy after this. I walked in slowly and I moved the chair from the wall to Harvey's bedside. I sat down at the edge of the chair and stared at him. I was looking for something, anything to tell me that this is all a bad dream. Harvey was only 41 and I was about to bury a husband at the age of 38.

I realize something about getting older: when you are in your 40's people say, "Wow! You are getting old." But when you die in your 40s people say 'They were so young?" People are strange.

Chapter 12

The wake and funeral was to be held at Walton's Funeral Home at 2 pm. August 14th. Harvey had everything laid out and we tried to make sure that we carried out all his wishes. He even picked out his headstone and what it should say. I really didn't have to do much because Trey and Zoë handled all the arrangements like Harvey suggested. I had no voice in anything; not what he was to wear, how the services were supposed to go not anything. It was a big help to me because I wouldn't know the first thing to do. I stayed upstairs in my room most of the day until it was time to go. There were so many people in the mansion that it gave me a headache. I called down to Myra and asked her to make sure that Mr. Wilcox's suite and office was locked. I didn't want people creeping around the house. I also made sure that security was all around, in plain clothes of course. I didn't want to make anyone uncomfortable. It was important to Harvey that people felt welcomed.

I don't really remember too much at the funeral service but I do remember D'Kyra walking in with me. JaVon was in Canada touring at least that's what her manager, Vivian said. I called her cell but Vivian answered and said that she would give her the message but after the tour which would be in another two months. She didn't want anything messing with her head or risk her losing her focus while on tour. I hated that Vivian bitch sometimes. I wanted to tell her to take an enema so that we'd all could feel better but then she would stop taking my calls.

Anyway, I do, however, remember Ethel's ole drunk ass trying to sing at the funeral. She was drunk as a skunk that smelled itself. I wasn't sure what I was feeling at the particular time, but I know I wasn't feeling like hearing Harvey's ole drunk ass mother mess up another hymn or her at my husband's funeral. She walked up to the podium and over the microphone actually asked the organist if he knew "TIE A YELLOW RIBBON". I was so embarrassed. She wore a hot pinkish magenta looking pill box hat that matched absolutely nothing. She said that her son bought that hat for her from Switzerland when he was on a business trip. She stood there saying how proud she was of her only boy because he stayed in the family business but said that the Wilcox name vanished when he die because 'his wife couldn't give him no children." I was like, this woman really needs to do that lady sings the blues faint on stage thing right about now because everyone know she's Odessa Campbell. H C just looked all poker faced like this is second nature and he didn't even try to calm her down or nothing. I guess he felt that she'll talk until she runs out of gas and them she'll faint or something. I hoped she would hit her head in the process.

I couldn't take it any more so I asked Dee if she would sing or fart or do something because these Wilcox's are turning Harvey's funeral into a for real drunken country-bama dysfunctional family reunion. She walked over to the organist and asked if she could honor the request of the deceased's wife to sing now. The organist nodded. D'Kyra walked over to Ethel while she was still at the podium and gathered her by the shoulders and guided her away from the podium. Harvey's two sisters, Cookie and Rita walked up to get their highly intoxicated, highly flammable mother and made her sit down before she made a bigger scene or a bigger ass outta herself.

D'Kyra belted out "More Than Anything". Talking about music calming the savage beast? Not Ethel. She tried singing with D'Kyra. I don't know what Ethel's ole drunk ass was thinking. D'Kyra wrote that song (she use to sing back up for CRUZ) and I don't even try harmonizing with her because she can blow. And to top it off, Ethel screamed like someone found all her stash and poured them out. Again, H C just watched. I needed to leave. I sat there with my eyes closed until D'Kyra finished then I asked Trey and Zoë if they could just wrap this up so I could go home.

At the grave site, after they prayed and finished with everything, Ethel actually took her flask out, wobbled over on her drunk ass legs to Harvey's casket and literally pour some of whatever was in the flask on the casket and said, "For my boy." I can't believe no one had a leash on her or something. I was about to say something to her, I mean I had taken steps toward that fool BUT God stopped me. Just then Ethel tried to turn and walk away but she lost her footing in the green tarp and the loose soil underneath aggravated the situation further. She fell. People started laughing. I mean, it was a bit mean to laugh but the old bat had it coming. How you gon just show up already drunk at your only son's funeral? That's trifling. She should have fell in the grave. That would have kept her from saying, "Take me now, Lawd. Take me now."

The only people that knew the true cause of his death was me, Trey and Zoë, not to mention the doctors who also came to the mansion. Most of the time, I felt weird and out of place. Trey and Zoë never left my side. They were a huge help because I didn't know half of the people that were there except for his family and most of them were just as baffled and dumbfounded as I was. I really was afraid that they would blame me for his death. He had two sisters, Cookie who lived in New York who was married but didn't have any children. She always found fault in whatever I did. She called me lazy once because I didn't work, she thought I married Harvey for his money. She would really have a bull, horns first, if she knew that Harvey left me everything. His other sister, Rita, was so mean; she had enough meanness for two people. Plus, she was blacker than six midnights. She was so pinched in her face that it looked like she smelled something all the time. She wasn't a pretty woman, I guess it was because of the bitterness in her face but whatever it was she needed to stop it. It's amazing how some wealthy people that grew up looking down their noses on others who aren't as well off as they are.

I didn't want to tell his family anything unless they had already known something. Then, only then, would I feel comfortable enough to talk to them about it. I hope that Harvey told them something because if they knew that he contacted AIDS from being unfaithful the night before we were married, then I would have to tell them that we never consummated the marriage, then they would have to know about the attack and I really don't wanna go there with them. They would somehow blame all this one me. In Harvey's letter, he said that no one knew and he wanted to keep it that way.

Zoë invited herself to stay at the mansion to handle everything as well as Trey; after all, there was more than enough room. They were a big help. They even got in touch with D'Kyra and JaVon but JaVon was in Japan and couldn't come.

Ethel, Harvey's mother, was normally a cold woman when she drank so I really didn't know how to address her. Ethel came looking for me while I was sitting on the balcony from my suite. She was in rare form that day and actually embraced me and said, "Harvey loved you so much." She looked around the bedroom suite with her nose up it the air like we were trying too hard. She was a tall, oddly shaped woman. Her face was square and she wore her hair in a man's pompadour that made her look like a man. She opened drawers, pulled back curtains, opened closets, you name it, and the busy body did it.

"Well, we always thought that this house was too big for two people. Why y'all never have children anyway? You, know, I think that would have made my Harvey happy." She asked.

"We never got around to it." I answered. Ethel was really beginning to piss me off, talking about things she didn't know about. She was trying to be the quarterback after the game was over.

"When women don't give her husband children, it means that there's something wrong with the woman, *not* the man. A woman who can't give birth is less than a woman. In some countries, those women are banished like she had a foul odor in her **secret**. My son made the worse mistake of his life when he married you. I don't know what he was thinking. You put some sort of root on him, I know it. He never would have brought this house with a clear head. I don't trust you." I listened but I really didn't hear her. My mind was on D'Kyra. I pretended that Ethel wasn't even there. I was in my robe and house slippers as I walked back and forth getting ready. Ethel helped herself to the chaise lounge and I heard her talking but it only sounded like *blah, blah, blah, blah, blah*. She reached down to remove her orthopedic shoes which revealed her bunions. Her feet almost looked like hands. I almost asked her how she got the shoes on her hands. Then I thought about tossing her a piece of chocolate and yelling out, "CATCH, MONKEY!" But that was Harvey's mother and I had to respect her as such so I decided on wearing Harvey's favorite color, blue. I also wore a hat with a veil so no one could see my face.

Harvey's Dad, H.C., was always nice to me and would always address me as 'baby girl' because he said that he could never pronounce my name. H.C. cried all day. He was always so charming and funny. This is how Harvey was when we were dating. As a matter of fact, Harvey looked a lot like H.C. (thank God)

Suddenly there was a knock on the door. Ethel was still sitting there and talking. At least I think she was talking. Her mouth was moving and nothing was coming out unless she was praying. I really tried to ignore the ole bat because she was getting on my nerves. "Khy? It's me, D'Kyra. Can I come in?" she yelled from the hallway.

"Yeah, it's open." I yelled back. D'Kyra rushed through the door said, "Hey, Boo. I sorry I'm just now getting her. What do you need me to do because—" She stopped in mid sentence because she caught a glimpse of something in the corner of her eye. It was Ethel.

"Oh!" D'Kyra gasped and put her hand over her mouth with eyes open wide. "Girl, I'm sorry. I didn't know you had company. Want me to come back?

I jumped up and ran over to Ethel. "No. Ethel was just leaving. Ain't that right, Ethel?" I grabbed her shoes and put them in her lap. "Are you kicking me out?" Ethel asked.

"Well, I just think you will feel more comfortable if you were downstairs making sure that H.C. wasn't trying to 'lay hands' on any guess." I said.

"Alright. I'll go but remember, my son was a good man and he would have loved being a father."

"Ah huh. I will remember that. Thank you, Ethel." I literally had to push her out of the room before I had to kick her in her ole wrinkled throat. I slammed the door behind her and rested my back on it and let out a heavy sigh. I stood there for a minute cupping my face in both my hand shaking my head. D'Kyra walked over to me and put her arms around me and asked if I was okay and that whatever I needed, she would help me. It was weird because I was no longer thinking about Ethel or Harvey but that incredible bulge that was pressed against my abdomen. I snatched away from her and looked down and actually saw just how much the baby has grown. D'Kyra was actually showing. It was so cool.

"Oh! My God." I screamed. "Look at you." I said as I touched her belly. I kneeled down to talk directly to her stomach and said, "If you know what's good for you, you won't come out here. People are *crazy* out here."

"Girl, you are crazy" She screamed as she playfully hit me in the head. Then reality sat in. I fell to the floor and screamed in my hands. She sat on the floor with me and said that she was going to help me through this.

"You know, the funny thing about this is that I really don't know why I am crying, D'Kyra." I said.

"Look, you know I love you. You're my best friend. Whatever you tell me I can handle it. Hell, you were there for me when I was going through all of this stuff with Tony. I got you."

We talked for a long time. I told her everything; our wedding, the attack, and what my marriage was like. I even read the letter to her that

Harvey sent me. She listened. She didn't judge me. She heard every word and comforted me through the tears. It felt good to tell someone because as I had said before, my parents didn't even know.

Myra and Eva came to the door. "Senora, may I come please?" I nodded to D'Kyra indicating that I wanted her to handle whatever was going on behind door number one. She opened the door and walked in. By that time, I pulled myself up on to the bed and lay across the bed onto my stomach with a box of tissues. Myra and Eva walked over to me and explained to me that my mother was downstairs trying to 'give religion' to everyone (as Myra put it). They wanted to know if my parents were staying. Basically, Mom was alienating the house whole. When I asked about my Dad, they told me that he was outside looking for a barbeque grill so that he could cook out. When I asked about Travis, they told me that he was somewhere on the grounds with Pierre walking the dog. I apologized to them and I told them that I had the best house whole family that anyone could ask for.

After they walked out, Dee looked at me and said, "Girl, what's going on with your parents?"

"They are acting like they are the Duke and Duchess of Hazard County or somewhere. Girl, Daddy out there looking for a barbeque grill. I bet he bought his own cookout stuff. And Momma trying to give the Holy Ghost to everybody. This ain't the time or the place to witness to people. I bet, watch, I bet she asked them what they worship." D'Kyra was trying not to laugh but I guess the story was a bit comical. As she walked over to my mini fridge, took out a bottle of water and walked over to the chaise and sat down. She kicked her shoes off and twisted the top opened.

"I'm telling you, I bet she's on her way up here. Watch!" I scoffed. "She gon say something about my hair, my clothes, the funeral, wake and the program. I can just here her now: 'Girl, who catered the food downstairs? Do all your help got green cards? Is that driver a man or a woman? Do they wear gloves when they fix the food? I know one of 'em baldheaded but don't you think he need a hair net just the same? What about dandruff? You know they can poison people with that pool cleaner stuff. I just saw that program of TV about all those chemical? How come y'all didn't have no babies? Was he shooting blanks? You know, since he was such a young man, he may have had a back up in his colon. People have die with 40 lbs of 'be excuse" in their colons. How you know he was *born* a man?" I waved my arms and screamed. "Girl, my mother knows how to work a nerve." I added.

By then D'Kyra had laughed so hard, I thought her water was going to break but she was only 7 months and barely showing but showing just the same. You gotta love it! And just like clockwork, there was a knock on the bedroom door.

"Khylee? KhyLEEEEE? Khylee Niamiah Nadez`. This is your mother. Open the door."

"AAHHHH!" I bellowed. I placed my right fist fingers down over the wrist of my left hand palm side up. I moved my right hand back and forth as though I was cutting my wrist. D'Kyra continued laughing as she got up to go to the bathroom. "You gon make me piss myself. Stop it and open the door for your mother." I rolled my eyes at her as I walked over to the door.

"Hey, Ma." She stood there with her beautiful salt and pepper barely visible with that straw hat because she wore it pulled back. I've seen better hats on scarecrows. Mom also worked a pair of panty hose with opened toes sandals. Mom stood 5 ft. 2 and has the best singing voice you ever wanted to hear. Don't get me wrong, I love my mother more than anything and it's nothing I wouldn't do for her but she can be a bit worrisome at times and can work a nerve like nobody's business.

She carried a big bag, her bible and an umbrella with her all the time, everyday rain or shine. She wore a pattern that looked like it was made of quilt pieces but it wasn't and if I know my mom and I know my mom, she made her own outfit.

Mom's glasses were gold wire rimmed glasses and she had a huge white collar. She actually looked a bit like the Mother Bear of Bernstein Bears. Her bust line was at least a 46DD. I don't know how a shelf that short and small could handle a rack that big. "Oh, honey, I am so sorry about your Harvey. A young woman should never, ever bury a young husband. Why y'all didn't even get a chance to have children." She grabbed me and hugged me so tight that I couldn't breathe. She was crying so hard, I could never get a word in edge wise. I didn't want tears because I wasn't sure if I should cry. I was still sorting out my feeling. Then she began to pray and moan: *"Oh Lord, take this sister, my baby girl, under your wing and protect her. Bless her mind, Lord. Let her cast all her cares on you for you made her and you know all about her. Strengthen her and take the pain away."* Then, she started speaking in tongues. I would have wrote down what she said but I don't currently have the gift of tongues and I couldn't spell it anyway. D'Kyra slowly opened the bathroom door and peeked in the suite with her eyes and mouth opened wide. I wasn't quite sure what she was doing but she tried to sneak in the room without disrupting Mom's rejoicing. D'Kyra knocked over the lamp that was beside the bed and Mom, without missing a beat, screamed out, "SATAN, I REBUKE YOU!!" and went back into tongue. I had no other choice but to stand there until she was finished.

Amazingly enough, Mom did make me feel better. No matter how weird she is or how peculiar she dresses, she's still my mother and she only looks out for my best interest. I looked at the situation as though it was a positive thing and it helped.

When she stopped, she looked over at D'Kyra and walked toward her. Mom touched her stomach and said, "A belly full of sin and if you don't repent, this sin will be the death." Mom turned around and walked out of the door with that straw hat, carrying that Mary Poppins looking umbrella, wearing those socks and open toed sandals. Just as quickly she came, she was gone. Plus, I wasn't as confused either. The prayer really did help. I felt like a little girl for a few short minutes; and that 'belly full of sin' statement?

Chapter 13

*I*t's been a few weeks and I'm sure by now Harvey's resting place has settled into the ground. I only visited it once and that was because I wanted to make sure that the head stone was exactly like he wanted.

Harvey Chauncey Wilcox, Jr.
Jan. 26, 1964-Aug. 10, 2006

I was calmer and more settled now. I had made my peace with him and I got closure. I didn't pray to God for deliverance. I didn't pray for God to heal him. I didn't even pray to God to help me through this because I had stopped praying some time ago. How could a God that sit so high and look so low allow such things to happen to me?

I don't understand this. I don't understand how I was robbed of my virginity at gun point and my husband, who I had just married less than 6 hours earlier, only watch as he had a gun to his head as well.

I no longer prayed. I felt that there was no need so whatever happened from that point on, happened. Even with the situation with Harvey, I had to accept the fact that there was nothing more that I could do. I am thankful that, even though he cheated on me almost from day one, he cared enough not to want to infect me.

I felt mad and thankful at the same time. Did Harvey love me? I could look at this either way: YES; because he stayed married to me, showered me with every material gift imaginable and made me his soul heir. NO; He didn't come to me but instead told his personal secretary and his best friend and tell me the truth about his illness but had an affair all 13 years we were married.

Should I feel grateful? Should I feel appreciative? Do I still love him? I don't know what to think, feel, say or do but I do know one given factor: I will take Chaz Boomerang to my grave.

* * *

Someone once said that the best you can give someone is a chance. The only thing that beats a failure is a try. I wanted so much for that void to be filled in life that I thought it was Chaz. When in all actuality, it was my own salvation that was thirsting to death. It's almost like I wanted that two sides of everything lifestyle. I wanted someone to sweep me off my feet, someone to always, without fail, tell me that I mattered. I wanted, craved for that fairy tale love affair with Harvey, who I love but wanted to deeply be in love with him. His death really put things into perspective.

What happens when you try to love someone and they don't return that love? I understand the Harvey really thought that he was doing the right thing. I'm not there yet. I mean, okay. Here's the thing: As I write this journal, I wanted to keep up with my feelings and try to at least pen point what I felt and when I felt it. I needed to make sure that I wasn't going crazy and just in case I did somehow wake up in the Chocolate Macadamia Ranch, I needed to know why I was there and I will leave my writings behind so that everyone else knew why it was that I snapped. Plus, as I write, I was hoping that whatever lesson that I am to get from this, the words would jump out at me.

I had even thought that if I loved Harvey hard enough it wouldn't matter what his feeling were for her, that if she tried to control the emotional environment and set the tone, things would be okay. I thought wrong. Things got worse. At least, Harvey knew the outcome; I had no idea until it was too late. We lived through and survived the beginning, the middle of the present was blinding fog from day to day but the end, the final finish was cold and excruciatingly lonely.

Love is a process that sneaks upon you. Love is also an absolute animal that happens when you are looking, for something else. Love is so definite that if you love someone, you'll always love them. Broken hearts mend sort of like a broken bone. You can only feel it in stormy weather. You can only see it if you look at it through the X rays of your eyes. You can only hear it when there's pressure thrust upon it. But what happens when you fall in love with forbidden fruit? And what makes it *forbidden*? If love is good and good comes from God, is there such thing as falling in love with the wrong person, because they both belong to someone else? I believe it goes back Adam and Eve: The tree of the knowledge of Good and Evil. You can eat from any tree EXCEPT that one.

Some people say love is complicated. Some even say love is overrated. "No one really loves" anymore, I mean that forever kind of love. (Like my grandparents Big Daddy and Nan Maw (who stayed married for over 70 years) and my great grandparents Papa and Madea (who stayed married over 85 years.) They say, but it's only true if you don't know the ground rules but they stayed married until death did them part.

Even though I felt guilty after every physical encounter with Chaz, I knew that I couldn't stop myself from thinking of him. I wanted so much for someone to be with me because they loved me, not out of obligation.

Loving someone who only feels obligated is exhausting. I realized that I was in love with Harvey once but over time, I wasn't in love anymore. So how could this be? I knew that Harvey provided for me abundantly and for that I was grateful. I knew that there had to be more to life than this because I was so unhappy.

My mother, Hazel, is Anglo Saxon (named for the color of her eyes) and my Dad, Walter, is African American. That's right, readers! I am biracial if I didn't mention that already. Daddy had been a preacher all my life. He's the pastor of International House of Prayer. Yelp, the acronym spells IHOP. If I had a nickel, you know. Anyway, Daddy is the best pastor I have ever known. He was always humble to me and always took pride in his work for God. He always took his scriptures and his walk with God very serious but Daddy knew balance. He always made time for me and Momma, I don't care what was going on, he always made sure that me and Momma was second God first, of course. He'd say, "I don't ever want my wife and baby girl telling anybody that I was never there." He would delegate to his assistant pastor and the other ministers. He would make sure that when we were going out of town that the assistant and the ministers held things together and they never once let Daddy down.

Daddy isn't very tall. He is only 5ft 6. He looks a bit like Winnie the Pooh. He has a round face and with small round eyes. His voice is almost soothing, you know? But when Daddy is preaching and the spirit of the Lord hits him, he is truly a force to be reckoned with. Daddy walked like he is marching up hill. He always walked with is head up high. His smile is bright and I have his smile, his ears and his hands. He always makes me laugh, I don't care what is going on, and he always makes me laugh.

Whenever Daddy would sing, all is right with the world. His voice is so soothing. He would always tell me stories about when he use to travel and sing with his Gospel group called JONATHAN which means God's Gift. Honestly, I think he was a bit conceded. He would always pull his pants up to appear to have the high pocket look and would limp on one leg and sing something purposely to me off key and would yell out, "Khylee you don't know nothing 'bout this."

Momma, on the other hand, is white as I stated before. She is rather timid whereas Daddy was outspoken. But he said it was love at first sight and she didn't want to have anything to do with him because she had heard that he had a reputation with the ladies. They met in college in St. Louis. They both were raised in Holiness and Momma still to this very day has a problem with me wearing pants. She is, however, coming around.

Momma's hair is wavy. It's not very thick but it's always shiny. *(Sometimes Daddy would wash Momma's hair while he sang to her. I thought that was so romantic.)* I longed for a marriage just like my parents. In their world, everything is right. They are still so in love with each other that bees don't sting, roses don't have thorns and animals never bite. Momma does look exactly like she did when they first met. She is a bit taller than Daddy. Mom is around 5 ft 8 and only weighs 150. She is correctly proportioned. Nothing is out of place. She use to compete in pageants and was pretty good at it, too. She still has that smile and that stance. She use to tell me how homely and ugly she was growing up but I have a hard time believing that even after showing me the photos in Grandma's picture box.

Mom was prom queen, cheerleader captain, and class valedictorian. I never understood how because she was so quiet and never talked much. But I love my parent's relationship. There are always all over each other. I'm sure that they had their share of arguments and disagreements but they shield me of that. I sometimes wish they had slipped up and just argued once in front of me. It would let me know that life wasn't a fairy tale.

I got a call from Daddy saying that they won't be able to make the wake but will be there for the funeral but I didn't see them. When they arrived at the house, I was sitting in the kitchen nursing a cup of tea. I heard Daddy's voice first saying, "Wealth and riches is most definitely in this house." He marched into the kitchen where Eva gave him a cup and saucer and said, "Coffee, please?"

"Don't mind if I do." he said. I stood up and ran and jumped into my Daddy's arms and I sobbed softly. I saw Mom standing behind him.

I could see the look on her face as she hugged me along with Daddy. I could tell that with those red and hazel eyes, she had been crying too but didn't want me to know. We broke our embrace and Mom went over to Eva and asked for some tissues. Mom walked towards me and put her arms around me and softly asked, "How are you doing, Lady Bug?"

"Mom, it so hard, you know. I never thought that I would miss Harvey this much."

"What are you going to do?" she asked.

"I really . . . I honestly don't know."

From behind Daddy's cup of coffee, he said, "God has you, baby girl." He took a couple of sips and let out a disgusting 'AH!' and fanned his hand in front of his face. Eva quickly dashed to the refrigerator to bring out the cream for him. "Thank you." he said. Eva flashed him a bright smile.

"You know, me and your father can stay here as long as it takes. Do you still want the house whole to stay? We can handle whatever they can do for a few days."

Dad cleared his throat and whispered, "Ah, Hazel? Have you seen the size of this house?"

"Y'all can stay as long as you want but they stay as well. Some don't have any where to go or have anything else to do. They are loyal and that's why I call them house whole family rather than servants." I said.

"Well" Daddy said as he clapped his hands and rubbed them together. "I guess that settles it. Besides, Hazel, they have their own thing going on here. We don't need to disrupt that. Baby girl, do you have a place quiet where I can plug up my laptop?" He walked over the Mom and gently kissed her on the cheek. "Why don't you relax, Hazel, huh?"

The only place I knew that he would be comfortable is on the other wing where Harvey spent most of his time. "Daddy, there is a place where you can study upstairs. You can use any room upstairs you want." I walked over to the island where Eva was preparing a salad. "Eva, usted y Myra por favor tome el gran cuidado de mis padres. Déle el uso lleno de la oficina de Harvey y prepare el dormitorio de Harvey para lo que ellos necesitan." *("Eva, you and Myra please take great care of my parents. Give him full use of Harvey's office and prepare Harvey's bedroom for whatever they need.")* Eva immediately places the knife on the cutting board beside the cucumbers. I washed my hands at the sink in the island and dried them with a paper towel. I picked up the knife and started cutting the cucumbers where she left off. I love her salads. They are always so fresh. She kept an herb garden in the window over the kitchen sink. Each time she makes salads, they are never the same. I simply tell her what I don't like and I leave it up to her on what to cook unless I have a special taste for something. This time, she had cucumbers, cherry tomatoes, turkey bacon bits, honey roasted pecans and homemade garlic croutons. Don't ask me how she did it, but they're always delicious. (I always insist on the croutons.)

As I continued slicing the cucumbers, I started thinking about Harvey and how he loved Eva's salads. I started thinking about how I still had mixed emotions about our marriage. Seeing how he left me everything, including the companies, I can't help but think that I really need to make sure that I keep Zoë happy. She is the only person that I know of personally who knows the company inside and out. I needed to make sure that she has no plans in leaving.

Suddenly, Mom grabbed my right hand and forced the knife from my hand. "Didn't you hear me calling you? I have been calling you for a few minutes. Are you ok?" I didn't answer, I just stared at her. "Come on. Maybe you need to go upstairs and take a nap or something." She called out for Myra. "Coming!" Myra answered from the laundry room. "Sweetie, can she speak English?" Mom asked in a whisper. I looked at her like I can't believe strapped on a pair of balls and asked me that in front of her. "Yes, she can. It's Eva that is not too comfortable. So I speak Spanish to her just to make her comfortable."

"But why? Does she know any English at all?" Mom asked.

"Yes, she can speak some English. I don't always speak Spanish to her all the time."

Chapter 14

I guess I was more exhausted that I was thought. I don't know how long I was asleep because I lost all track of time. The last thing I remember, I was talking to Mom and something about cutting cucumber. I laid there in the bed for a few minutes. I looked around and the clock read 5:36 am. Wow! But what day was it? I reached for the remote and click on the television. It was Sunday. It all came back to me now: Harvey's funeral, his family was here and so were my parents. I immediately closed my eyes and sunk deep inside the covers. My chest ached and back burned. All I wanted to do was scream. I didn't want to hurt no more. I didn't what to remember all that had happened because I knew in my mind that I needed to go forward but my heart housed this piercing pain that shot through my whole body. I tried to take a deep breath but I couldn't. No matter if I inhaled or exhaled, I felt that it was my last breath regardless.

I never understood how people could have people all around them but still felt alone until that very moment. Harvey was more than my estranged husband. He was a major part of my sanity. Even before all this madness manifested, I knew who I was even thought who I was wasn't who I wanted to be. I felt aware. I had ignorant peace rather than blessed assurance.

I didn't want to talk to or see anyone. I felt the side of my head starting to produce a headache. I heard a knock on the door and a muffled voice. The door opened and I felt a presence in the room that sat on the side of the bed. It was Mom. "I know you not sleep. You forget I was your mother?" she announced. I slowly pulled down the covers and saw my mother standing there in her pink pajamas and matching robe and slippers. Her hair cascaded down her face. She had two mugs of tea on a serving tray. It was my favorite, peach. I smiled as I sat up. She sat the serving tray on the table next to the bed in order to get in bed beside me. Once inside the covers comfortably, she reached for one mug and handed it to me. She waited for me to take that first sip.

"Mmmmmmm. Mom." I said with a smile. It reminded me of the time when I was living at home and I had just met Harvey. I didn't want to tell Daddy because I was afraid that Daddy wouldn't let me marry him. So, for a while, Mom only knew. She said that we would tell Daddy when the time was right.

"You know, Lady Bug." she said as she sipped on her tea. "I know you just lost your husband but I know that there's something else bothering you. What's wrong?" I knew it was inevitable and I also knew that I could trust her no matter what. I sat my tea on the night stand and opened the drawer. I pulled out my journal and flipped to the back and pulled out a yellow manila envelope addressed to me. I handed it to Mom and then I picked up my tea and continued sipping. It was Mom's special blend of real dried peaches. That's why it made me feel melancholy. Mom sat her tea on the night stand next to her and silently opened the envelope. She pulled out the letter of explanations from Harvey. I couldn't look at her while she read the letter so I looked at the television. Soon enough, Mom cleared her throat and calmly but slowly placed the letter back inside the envelope. She picked up her tea and asked, "Who else knows?"

"Only the ones mentioned in the letter and now you and I'm sure you're going to tell Daddy."

"Not right now, I'm not. How did this make you feel when you read this?"

"I was with him when died, Momma. He told that he loved me and he asked if I would forgive him and I have. It really wasn't that cut and dry but I had to think about the fact that he could have been selfish and not tell me. He could have had sex with me and your only Lady Bug would have AIDS right now and not know or worse, dead. Oh, and I did tell my best friend."

I added.

"Are you talking about Delia?" she asked.

"Her name is D'Kyra, Momma." We laughed a little.

"What happened on your wedding night?" She asked as she put her empty cup on the night stand. I think the reason I didn't want to tell her was because I didn't want Mom to think different of me or be disappointed in me.

"I didn't want you or Dad to find out because I wanted to give myself to Harvey first. I saved myself just like you and Daddy taught me." I stopped for a minute because I didn't want to cry. I felt my heart racing and my throat close up.

"But, Khylee, what happened?" she asked.

"Mama, he really did try to save me. Harvey tried but when they shot the driver in the head and killed him, I screamed." Mom repositioned herself in the bed and grabbed me by my shoulders. By this time, I was sobbing uncontrollably.

"WHAT HAPPENED?" she screamed.

"One had a knife at Harvey's throat and the other one had a gun at his head while the other one . . ." I stopped. I couldn't tell her. What would she think?

"Khylee? Sweetheart? I love you. I'm your mother and there is nothing, NOTHING that is going to change that. Let me help you. What happened, baby? What did the other one do?"

"He . . ." I began as she took my face in her hands and looked me square in the eyes but I saw tears in her eyes. Then, I think it was at that moment I knew that she figured it out.

"NO! No way, Khylee. Oh, please, God, NO!!!!" She grabbed me and hugged me tightly as if her embrace would erase all the pain and humiliation of the rape. She pulled back and kissed my forehead and embraced me again. "Oh, honey, I'm sorry. I am so sorry."

Mom repeated this for a few minutes. Each time she said it, it was like a little more of the puzzle fit perfectly. She cried. I cried.

"Does this have anything to do with why I am not a grandmother?"

I nodded while saying, "The trauma was too severe. Harvey kept taking me to the doctor and paying for all these test to make sure that I hadn't contract any kind of STD when all the time . . ."

" . . . when all the time he was the one who was screwing around and got the STD instead." She broke free of the embrace and asked, "But honey, why did you stay with him?"

"I really don't know, I mean what was I suppose to do, Mama?" She picked up the manila envelope and held it over her head and asked, "Is this the first you heard about this Annabella person?"

Reaching for a tissue, I blew my nose and put the tissue in the waste paper basket beside the bed saying, "I always had some suspensions but Mama, I couldn't prove anything. He was just never home. He would always call and tell me where he was. He always made sure that I had the best of whatever I wanted. The house whole was at my disposal. I could go and come as I pleased. I remember once I asked him why he wouldn't spend any time with me. He said simply said, "All of this will be yours. I promised to take care of you and that's what I plan to do." He never looked me in the eye but I kept telling myself that he loved me. Eventually, I fell out of love with him but I still loved him. Does that make since, Mama? Please tell me I did the right thing?"

Mama reached for a tissue and blew her nose. The more tears she wiped away, the more tears fell. She slowly shook her head with a twisted frown on her face. Mama's hazel eyes were so red and puffy and for a moment, I hated Harvey for making my mother cry.

"I don't know what you want me to say, Khy?" she blew her nose again. I walked over the fridge and pulled out two 4 ounce bottles of water. I popped open the first bottle and handed it to Mama. Then I popped open the other one and took a few gulps. I sat down on the bed and said, "Mom, don't say anything. I was with Harvey when he died. He was very coherent and he asked me to forgive him. He never wanted me to leave or divorce him because he promised to take care of me. He just wanted to make sure that after he died, I got everything and I do mean everything. Mom, I now own every Wilcox Pharmaceuticals. I own this debt free house and every dime that he has is now mine. He wasn't in any debt at all. So, I still haven't really wrapped my head around this yet but I have to forgive him. I have no other choice." Mom looked at me. It was like she was seeing me for the first time. "You're better than I am." She said.

"You taught me better than that. You taught me that the best gift you can give someone is a chance and that's what I gave Harvey. He was my husband and I couldn't tell him no."

I sat closer to her and whispered, "See, he protected me the best way he knew how. I could be bitter for the rest of my life about him being with Bella but look at all I would have lost."

* * *

Later that day, I called Zoë and asked her to give me pointers on the business. Seeing how I never went to college, it was really going to be a challenge to learn the basic things. I talked to Zoë about being my VP while I took the role on as President. We needed to hire a replacement for Zoë's position which was going to be a hard task. We decided to start the first thing Monday morning and work until we found the right person.

When I finally went downstairs, the foyer looked like a flower shop. It smelled of freshly cut grass and honeysuckles. I was amazed to see so many flowers and that all these people wanted to send their condolences. There was an envelope from Amanda that has a single red rose attached. I smelled the rose and smile. When I opened the envelope there was a single sheet of paper with a handwritten note on it. Amanda is so comical that I almost started laughing before I read it. I just know that it was something that would cheer me up. The note read:

Khylee,

Remember that bald repairman that would come to do maintenance on the sound machine? Girl, he owns this building! Did you know that? Call me.

Love you,
Mani

Wow! I said to myself. I had no idea that Chaz Boomerang *was* Blu Sky Repair. I realized that I hadn't thought about him in a while and I really don't know what Mani thought that little bit of information would do or how it was suppose to play out. I looked around the foyer at all the flowers, plants and arrangements. Eva came and stood beside me. She sighed, beamed a bright smile and waved her hand in the area of the flowers and said, "I put away?"

"Yes. Please." I noticed a floral arrangement with tulips and roses with a card attached. The card was 3 x 5 blue and white. As I got closer to the card, I noticed that it was a picture of the sky with clouds. My mouth dropped. Please, Lord, tell me . . . . it couldn't be. My heart was beating so fast that I thought it was going to bust out of my chest onto the floor. I started sweating and apparently, my face looked flushed because Eva asked with a twisted frown in her thick accent, "Is ok?" I nodded slowly and with the fingertips of my right hand, I pushed my chest as I took and deep breath. "Yeah, I'm fine." I said. "Girl, please."

"Ok." she said as she walked away with an arm full of arrangements. I watched her walk away and as soon as she was out of sight, I turned quickly to the blue card. I leaned over and quickly snatched the card from the arrangement and went into the half bath and locked the door. I pulled the lid down on the toilet and sat down. I sat there for a few minutes with the card in both my hands shaking. 'Oh my!' I thought. I turned it over so that the flap side was up, took a deep sniff with my eyes closed and opened it. I slowly pulled the card out. It matched the envelope. I placed the envelope on my lap and opened the card. It read:

Khylee,

I really don't know what to say but I have to say something. Since I haven't heard from you, I figured that you were going through a rough time because of Harvey's death. I'm here for whatever you need.

You will always be my girl so fold your arms and squeeze. This is me giving you a hug.

Chaz

I read it over and over again. It was really sweet of him. I really wanted to know what happened between him and Bella. All my daydreaming was soon cut short when I heard Ethel's voice. It sounded like fingernails on a chalk board. 'KHYYYYYLLEEEEEEEE!"

I wanted to stay inside this bathroom until they left but knowing her, she wasn't leaving until she insulted me just one last time. I put the card back in the envelope and stuffed in the pocket of my robe. I stood up and opened the medicine cabinet over the sink. The only thing that was in there was a first aid kit. I was looking for something sharp.

"Baby girl?" I heard H.C call out which seemed like right outside the door. Ethel's voice was upstairs now. I quietly opened the door and peeped out and saw the back of H C's head. I reached over and flushed the toilet and turned on the water faucet and wet my hands. I got the hand towel, dried my hands, opened the door and walked out.

"Oh. Baby Girl, how you feeling this morning?" H C asked. He reached out to give me a huge. "I'm good." We walked toward the foyer where Eva was clearing out the remaining of the floral arrangements. "Oh, H C, do you think you and Ethel may want some of these. I have more than enough. Take the flowers because I want to keep the plants."

"I don't but I'm sure Ethel may want something." he said. "Well, we are leaving and if there is anything you need, please let us know, okay?"

"Sure. Is Travis taking you to the airport?"

"No. We can take a cab." he said

"You don't have to, Travis will take you." I insisted.

"Sweetie, if you want to keep your driver, don't let him near Ethel. You know how judgmental she is. She'll drive him nuts before we get to the airport. A cab is fine, okay?"

Next to depart were my parents until Mom had to **Hazel** things up. I didn't see much of Dad because he was busy trying to barbeque. It was very successful but we kept trying to tell him that everyone don't eat barbequed chitterlings. Daddy stayed outside for a while with Hector and Eduardo who wanted to learn the art of barbeque whereas Dad learned Spanish. Dad's dialect was horrible. He didn't roll his 'R's' like he was suppose to. Personally, I think he sounded silly. That was Daddy; he loved a challenge. I hope he don't go home and tell his congregation that he *knows* Spanish because he has Latino and Cuban members. But knowing Dad, he will.

Mom, on the other hand, decided to rest on the lawn chairs by the pool yesterday and fell asleep in the sun. Sometimes I wonder about my mother. (Did I say I love my mother?) If intelligence is the key, she'd be locked out. Her hamster fell asleep at the wheel long ago. I wondered if you put her brains in a cat, if the cat would bark? (Did I say I love my mother?) Mom was sun burnt on her back. She was the color of that Grilled Salmon Filet I had last night. My parents! I have always wondered why I was an only child. Now I think I know. First: How you gon barbeque chitterlings and Second: How you just gon fall asleep in the sun? C'mon! But what's really sad is that Daddy has about 1000 member congregation, well when I was at home it was 1000 or so. Anyway, the saints look up to his leadership. I do admire my parent's sense of humor but I am now convinced that the funny things they did when I was growing up was due to clumsiness and being accident prone. The thing about being a leader is that you don't know if the people are following you or chasing you. I love my parents. We use a whole bottle of that sunburn medicine stuff on Mom. There was no way she was going to be able to sit comfortably going home so they had to stay until she was better.

After a long, hot, bubble bath, I realize that it didn't make me feel better at all. I only wanted to go back to bed but I couldn't. Today was the day I had to sign everything. I'm supposed to go the Wilcox Headquarters but I just wasn't feeling up to it. I dried off and put on my terry robe and crawled back into bed. I laid there and I cried for a few minutes. Later, I reached for my cell and called Trey but I only got voice mail. I left a message and decided to pull my laptop out. D'Kyra always encouraged me to write whenever I start feeling depressed. Maybe depressed is a strong word. I just don't want to be bothered with anyone right now. I know there are important things I am suppose to do but I just can't handle them right now. As long as I owned everything, why can't Zoë and Trey keep handling everything, especially if I'm signing there paycheck?

Chapter 15

*O*n October 3rd, I got a call from Stanley. He sounded really rushed and a bit preoccupied. "It's Dee. She's in labor. Can you meet us at the hospital?" I could hear her agonizing screams in the back ground. I panicked and paced back and forth. "Okay, but which hospital?" I asked.

"Ah . . . . the one on Hancock, hurry." Stanley hung up and I panicked. I grabbed a pair of sweats from the drawer and a white tee and slipped on a pair of shoes. I also grabbed a jacket and my ready purse. (It's already filled with the things I need just case: money, comb, hair clips, lip gloss, you know, the ready necessities.) On my way out, I told the house that I was on my way to the hospital because Mrs. MacAfee was in labor. I didn't wait for Travis, I drove.

When I arrived to the floor where she was, they were dressing Stanley complete with mask, shoes, scrubs, and the whole nine. I ran up to him being careful not to touch him and I asked, "What's going on? How is she?" I could see that he had been crying. He wouldn't even look at me. He said in a low sad voice, "It's bad. They think that the baby is breeched. They may have to take it."

"What can I do?" I asked. Stanley turned around and looked over his shoulder and said,

"Take my cell. Call Danita. She's Dee's sister. Make sure you tell her that Dee said NOT to tell their mother." I took the cell from his back pocket and strolled down the contacts and found Danita's number and called but it just kept ringing. Right before I was about to hang up, I heard a faint, "Hello?"

"Ah yes. Is this Danita?" I asked as I walked down toward the waiting room.

"Yes it is. Who is this?"

"Ah, my name is Khylee. I'm a very good friend of Stanley and D'Kyra's and we're at the hospital here in Diamond County, on Hancock. Girl, she's in labor and Stanley said that the doctor told him that it didn't look good." In between every syllable from my speech, Danita kept saying, "Oh, my God."

"Okay, I'm on my way." she said.

"But wait. Hello?" I called out.

"Yes, what is it?" they said not to tell your mother yet, okay?" I said.

'Okay. Okay. I'm on my way." she said. As I closed the flap, I took a deep breath and sat down. It was then that I realized that in my haste, I didn't tell her what floor not to mention the fact that I don't even know what she looks like. This was a blind meeting so I sat.

I hated waiting. I looked at magazines, I looked through all the newsletters and I tried calling JaVon but she was in a photo shoot. Suddenly, Stanley walked slowly through the double doors pulling off his beanie hat they gave him along with the mask and the gown. He looked at me sadly and asked, "Did you talk to Danita?" I walked over to him and nodded. He didn't say anything and I really didn't want to bombard him with questions so I sat there beside him. "She said that she was on her way." I added.

An old classmate of Stanley's, Ivan Wojohorowitz, was the specialist on duty that night and to Stanley's surprise he walked out for a consult with a nurse named Paige.

"Mr. MacAfee?" asked Paige. Stanley stood up and saw that she wasn't alone. The doctor looked at Stanley and his face lit up. "Mac?" he asked. "Wojo?" Stanley responded. They hugged each other while me and Paige looked awkward.

"Man, I didn't put two and two together on the name, Man." said the doctor.

"That's all good man. Tell me something, Wojo? How's my wife? What's going on?" Stanley asked. Dr. Wojo walked over to the seat across from where Stanley had been sitting and motioned for him to sit back down. "Mac, I'm not gon lie to you. There's no easy way to say this so I am just gon come right out with it." Dr. Wojo, stopped and took a deep breath and said, "We had to put you out because D'Kyra's lost a lot of blood too rapidly and she is in a coma." Dr. Wojo's face lost color and I could see that the next thing that was about to come from his mouth wasn't going to be pleasant. We jumped when Stanley's cell rung. It was Danita.

"Hello?"

"Where are you?"

"Still in ER." She hung up and I looked up to see a woman dressed in green walking toward Stanley who looked a lot like D'Kyra. It was scary. Stanley jumped up and they embraced.

"What going on? How is she? Did she have the baby yet?" Danita asked.

"Danita, this is Dr. Wojo, Wojohorowitz. He was about to tell us what's going on." He then looked at Dr. Wojo and said, "This is Danita, D'Kyra's sister."

"Please," said Dr. Wojo as he motioned for her to sit next to Stanley while I sat next to Dr. Wojo whereas Paige was on his other side.

Once again, the Dr. Wojo took a deep breath and closed his eye tight. Everyone knew that he was stalling and really didn't want to say anything. "We had to perform an emergency cesarean because the baby, your son, was breeched. Not only was he breeched, he was partially conjoined."

"What? What do you mean *conjoined*?" Stanley asked nervously as he leaned back in his chair.

"Some things don't show up on the ultrasound. I just assumed that your wife told you." Stanley shook his head and frowned. "The baby has a third leg and a third arm protruding from its abdomen." Dr. Wojo added.

"She never told me. She would always go to her appointments alone." Stanley said.

"When I asked her about telling you, she said that she would tell you. I had always hoped that I would meet with you together but she always said that you were working and couldn't get away. I'm sorry, Mac, I thought you knew." Dr. Wojo looked so hurt.

Danita gasped with her hands up to her mouth. I sat there for a moment and tried not to cry. I started thinking about how the baby wasn't Stanley's and wondering if this was her punishment from God for sinning and for caring another man's child and deliberately trying to pass this child off as Stanley's. A belly filled with sin literally crouching at her door. It was at that moment that the 'airplane circled around the airport': I'm just as guilty. I am aiding and abetting. This is when the migraines began.

"But that's not all." Dr. Wojo added with another deep breathe. "There was some sort of growth about the size of a soft ball attached behind the right ear which made the poor thing look as though he had two heads."

Stanley looked up and said, "Wojo, that poor thing is my son. His name is Isaiah. Please refer to him as such." Tears flowed as he spoke softly but firmly.

It was very quiet in that waiting room except for the distant stat paging of doctors and nurses. A few beeps, elevator dings and bongs from the patients at the nurse's desk, "Can we see either of them?" asked Danita.

"Sure, you can see D'Kyra but I wouldn't recommend seeing the . . . Isaiah." Dr. Wojo cut his eyes over at Stanley. The doctor stood up and looked at the Paige and said, "Go make sure that Isaiah is stable enough for a visit but only for these. No one else." He then turned to Stanley, Danita and myself and said as he shook his head, "Isaiah is not going well at all. He has a tracheotomy and also hooked up to a heart monitor." He cleared his throat and continued, "Isaiah has a deformity and a conjoined severely under developed twin. He has a third leg attached to his left side, a third arm attached to his abdomen and . . ." with a heavy sigh, "if he survived, his brain would be so ill deformed that he wouldn't make it past his first birthday if that long. If you'll excuse me, I need to get back to Isaiah." As he started to walk away, Stanley caught his arm and asked, "My wife? How is she?"

"She's stable and holding her own right now. It's possible we can take her off respirator as long as she remains stable but I really need to get back to Isaiah."

"Please, do whatever you can, okay?" said Danita.

D'Kyra never saw him because she slipped into a coma shortly after Isaiah was taken. The cause for the comatose wasn't really expected. It was like the whole thing was a bad dream. My best friend was in trouble and I couldn't do anything about it and I had no one to talk to about this but the one that I needed and I needed D'Kyra. Plus, I still haven't heard from JaVon.

We decided to go to the chapel and pray. I only went with them just for the company but I felt that God stopped listening to me the day I was attacked. I felt he didn't care about me so why should I pray to someone who stood by and watch me and not help? And yes, I still held a grudge. I still don't understand why I had to go through what I went through.

I felt my pocket vibrate. I reached in and pulled out my cell phone and to my surprise, it was JaVon. 'Saved by the bell', I thought. I excused myself from their prayer service and walked out in the hallway.

"Hello?"

"Hey, girl. What's going on?" He asked.

"Hey."

"You okay? Sorry I haven't been available. I'm on my way now to Beijing. How's everything?"

"Remember D'Kyra?"

"Yes. She okay?" asked JaVon with a concern whisper. "Wait, turn that down." she said to someone in the car. "Okay, what happened?"

"She's in a coma after giving birth through an emergency C-Section but the baby is not doing so good and . . . Harvey died."

"WHAT?????? Wait. Y'all shut up." She said to whoever it was in the car with her. "Did I just hear you say that Harvey died?"

"Yeah and then this thing with Dee, I don't know what to do. The baby is morbidly deformed and they are examining him right now to see the best alternative."

I heard her say, "James, I need to get back to home. Postpone everything. Okay, hello? Khy? You still there?"

"Yeah."

"I'm on my way. I should be there in about . . . an hour. Where are you?" she asked.

"I'm a still at the hospital, the one on Hancock. You know the one?"

"Yeah. Hold on a minute. How soon will be get there with the chopper or the jet?" I could hear James' muffled voice but couldn't make out what he was saying. I looked at my left hand and it was shaking. I took a deep breath and was determined not to cry because Stanley needed me and I felt that I was the only person who could shed the real light on this situation.

"I'll call you as soon as we get in the area, okay?" JaVon said. She sounded very panicky and I didn't want anything to happen to her trying to get to me.

"Be careful, okay?" I said as my voice cracked.

"Look, you don't worry about me. I will be there as soon as I can and you stay strong and I love you. I will be there for you, okay?" She hung up and all I could think about was the fact that I had a lot of explaining to do to her about Harvey and how he died. Plus the fact that I have to bear the sinful secret of D'Kyra's. I was mentally exhausting.

As we journeyed back to the waiting room, we got word from Paige that Dr. Wojo wanted to talk to Stanley about the progress of Isaiah. She also bought sandwiches and drinks which was a welcomed sight because I hadn't eaten anything in a while.

The waiting room we were in wasn't the usual room. It was more like the resident's lounge on the 4th floor. This is where they wanted to do the operation and they moved D'Kyra to the room down the hall from the lounge. Actually, it was all handled by Dr. Wojo as a favor because he knew Stanley. It was small but more private than the regular waiting room. It was like a cross between a small locker room and a dorm about 20 x 20. There were two sets of bunk beds with only one pillow, a fitted sheet, a flat sheet and one of those tan warming blankets. There was a small white refrigerator in the corner of the room with a small table that looked like a large card table with two microwaves on it that also had a coffee pot between it. There was also a day bed there with only the seating that came with it. In the corner was a pantry looking closet with no doors or curtains or anything that separated it from the other part of the room. The room smelled of rubbing alcohol.

There was a wall filled with medical books and two desktop computers that were next to a wall of about 10-15 lockers and the lockers had names on them that read: Gomez, Wilkerson, McIntosh, Clark, Grier, Bullock, Whipple, Campbell, Ball, Norton, Krueger, Jackson, and Flowers. There were more but they didn't have names on them.

The sandwiches were in clear covered containers that were cut in half with those long tooth picks sticking through them and the colored flagged on the end. There were a pack of chips sitting in the middle with a pickle, too.

As we settled to eat, Paige returned with a clip board with a lot of papers attached. "Mr. MacAfee, Dr. Wojo wants to operate on Isaiah. He wants to remove the third arm and leg." She flipped through the papers and said, "All this says is that you give us consent to do the operation." She hands him the clip board.

"What about Isaiah's head?" Stanley asked.

"This only states consent for the other, not the head. That's more intense and, well, I really need to let the doctor tell you the rest. Please, I'll just sit the papers here."

"I don't wanna do anything to Isaiah until I talk to my wife." announced Stanley.

"You do understand that we can't guarantee when that will be, Mr. MacAfee?"

Stanley said nothing.

"You don't have to do anything right now. Just take your time. Can I get you anything else right now?" Paige said softly.

"Yes. There's another person that's going to be looking for us. Her name is JaVon Tipton. Will you bring her in here when she gets her?"

"No problem. If I can do anything else, please, let me know, alright?" she asked with a really warm smile.

"No. Thank you, Paige." She walked out of the door and I pulled out my purse and took my brush and a band to put my hair up.

I walked over to where the clip board was sitting and picked it up and scanned over it. I went over to where Stanley was but he was just staring into space. I don't even think he was listening to anything Paige had said. I looked at Danita and shook my head. She hunched her shoulders.

While Danita and Stanley were sound asleep, I kept thinking what if Isaiah needed blood. Stanley couldn't do it because he wasn't the father and then he's going to look at me. What am I suppose to say? I think this is when I actually cried for the first time about D'Kyra.

When JaVon arrived, I jumped up from the bottom bunk and pushed her into the hallway. She grabbed me and hugged me so tight. It had been 19 weeks since Harvey's death. I was okay; I mean the thing with D'Kyra helped keep my mind off Harvey. I just kept telling myself that he is away on business and that Trey and Zoë were handling his calls. Call it denial? Well, people mourn in their own way and in their time and this is how I chose to deal with this.

"Well, I don't really wanna talk about Harvey right now. How long are you here for?" I asked.

"As long as you need me to." She said as she played with my hair. She pulled my pony tail and sang, "My little pony." It made me smile a little and I think she knew that it would.

"I want you to stay with me, Okay?"

"Sure, but what happened?" she asked as she sat down in the general waiting area.

"Her husband, Stanley, called me and told me that she had gone into labor. I could hear her screaming in the back ground over the phone and it even sounded like something was wrong. Well, when I got to the ER, we found out that she had to have an emergency C-Section because the baby, who he named Isaiah, did I tell you this already?"

"No."

"Anyway, Isaiah was not only breeched but morbidly deformed and conjoined. Something happened; she lost too much blood at an alarming rate and slipped into a coma. It's been almost 24 hours now and we've been here with him."

"Who's *we*"

"Danita's here, that's her sister. She looks just like her, too. D'Kyra knew all of this but didn't tell her husband. She kept telling the doctor that she would tell him when at the same time; she told her husband that everything was fine. I guess she didn't want him to worry and she believed God." I really didn't believe a word of what I just said. I knew the real reason why and I couldn't tell anyone. I hated knowing and I wish I didn't know but I do and I have to live with this.

"What are they going to do?"

"It's possible that they can remove the extra limbs but we don't know about his head."

Dr. Wojo came from around the corner with Paige and had a piece of paper with him. He was headed in the lounge so we followed him.

"Mac?" He said as he walked through the door. Dr. Wojo walked over to where he was sleeping and nudged him a bit. Stanley jerked awake. His eyes were blood shot. He looked confused and the first thing he said was, "Oh, God. I thought this was a bad dream. But it's not." He sat up from the bunk bed and held his head cupped in his hands. I touched Danita on her arm and nudged her awake. I opened the fridge and gathered bottles of water. The sandwiches that were given to us earlier were sitting in the fridge on the second shelf. Someone made a really nice gesture.

"Okay," said Dr. Wojo, "I got the labs back and we have good news and bad news." We all looked at Stanley and with his face still in his hands; he said in a muffled voice, "What's the good news?"

"The good news is we can successfully detach the extra limbs." I cringed and braced myself for the bad news. What if they needed blood? Stanley's won't match. I passed out water to everyone when at the same time I felt like I was going to pass out.

"And the bad news?"

"The bad news is that Isaiah's growth on his head is a medical mystery and a challenge because there were two heads and two ears. One of his heads has two eyes, one nose and one mouth. The other was only a lump of soft tissue with no bone which means that the seemingly normal head had an opening to where the second head was attached wasn't secure. The second head is exposed brain with skin over it."

"Then you can just remove it, right and then reconstruct his head because there is no skull to cut, right?" ask Stanley hopefully.

"Simply removing or cutting off the extra soft tissue isn't so cut and dry. It could kill Isaiah. Most of the brain was the morbid part. The part that is intact in the brain wasn't his brain at all. It's like the part that's in the skull is dead tissue and the part with no skull protection is where the brain is, all the nerves and everything. It's going to be a challenge to reverse the process."

Stanley stood up and asked, "What will happen if we do nothing?"

"If we do nothing, Isaiah won't live to be productive. There's nothing to protect his brain."

"Are their papers to sign for this part of the surgery?" asked Danita.

"I have them right here." said Paige as she held up the clip board.

"What happened to the other papers? The first ones?" asked Stanley.

"I signed them." said Danita. "I *am* her sister. I should have some say so."

"Okay. Let's do this." said Stanley as he reached for the papers and took the pen from Paige's hand. He then gave the pen back to her and said, "Go take care of my son." Stanley's tone changed to an almost doubtful tone. "I really would rather make this decision with my wife. I mean, she don't even know what's going on."

"Stanley, just tell her that we did it. If she wanna be mad at someone, have her mad at me." Danita said. "This won't be the first time she's been mad at her sister.

"Alright." Dr. Wojo said as he rummaged through the papers. "I have everything I need." He turned to Paige and said, "Have them prep Isaiah for surgery."

"Why don't you let me call Pierre and have him bring some clothes? You go back in the lounge and get some rest and I will let you know when Pierre gets here." I suggested. "You can't do anything right now but wait. I'm going to go see Dee, okay?" Stanley turned and walked away. I haven't seen him eat anything since we've been here. As a matter of fact, I think his sandwich is still in that little fridge.

It seemed like it took forever for them to operate of Isaiah. I went down the hall to see if I could visit D'Kyra. You know they always say that patients that are in a coma can hear and are aware of their surroundings. I really needed to talk to her.

Me and Von went to visit her. The room was behind a glass sliding door rather than wooden. It was a nice room. There was a TV and a sofa sleeper. I knew that because you could see the directions on the side of the sofa on how to use this bed. The top of the door frames had drapes that you could pull together for privacy.

I sat my purse on that sofa and walked over to her and sat on her bed like I sat on the bed next to Harvey. There was no tubing in her. She's asleep and she looked as such. She was so peaceful looking it was shameful. It brought back memories of Harvey and I choked. I took a few deep breaths and Von took me by the hand and asked if I was okay.

"No, I mean the last time I was in a hospital, I watched Harvey die and this is one of the two best friends I have in the whole world. She was there for me when I lost Harvey. What am I going to do? Whose gonna be my best friend now when you are on tour again? Oh, God." I sat on the sofa and cried. "You two are all I have. I have no children and no family here. It's just me and the house whole in that big ole mansion."

I walked over to Dee and whispered in her ear saying, "You are going to have to wake up. You have a little boy, named Isaiah and Stanley really thinks this baby is his. I can't keep covering for you." It was in a joking manner, hoping that it would cause her to flinch or jerk or something. But, there was . . . nothing.

I stepped out of the room and called Myra and asked her to bring a couple of pairs of pants and a couple of shirts and the toiletry bag in the bottom of my closet. When I got back in the room, JaVon was holding her hand, singing and praying in tongues. I stood there for a moment watching and listening. At first, I thought that it was a waste of time because she didn't make a move or even acknowledge that I was there but when JaVon was there, it was different.

JaVon's voice is so sultry and so heartwarming that I notice something miraculous. You could almost see a halo . . . no, not a halo. It was like a mixture between orb lights and florescent lighting. As I started walking closer to her bedside, D'Kyra's breathing altered but only slightly. I sat in the chair next to her bed while JaVon continued singing and speaking in tongues. Then I noticed a thin but steady stream of tears that cascaded down the side of D'Kyra's face. I was blown away. I didn't know whether to run and go get Stanley or to just stay there and continue watching but I was amazed.

The melody was one that I recognized but couldn't quite put my finger on it. I didn't worry about it at the time; I just wanted D'Kyra to wake up. But she didn't.

Chapter 16

On Thanksgiving, Stanley let us all know that he was going to make arrangements to move D'Kyra home. There will be three nurses assigned to her, one for each shift. They want to make sure that she has round the clock care because her muscles need to be exercised even though she's not aware. Stanley did say, however, that she did squeeze his hand a few times. That's remarkable.

Their pastor, Aaron Phillips, visited them in the hospital a few times and he really seemed to be a really attentive Pastor. He managed to get her to squeeze his hand, too. This made Stanley hopeful, on the other hand, they went to visit Isaiah but he was still the same. Stanley still had faith that she would wake up in time. He didn't want to listen to reason. At least no blood was needed.

It was around 10 am when the ambulance brought D'Kyra home. The children were aware that their mom was sick and she was sleeping and that she need rest. They were also aware that their little brother was really sick and still in the hospital so that the doctors could make him well. Deuce was about to turn 11 and was very brainy. He went online and did his own research about everything. Deuce was the spit of his Dad. He was nearly as tall as his Dad as well. He was slender, his complexion was caramel and he finally got his Dad's permission to get those twists in his hair but the texture of his hair was more like his mom's and it wouldn't 'nap up' enough so, he had to keep it cut short. I teased him all the time saying that he had cat hair. Lisette was almost 9 and she was very smart for her age and she did the same as Deuce, consulted the internet for her mom's and little brother's condition. Lisette went one step further. She clicked on photos. There was blood curdling screams coming from her room which was just across the hall from Deuce.

"Deuce! Come here, quick!" she screamed. She was about to click print as Deuce burst through the door.

"What is it? Lizzie, what's wrong?" he asked. She sat there crying with one hand over her mouth and the other one pointing at the printer. "Is this Isaiah? Is this what he gon look like?" Deuce reached over and pulled the paper from the printer tray. It was a picture of a baby with vertical craniopagus malformation. The baby on the net was severely disfigured whereas Isaiah wasn't.

"Lisette, don't look at this." He said as he logged her off the computer. He reached over and embraced her as she sobbed uncontrollably. Ms Connie walked in the room. "What's wrong, sweetheart?" she asked as she went over to Lisette.

"I want my mama." she said. "I wanna see her right now." Ms. Connie went across the room into the bathroom and reached for a white hand towel. She turned on the faucet and ran cold water onto the towel and squeezed it out. Ms. Connie then took the towel over to Lisette and offered to wipe her face. "Now you don't want your mother to see that you have been crying, do you?"

"No, ma'am." she stuttered. Deuce smiled and said, "Thanks, Ms. Connie." He pulled Lisette's arm and said, "Get up, girl. Let's go see Mama."

"Thanks, Ms. Connie." Lisette gave her a huge bear hug. As they walked out of the room, Deuce decided to linger and take that picture that printed and fold it. He'll throw it away later.

The room that D'Kyra slept was downstairs on the first floor. It was easier for the house whole and for the nurses. Nurse Linda came in the mornings at 7 a.m. She made sure that D'Kyra got her morning feeding and her lunch at 12 noon. By 3 p.m., Nurse Amy came a little early to help Nurse Linda with her exercises before Linda left for the day. They also worked together in turning D'Kyra to keep the bed sores away and they gave her sponge baths. Then at 7 p.m., Nurse Betty came a bit early to do basically nothing. This shift worked out find for her because she was older and all her children were grown and away from home with lives of their own whereas Nurses Linda and Amy were younger. Linda was in her mid 30's, married with 3 children of her own and she was delighted to leave the hospital for a while. Nurse Amy wasn't married but had two classes in the morning. She wanted to be general practitioner.

The nurses all share one bedroom and bathroom (not at one time of course) which is adjoining D'Kyra's room that it overlooks a small maze garden park that was build for the children. The secret thing about his maze is that you can't get lost because there are arrows pointing the direction out. How sweet.

D'Kyra's room was well lit in green and white. It was beautiful. There was a small table fountain of water and rocks that set the mood at peaceful. It was sitting on a table next to the bed on an antique oak table. The matching table was occupied with a humidifier. There was a small kitchenette on the other side of the bathroom (which was a walk through) and the kitchenette held all the necessities for D'Kyra.

They put a rocking chair in the corner next to the bed and it was very comfortable whenever I was there. Sometimes, Faye would sit in it when she would read Zuaenette a bedtime story. It would seem to calm Zuaenette down to see her sleeping mother before going to sleep herself. One particular night, Faye brought Zuaenette to D'Kyra's room and Zuaenette ran over to her bedside, "Mommy Lady!!!!" She tried to climb into bed with her but the feet in her neon green footy pajamas were slippery and there wasn't much traction on that polished hardwood floor. Her feet moved to no avail, almost like watching a cartoon run in mid air. Faye ran over to help her crawl in the bed and cuddle next to her mother.

"Shhh!" Zuaenette's tiny hands didn't get the fingering quite right. She spit mostly on her hand rather than actually giving the shush. "Mommy Lady seeeeeping."

"That's right, love." agreed Faye. "Now do you want to be sitting in my lap or lying next to your Mum?" Faye tried to sway her from the bed in order not to disturb D'Kyra's rest by patting her lap.

"No, love. Mummy Lady." Zuaenette folded her arms and leaned over on D'Kyra's chest. Zuaenette has been picking up the British dialect from Faye as well.

"Very well then." Faye said as she made herself comfortable in the rocker. She opened the book and thumbed through the pages until she found just the right story. "Ah," Faye said. "Sleeping Beauty. Would you be liking that story, Love?" she asked Zuaenette.

"YEAH!" cheered Zuaenette as she clapped her hands and laughed. "Mommy Lady *Seeping* Beauty?"

"That's right." agreed Faye. "Your Mum is Sleeping Beauty."

" . . . and we *pup* and *pup* and **bow** the hoss down?" Asked Zuaenette innocently confusing Sleeping Beauty and the Three Little Pigs. Faye laughed at the language of a three year old. "That's right. "bow the hoss down."

As Faye started reading the story, Zuaenette pulled out a pink doll's brush from her pocket along with a fist full of barrettes which in her case were only three. She crawled up on her knees and brushed and styled her mother's hair by adoring it with a yellow, red and green barrette. Faye happened to look up and saw the monstrosity of her hair and didn't have the heart to take it down, lease way not in Zuaenette's presence.

Nurse Betty was settling in the bedroom and came in just in time to see Zuaenette yawn and snuggle next to her mother. They usually let her sleep for a few minute until they remove her and take her upstairs to her crib but this time, they took her immediately.

Nurse Betty walked over to the bed to collect the baby and offered to take her to give Faye a little rest. Faye scooted down from the rocker and followed Nurse Betty to put the baby to bed.

Lisette couldn't sleep. She was worried about her mother and brother. She looked at the time which was shone on the ceiling of her room from the clock. It was a present from her Dad on her 8th birthday. It was a stuffed frog that sat on a lily pad and in the stomach of the frog was clock. If you look at the stomach where the clock was, the time read backward but if you sat the frog on its back in a clearing, it would shine on the ceiling like the batman symbol.

It was 9:27 p.m. and she peeled the covers partly back and kicked them off the rest of the way and rolled over on her knees beside the bed to pray. At first she didn't know what to say, so she kneeled for a few minutes and sobbed lightly. She reached for a tissue from the night stand and resumed the praying stance. She cleared her throat, wiped her tears and began to pray:

> *Dear Jesus. We have lots of things. We may even have more than some people so I don't really feel right by asking you for anything else but I think it's okay because I'm not asking for myself but for my Mama and my little brother, Isaiah. I looked it up. Isaiah means, "The salvation of God". I'm asking for you to give Mama and Isaiah your salvation. Please save them. Let Mama wake up and be normal again and let Isaiah be alright so he can leave the hospital. Amen."*

Instead of Lisette going to bed, she pushed up on the bed, reached for her purple terry robe and put it on over her white pajama. Slipping on her purple house slippers, she walked to the bedroom door. She put her ear to the door to see if she could hear anything or anyone. Nothing. She slowly opened the door and peeked out to see if anyone was coming. She didn't hear or see anyone. The coast was clear. She walked out into the hallway and gently closed the door behind her. She walked down the hall and could hear Faye softly humming an English lullaby to Zuae. She quickly walked past her sister's room and reached the top of the steps. As she traveled down the main stairs, her heart raced. Half way down, she heard "BONG!" "BONG!" She let out a mousy squeal but soon realized it was the Grandfather clock that was in the corner beside the banana tree on the 2nd floor. It bonged 10 times. She ran to the rest of the way down the stairs (sort of like Cinderella leaving the ball) and didn't stop until she got to the outside door frame of her mother's temporary bedroom. She stood there for a few minutes to catch her breath while her breathing became regulated; she heard voices coming from the room. The door was partially opened and in her excitement, she opened the door being careful not to disturb anything because she wasn't sure where Nurse Betty was.

Nurse Betty made it a habit of talking to D'Kyra as if she was participating in the conversation. Betty had a lot of experiences with comatose patients and she knows that talking and treating them as if they can talk back helps with recovery. So, as Betty watched the late night talk show, she would laugh and talk to D'Kyra as if she was wide away and talking back. These are the voices that Lisette hears. She stood there for a few more minutes outside her mother's bedroom door and looked in and listened to the nurse talk to her mother and the television.

The only light that was in that bedroom was from the two lamps, the TV and the faint lighting in the bathroom next to the bed. In all honesty, Nurse Betty saw Lisette when she first got to the door by way of her shadow on the wall. She just pretended not to see Lisette because she knew that the children were worried about their mother and Lisette was curious.

Lisette stood there silently watching as her mother sleep. She learned all about comatose patients from internet and she knew that some may not wake up. This is why she didn't understand why her mother looked like she does when she was upstairs laying next to her Dad sleeping. Her cheeks weren't as rosy but her hair was just as shiny and beautiful as always, she thought. She also thought that she could wake her up if she said something that only she and he mother shared.

D'Kyra was lying on her left side which means she was facing the door. Her hair was braided in two braids that draped down her shoulders. They dressed her in a pair of red pajamas and made sure that everything was as normal as possible. The nurse also made sure that her favorite music was available as well as smells, sounds and any items like blankets or even stuffed animals.

Lisette looked around the room and saw all these things and it made her want to cry. She thought, "Why can't you just wake up and see all these things in your room, Mama?" Nurse Betty was straightening D'Kyra's bed and humming and talking to her all at the same time, sort of like singing to her. She brushed away any wrinkles in the spread with her hand and made sure that her pillows were just so. Lisette pushed opened the door and said, "Nurse Betty?"

"Yes, baby?" She stopped and smiled.

"Can I come in a talk to Mama, too?" Lisette asked while walking toward the bed.

"Oh, you sure can." Nurse Betty said. "Now you just bring your pretty self right over here and keep your mother company while I'll go get her something special. I'll be right back."

"Yes, ma'am." Lisette said. She stood there at the foot of the bed and watched as her mother's chest rose and fell. Lisette couldn't get over the fact that it just looked like she was asleep. She walked slowly around the side of the bed so that she could face her mother. There were two pillows supporting her back and Lisette crawled in the bed in front of her. She sat there for a minute and as she reached around and grab her mother's hand to hold. They were swollen and her rings were missing. She replaced her hand where it was previously resting and leaned closer to her face and took her thumb from her right hand and lifted her mother's left eyelid, whispered and asked, "Mommy, are you in there?"

Lisette paused for a moment. I guess she was expecting her mother to answer but Lisette is only 8 and a half and she wanted her mother to wake up.

She released her lid and lightly rubbed her mother's face and kissed her cheek and said, "I love you, Mommy. I know you're in there. You just rest and I'll be right here when you wake up, okay." Lisette curled up and cuddled next to D'Kyra and fell asleep.

Deuce, Stanley Ellis, Jr. was born in Nice, France weighing in at 7 lbs even. It was a fairly smooth birth. D'Kyra use to model a little. After she became pregnant with Deuce, she modeled maturity attire but after she gave birth, it became a little much and she didn't lose the weight quick enough for the agency so she gave it up.

Deuce looks just like Stan especially when Stan was a boy. He has his Dad's burnt auburn hair and everything. For the past couple of years, Deuce started wearing glasses, they are black rectangular shaped that were very flattering. He always wanted contacts because he wanted to cover up his natural green eyes with brown contacts. Go figure. His round face housed a complexion that was fair and this birthmark was on his right temple, just like his Dad's.

Lisette Cerise looks like her Dad and his side of the family. Since Stan was bi racial (Mom, Iris being white and Dad, Ellis, being Hispanic and Black), Lisette took more of the darker features. She was actually a premature baby weighing in at only 3 pound 6 ounces. By the time she was 4 months old, she no longer wanted her pacifier. She walked 3 days before turning 8 months old and was putting full sentences together by 18 months. She started reading at 2 and a half. Though she's only 8, she's in her second semester of 5th grade. She tutors middle school students Science and Algebra and some high school kids Geometric. Her rate is $5 an hour for Middle school students and $7 for the high school kids.

Lisette was named after D'Kyra's sister who died of breast cancer, the same day that Lisette was born. D'Kyra's sister, Lisette, was the life of the party. She was open-minded and with that open mind, she didn't hesitate to give you a piece of it. She and her sister were 22 months apart and most people thought that they were twins because they looked so much alike; more than she and Danita. They were as close as twin. She never married but had one child, a boy named Tomas de Silva Goldstein, who lived in New York with his Dad. Yelp! You guessed it! He's not only white, but Jewish. Nothing bitter to say, I just wanted to point that out because almost everyone in this book is bi racial and maybe even tri racial. True love covers a multitude of color. It's just that sometimes Lisette would be a bit sensational at times. She once went to the kids' school to bring Deuce his report card. She wore pink rollers, a short white silk robe with black patent leather stilettos. She didn't drink but she would always keep different types of drinks in her home for the company she'd keep, you know, just-in-case-beverages. She took a flask in the car with her to the school and parked in the handicap spot. (Not handicapped!) After she parked the car, she unfastened the seat belt and reached for the flask, being careful that no one saw her. She popped the top, smelled it and sighed. She sipped a little but didn't swallow; instead, she gargled while opening the car door and spit it out. She sucked air through her teeth and blew out air with her lips in a whistling stance. She gargled two more times, being careful not to swallow but she deliberately let some spill on her. Showtime!

Lisette grabbed the report card and took the keys and just before opening the door, she leaned on the horn for attention. She closed the door and staggered up to the school.

Now, Lisette was a very beautiful, runway looking model. She tried the modeling thing like her sister but she didn't like the lifestyle. When she reached the door, there was a button that you have to push in order for the secretary to let you in. She pushed the button and immediately started talking. It wasn't that type of button. After you buzz, you were to hear a click indicating that the door was open but, Lisette, really trying to make it look good, she started talking to the button. "DEUCE?" She screamed. "Juicy deucey?"

"Ma'am, you have to pull the door in order to open it." the lady said over the speaker.

"AHHhHHhh!" Lisette screamed. "Who dat? What I hear? Is that you, April? Girl, I saw Fred last night and I'm talking, woo!"

"Ma'am?" the voice said. "Please open the door and come inside." Now mine you, these people have no idea what Lisette look like much less what she is *almost* wearing.

"Oh. Okay." she said as loud as she could. The door clicked and clanked then as Lisette pulled the handle towards her, a cool breeze brushed her face and welcomed her. She nearly forgot that she was supposed to be intoxicated.

As she walked in the building, her three inch heels made a hollow echo against the floor. The office was the first door to the right and there were at least three people standing there looking to see who the hell that was yelling outside like they were from the east side of Mudslide, Alabama. She opened the door and zigzagged in and walked toward the front and slapped the report card on the counter and said, "I need to see Deuce." She stood there making sure that they felt the full affect of her breath. A tall black woman who was very well dressed walked up to Lisette and said, "Hi. My name is Ilene Collier. I'm the principal. Can I help you?" Lisette took the report card and handed to Ms Collier and said, "I need to see Deuce."

"Who is Deuce?"

"Oh. My bad. I bet y'all call him Stanley, don't you?'

"What's Stanley's last name, Ma'am?"

"Deuce's name is Stanley Ellis McAfee the second." Lisette said and nearly laughed. "Don't his name sound like a serial killer or at least someone who can fix your computer?" She didn't know how long she could do this. "Look, I gotta pee. Can you give this to him, please? I paid too much for these shoes to pee on them." So as she walked out of the office, she pulled her pretend panties from your butt. I say pretend because Lisette didn't have on any. When she got to the car, she called her sister and told her what she did.

Zuaenette, on the other hand, was named after 2 people. When D'Kyra was younger, she lived in a very small village near Nice, France. She went to school there when she was in 5th, 6th, and 7th grade. Her two best friends were LeZuae DuPont and Da'Ronette La Moiré. She still keeps in touch with them and they were even in each other's wedding and everything.

Zuaenette Moiré (*pronounced MO-hair*) complexion was fair and her eyes were gray and sometimes deep turquoise. Her face was round with wide eyes with dark lashes. Her hair was thicker and more wavy and kinky but of good texture especially if it's wet, it'll wave up. She hated her hair being combed. Her laugh was high pitched with a nervousness to it always sounded inviting. It's something about this child that she won't keep clothes on. No matter what Faye puts on her, she'd rather be 'bucket naked'. She would pick up anything outside and try to save it. She reminds me of myself when I was younger. I had a cat named Kit Kat. Daddy preached Hell, Fire and Brimstone for three Sundays straight. I went home and baptized the cat but she drown.

Chapter 17

Stan decided to agree with Dr. Wojo that it was time for Isaiah to be put out of his misery. Stan really wanted to wait until D'Kyra woke up but he just couldn't take that chance. He knew that there was no way that they could operate plus his head kept swelling. There was nothing else they could do except let him go. Isaiah was connected to a respirator and a heart monitor.

Stanley decided that it was better for Deuce and Lisette to see photos of Isaiah rather than come up to the hospital. He let them know what was happening and they seemed to understand.

At 4:08 p.m., Isaiah was pronounced dead. They decided to let the county take care of his body. To Stanley, it was an absolute annulment of birth.

Six days later, I went over to the MacAfee's Mansion as usual. Stanley was working as always and the kids were at school. Faye was chasing Zuae around the house with a pull up and a shirt. (I hope this isn't an early sign that Zuaenette won't be a pole dancer trying to make it rain somewhere.) I waited outside the bedroom door with my bag and laptop until the nurse finished with giving D'Kyra her bath, changing her linen, brushing her teeth and changing her pajamas. She opened the door to take the gathered linen and clothes to the laundry room.

"Oh'" Nurse Linda greeted me with a huge smile. "Good morning, Ms. Wilcox. How you doin'?" She said as she obviously struggled to hold the linen in her arms. I jerked forward to help her.

"Here. You need help? I got it." I offered as I walked forward but reached down to catch the slipping linen from her arms.

"Thank you." Nurse Linda said with a nervous laugh. I followed her to the laundry room where she met Myra. She was finishing up with the laundry until Nurse Linda came in with a small load. "Hi, Myra? Do you mind?" Nurse Linda asked as she squinted and pushed the armful of linen toward her. "I'm sorry but I didn't realize you were doing laundry." Myra smiled and said, "Is ok. I take do for." Myra took the load from her arms and I gave her mine. One of these days, I really need to teach her better English. Her vocabulary is like she was raised in the woods, and when humans found her, they shaved her down and taught her how to speak.

As we walked back toward the bedroom, I asked, "Is it anything you need me to help you with, I mean with Mrs. MacAfee?"

"Oh, no. Girl, I been doing this for a while. All I gotta do is comb her hair and fix her breakfast."

"Well, I can comb her hair for you." I offered. We stood there in the bedroom doorway for a few seconds as she looked around trying to figure out what to do. I mean, seriously, it wasn't an SAT question. "Well, okay." She walked over to the locked cabinet where D'Kyra's meals were kept. They were mostly these smaller looking IV bags filled with different colors of stuff. "I'll be right back. I'm gon take these and put them in the autoclave."

I took the comb from the nightstand drawer and I picked up the remote that operated the bed and raised her head. Then I grabbed the remote that operated the TV, sat on the side of the bed and pushed the power button.

"Ok, Dee. What do you wanna see today?" I asked as if she could contribute to the conversation. "You know, Gail? The girl who does my cousin's hair? You won't believe who she's messing with now. I saw Gail coming out of the Geyser Inn over on East Mountain Blvd down the street from your doctor's office. I was at the light and I started to blow at her until I saw, Pastor Phillips's brother, Raymond coming out behind her. He married Vera, remember? They got married last April, no it was last March, I think because it was cold but the trees were budding. Girl, I thought I was seeing things." I never turned my head towards her, I only surfed the channels to find something that I thought that she would like. "Oh good. **WAIT FOR TOMORROW** is on. Believe it or not girl, I got hooked—again! I was at home once looking for something to watch and I accidentally clicked on the Love Channel and there was Vincent and Cynthia and Marianne, and Larry and Richard and . . . that rich woman who has all that money . . . you know, she's been married at least nine times. What's her name?" I walked over to the side of the bed, removed the bands from her plaits and combed gently through the tangles. "Anyway, how you just gon keep marrying people? That's just straight up nasty! Can you really be in love that many times? Ok, now: Richard and Marianne are still together and girl, Larry is old and fat. Most of the other people on there are new and I didn't recognize. Well, you know I started taping it, right?"

I brushed through her hair and turned her head slightly to part it straight down the middle. I sat the comb and brush down on the bed and created one big braid on that side. At the end of the plait, I attached one of the two bands to the end so that it would not come undone. Then I walked on the other side of the bed to recreate the same braid on the other side of her head. "Girl, next time you fall asleep, cut her hair. It's too long and too thick for people to be spoiling you like this." As I finished her hair, I continued with my story about the pastor's brother. "Okay, so anyway, Raymond was married to Mufaro whose father is this president person named Obobo Umforo, or something? He's in trouble with the American Embassy; something about drug trafficking. Anyways, she always wore those weird looking clothes and that hair; it looked like the bottom of somebody's purse. She didn't believe in chemicals but she wouldn't get no braids. I bet she don't even shave her legs. She looked a hot mess, girl. At least get a press and curl, you know, I mean seriously. Maybe that's why Raymond was meeting Gail at the hotel. That's still something, I mean, how you just gon do this in broad open day light where there is an intersection? People can see all kinds of stuff at that light." Putting the final band on her hair, I said, "If I ever get in a 'comma', please make sure you take real good care of my hair like I am doing you." I returned the comb and brush to the drawer and said, "Be right back, gotta wash my hands. Girl, you got enough oil in your hair to fry a whole chicken. Who did that?"

When I returned, Nurse Linda was finishing up with D'Kyra's meal and I asked, "Do you mind if I sit with her?"

"No, come on in. I'll use the phone in the kitchen to call Dr. Wojo with my reports of her, okay. I tried while I was fixing her meal but I couldn't get through."

"Why don't you just fax them? I asked.

"Well, I would, but I wanna make sure that he gets them personally. I'm trying to call his cellular. Don't worry. I'll be right back."

"Take your time. It's okay. I'll be right here."

"Thanks, Mrs. Wilcox." I sat back down and turned the volume up and started watching *WAIT FOR TOMORROW* and talking to D'Kyra to catch her up. "Okay, see this guy? Well, Maggie thought he was dead and she remarried . . . ah . . . that guy!" I said as I eagerly pointed to the screen. "You know, I wonder if those people on the stories take routine STD tests? I mean, seriously, they kiss everybody all the time."

Then, that's when it happened. I heard a faint, hoarse, slurred voice asking, "I thought he was dead?" I snatched my head toward D'Kyra to see if she was the one how spoke. I stood up with my mouth open. I tried to take a step forward but my knees wouldn't cooperate with my brain so I fell back into that chair as if I was dead. Her frowned face was slightly pinched and she seemed to struggle to focus. She looked around the room and I tried to stand up again. This time I had a little momentum. I didn't know whether to run and yell for Nurse Linda or to grab her and cry. Apparently, my mouth was still opened because D'Kyra looked at me and said, "Mmm, you got Zackly." She let out a faint hum before speaking as if she was trying to search her brain for the right words. Lying there, being asleep for so long, I thought she would be a vegetable but I never said it. I couldn't even speak such thoughts. I laughed and I wiped my tears away. She kept closing her eyes a few times really tight and she licked her lips and swallowed hard. She frowned as if there was a bad taste in her mouth.

"Oh! Um, can I get you anything . . . water . . . ah . . . ." I asked nervously but before I would let her speak, I jerked up and said, "Wait! Your nurse is here." I ran to the door and yell toward the kitchen. I didn't want to leave her side just in case I was imagining the whole thing. I didn't want to appear stupid.

"Nurse Linda!" I yelled again. I heard her say, "Thanks, Dr. Wojo. I'll check back with you later. Good bye." I heard papers rustling and footsteps approaching all while she spoke up, "I'm coming." I stood there in the doorway waiting for the nurse and watching to make sure she stays awake.

When Nurse Linda came to the door, she asked, "Is everything alright?" I stood there and only pointed towards D'Kyra. She smiled as she looked directly at the nurse and waved timidly. Very professionally and trying not to show too much excitement, Nurse Linda walked over to her bedside and sat her portfolio on the dresser. "Well, I'm glad to see those beautiful eyes. How are you?"

"Mmmm . . . . ah huh." D'Kyra nodded and blink her eyelids slowly. I wondered if she will ever be the same. I know I sounded selfish but I needed to know if my best friend would be 100%. I paced as the nurse checked her over. She checks all her vitals and everything was normal. She took out her stethoscope and checked her heart. "Ah huh." commented the nurse. "I need for you to roll over onto her side. Careful, now." Nurse Linda took the stethoscope and said, "Now, I need for you to take a couple of deep breaths for me." Then the nurse walked over to the dresser where her portfolio sat and she thumbed through D'Kyra's chart. She took the pen from her smock pocket and with her thumb, clicked the top to open it to write. She went back to the side of the bed and said "Okay! Follow my finger." D'Kyra followed. "Ah huh." responded Nurse Linda. Nurse Linda cleared her throat and started writing again.

I couldn't take it anymore. "How is she?" I asked.

"Well, all of her vitals are miraculously fine. I need to call Dr. Wojo. I'll be right back." Nurse Linda said while returning the stethoscope around her neck, she lightly touched D'Kyra on her foot. I waited for the nurse to leave the room before I thumped D'Kyra on the big toe through the covers.

Chapter 18

The disturbing truth about Chaz Boomerang is that he got shot because Bella caught him in bed with another woman, in the very act. His black ass was up in the air thrusting and grunting while she was holding her ankles. Bella shot him and the girl was, get this, Amber, her sister.

I can't believe that he lied to me although I don't know why I am shocked. He didn't want to tell me that part of the story. He conveniently left that part out. I mean, seriously. What was I going to do? I always told him that he didn't owe me anything because we had made the verbal agreement that there would be no strings attached. I guess he didn't tell me about Amber because he didn't want me to know that he was a lousy sack of pond scum that was sleeping with her too. Turns out, Chaz has children, all girls, by 3 different women and only married two of them. It really makes me wonder what was wrong with him that he couldn't keep a woman cause it didn't look right.

Chaz's body is so perfect, that it looks like dark chocolate porcelain. I know I sound bipolar. One minute I am singing his sexual praises and the next I am cursing his dysfunctional achievements. I believe that I would have been the perfect woman for him if we had met before Harvey and before Darlene. At least I believe Chaz would have tried to fight those men.

I've often wondered if all that he told me was true ~~ it just didn't make sense for him to stay with Bella if she shot him or for her to want to stay with him. His stories didn't add up or make sense until I found out about Amber. Huh! Let Harvey feel trigger happy! Now Harvey ignoring me is one thing, but he's never hit me. I would go straight to the police but knowing Harvey, he'd probably got them in his pocket as well.

I decided that picking a fight with Chaz would be the best thing to do because the novelty of Chaz had worn off so quickly that I didn't even see it coming. I didn't care anything about a key, really. I didn't even care if he'd left Bella. It was just the right amount of ammunition that I need to put my little plan in the action.

I could never call him until he called me and sometimes it got old. One particular day, I got a text from him but didn't read it until later that day because I had been busy with some business at Wilcox. I didn't realize that I even had a text and I didn't feel the vibration at all. The text read:

CN I SQUEEZE U? Now normally, that would make me swoon but the only thing I said was: LOL. This didn't set well with him because it was replied: U COULD HAV TXT ME EARILER?

COULD HAV BUT DIDN'T. This is when it all started. This was my out and I took it and for the first time I felt powerful. I felt like I could do anything. I felt control of something in my life. For the first time, I could have a say in what I wanted to do and say and be and everything. I took control of the conversation. I took the bull by the horns and rode all the way. I grew tired and bored because he no longer was that great and powerful super hero of a man to me anymore. He became a whiner. I remember that I called him once on Saturday and I set it up so that it would show restricted on his end.

"Hello?"

"If you can't talk, say wrong number." I said quickly and bluntly.

"No, it's okay. What's up?

"You busy?"

"Well, I'm moving right now. Can I call you back in about an hour?" Needless to say, I was excited. Since Harvey was dead, I felt that we didn't have to sneak around anymore.

He called and left a message on my cell. I don't know how I missed his call. Maybe he called restricted or unknown because if so I won't answer those calls. He hurt me and I wanted him to hurt equally as much if not more. Then it had occurred to me that maybe the reason he was acting this way was because he had nothing to bargain with. Initially, there were no strings attached and that we didn't want anything from each other. Now that Harvey is dead, he didn't need me anymore. There was no threat and the excitement and novelty wore off. He now has more to lose than I do. He has children, I don't. His message was:

"Hey, it's me. Look, I got a key for you, okay. I want you to know that I love you, too. I'm crazy about you. Okay, talk to you later."

You know, what's funny? I didn't want him but I didn't want to be without him either. Bella don't deserve him. I wanted to have something always available and ready to carry out my wishes. I lost my virginity as a result of a rape on my wedding day to a man who wasn't my husband. My first was as a result of an affair and I never had sex with my husband. This is so insane that you can't make this stuff up. Since the truth shall make me free: Well, this is the truth, the whole truth and nothing but the truth: The one thing I knew for sure is that I knew that I loved him. (Maybe that's why I mourned Harvey's death as sibling or a friend rather than a husband. I think I understand now: I was mourning Harvey for what could have been.) Most time, a woman will always love her first especially if your first was Chaz Boomerang. That explains all the apple seeds Johnny left behind.

I do know that something happened. He sent me pictures to my cell of the bruises. He asked if I would meet him later because he really wanted to talk to me (It was a Tuesday, I remember it well) because he really needed to talk to me. I had already made it up in my mind that I wasn't going to ever sleep with him again but I didn't want to hurt him either so I agreed.

When I got to the hotel, I was so nervous. I sat there in my car for a while trying to figure out how I was going to get out of that room without being fucked. I knew that once I saw him, smelled him, touched him, I would be in trouble. I had to think of something that would piss him off or at least pretend I was mad at him and leave dramatically. I opened the car door, took a deep breath and grabbed my bag. I clutched my bag as I closed the car door behind me. I played with the keys in my hands because I needed to mask the sound of my hollow footsteps. I felt like I was walking into a trap. Everything within me said, "Run. Don't do it," but I had a plan and that plan was to stick with the plan. When I got to the door, I took a deep breath and I knocked on the door. Three short little taps with my index finger knuckle. I heard the **click, clank, slide** of the door locks. The first thing I saw was that charming smile and that strong chin. *Khylee, you can do this. Stay strong, girl.*

"You look good. You smell good, too." he said in his own charming way. I usually greet him with a long hug and an even longer kiss but I only said, "Whew! I really gotta go to the bathroom." I sat my bag on the bed and walked into the bathroom. I closed the door behind me and stared at myself in the mirror and reminded myself that I could do this.

When I walked in, our eyes met. He was lying on the bed surfing the channels on the television. I walked over to him and looked at his head. "I don't see anything." He took my hand and placed it on top of his head where the knots were and I could feel it but not see it. I gasped as I snatched my hand back. I knew then that this was something that I could blow out of proportion. It was a bit upsetting but nothing that I couldn't handle. He had scratches on his face, too. Someone really worked him over.

I really didn't want to stay and still don't know why I went in the first place but I cared about him and I was afraid of it. After all, he knew where I lived and I didn't want to be hurt, missing or worse—DEAD! I knew I had to play it safe. So, I sat there on the bed nervously, try my best to bring water to my eyes. I figured that if I cried, I could over dramatize the situation and pre panic so I could make a ghetto fabulous exit. "AW, naw, she didn't hurt my man. I need to whip her natural black ass." He loved that. He fed off that. He smiled. It was more like a smirk. He actually was conceded enough to think that I would fight HIS WIFE over him? I know, Huh? I mean, seriously. I covered my face while rocking back and forth. "No, No, NO!" I kept saying. I felt him raise up and come toward me. He put his arm around me and asked, "Ah, baby. You okay?"

"No, I mean, I can't believe she did this."

"I know. I don't know what's wrong with her." I stood up and stood in front of him between his legs and cupped his face in my hands and lightly kissed his bumps and I leaned forward, trying not to hurt the healing gunshot wound.

I was almost sick to my stomach. I needed to make a fast exit. He couldn't make eye contact with me. That's when I knew that something was really wrong. Those wounds had nothing to do with what he told me. He had been lying all along. I can't believe I let him suck me into his black vortex of a lie. True, I cared about him but I wanted out. He was poison and I could no longer think straight. D'Kyra and JaVon use to tell me all the time to cut ties with him. I usually let them know when I was about to walk into the lion's den but this time, no one knew I was here. He could kill me and no one would know I was even there. I've seen movies like this before.

He kept telling me that he was leaving her and that when he did, he would give me a key and I would never have to ask to come over. As long as I had that key, I could come and go as I pleased. It sounded good, especially with Harvey passing but I knew that the key would ever manifest.

"When are you leaving her?" I asked.

"Oh, I already got a house. I'm just waiting to move the rest of my stuff in. Bella ain't gon know shit when I do." He bragged.

"I don't believe it. You just selling woof cookies. You got 'em in your pocket right now. You ain't going nowhere." I barked and hoped that it ticked him off. He leaned forward and pointed his finger in my face and said, "You sound just like Sam. He said the same thing. He said I wasn't gon leave either but I got news for both of y'all." He said. He was getting heated. My scheme was working.

"Who are you trying to convince, me or you?" I asked. I looked at him straight in the eye and he looked away reaching for the remote. "See, you ain't trying to talk to me about this cause you know you wrong. You love it. You love all this drama. What's really going on? Why are you even staying with her after she kicked your ass, she shot you for Christ sake. Something ain't right about this." I said.

"Oh, so you think I'm lying? Is that it? You know you upsetting me, right." He yelled as he turned the TV off. He looked at me with a deep frown on his face. I was getting a bit scared but I couldn't let him know. So, I took a deep breath and someone said, "Chaz, I'm not Bella and you betta watch who you are raising your voice at." It was me. I strapped on a big pair of balls and continued, "Now, I ain't done nothing to you. I have been there for you, when you wanted to talk, I was there. When you wanted to meet, I met you. Now, I'm not the one you need to be raisin' your voice at. You need to watch your mouth before you say something you can't suck back up." (This was my out.)

"You've changed. You use to find ways to spend time with me and you couldn't wait to be with me. I got your key I my pocket." He said sadly. It was true but I still couldn't admit it to his face. I couldn't make a clean break. There was no such thing as a mutual break up with me. I needed for him to hate me so that way, I wouldn't be tempted to crawl back to him.

I hadn't changed I was only torn. I went from a husband not paying any attention to me to particular dear friend who paid attention to every crevice of my body. I loved him and wanted him but really didn't know how to handle it. He was the ***only*** thing that made me feel alive and loved. That feeling right there scared me more. I was more afraid of what I was feeling for Chaz rather than Chaz himself. I just lost all interested in him and that scared me. He was merely a temporary inconvenience for convenient situation.

I snapped up from where I was sitting and grabbed my bag.

"Where's the key? Where? You said you loved me? And why do you have to wait for the right time to leave especially if you don't care nothing about her. Something don't add up." He looked at me. I looked away. I had to save face. What the hell was taking him so long to end it? I opened the door and left. Walking to my car, I felt horrible but I felt in control.

That night was long. The next morning was empty because I couldn't even remember much of last night but I kept trying to replay the conversation that I had with Chaz over and over again in my head. It didn't go the way I had planned. I laid there on my side staring at the wall. The house phone rang. I looked at the monitor, it was Eva and she wanted to know if I was ready for breakfast. Well, that's what she always wants at this hour every morning. I sighed, stretched and picked up the phone.

"Hello." I answered groggy.

"Hola. It is breakfast?"

"No, Eva. I'm not hungry. Okay?"

"Ok. No hungry."

I looked at the clock and it read 6:39 am. I wanted to sleep, no. I wanted to hide. That's it. I wanted to be someplace where time stood still just for me; a place where no one knew me and I didn't know them. But in this place, everything was the same. I mean, I could still buy things. I could still watch TV and I could still drive places. I just didn't want any responsibilities. Then, my cell buzz. I stared at it for a moment. I knew who it was. I stretched for it and I tried to squint to focus. It was Chaz. Dam!

"Hello?' I tried to sound like he woke me up, you know that yarn talk.

"Good morning. You still in the bed" He asked in that same sexy voice like nothing even happened last night. Maybe *he's* bipolar.

"Yeah. What's goin' on?"

"Nothing. Look, last night was really weird . . ." He started, "Hold on. It's one of my employees. I'll call you back in about 10 minutes, okay." I sighed and smacked my lips because he always says that and never does so I took it for what it was worth and said, "Okay."

"Bye" I'll be damned if he didn't call back in about 15 minutes. Still lying in bed, I answered my cell.

"Hello?"

"BAM! You thought I wasn't gon call back, now didn't you?" He smirked.

"Of course." I said.

"You know," he chuckled. "You upset me when I got off the phone earlier. I told you I would call you back."

"Yeah! But you always say that and I don't hear from you for days. You can call me or text me anytime. But I can't contact you, remember?" I snapped.

"When?"

"You always say that you'll call me back and never do. Remember that Saturday when I called and you said that you were moving and that you would call me back in an hour? You never did?"

"You right." He said with a sigh "I do *do* that, don't I? I'm sorry." I was alone. I was ultimately alone and it was excruciatingly painful. Plus, I just opened myself up to all kinds of heart sores. I had no one, not even Harvey from a distance. Pretending that Harvey wasn't dead wasn't working for me anymore. I kept trying to tell myself that I could handle this by saying that "Harvey is gone on another one of his trips again" but it wasn't working. The reality was about shine through like daybreak through a sheer curtain at sunrise. Now, I was free to be with Chaz IF he's left Bella but I don't think he did. See, he told me that I could call him anytime after the shooting because he had moved in with his grand Dad until his place was ready. He just didn't tell me when I could no longer call.

"At the risk of sounding like I am brushing you off, which I am not, I do have to go. I have a situation with one of my employees. I just wanted to hear your voice, okay?"

"Okay."

"I will try to call later." Then there was silence.

One morning, I called and he pretended as though he was talking to an employee. I didn't get it at first. This went on for a couple of days until I just thought that he had a girl spending the night with him in his new place. I didn't get upset or anything. I actually was a bit relieved and confused. He told me that I could call him anytime or so I thought. Things were getting as confusing as that boy with the helmet and special shoe trying to put a screen door on a submarine.

He called me back a while later and tried to explain what was going on.

"Don't worry about it," I said. "You don't owe me anything and I don't want anything from you. I've been honest with you and I just want you to be honest with me. At first I didn't catch it when you were pretending that you were talking to your employees or something. I thought it was that half sleepy talk thing that people do but I just thought that you have a girl sleeping over."

"Hey, what do you take me for? Who do you think I am Big Daddy Mack or somebody? You really thought I was seeing somebody behind your back?"

"Well, you're seeing me behind Bella's back. You cheating on her with me, you could cheat on me with someone else."

"I could think the same thing. I could say that you could be seeing someone else besides me. You're free to see whoever whenever now."

"Chaz, things started getting complicated after we started sleeping together. It's wasn't supposed to be this hard. We said **no** strings attached, Chaz."

"I'm crazy about you. I think about you all the time. You wanna know if I have been sleeping with anyone else?"

"No. It's really none of my business." I said and by saying that I knew he was going to tell me.

"Look, Khylee, I moved. I got my own place. We got in an argument when I was trying to move out and she took the kids and left so I finished moving and setting my stuff up. She called me on my cell and told me that she didn't have anywhere to go." Any blind person could see where this was going. This big dick, smooth talking, charming, sexy bald headed man was a wuss. He was afraid of Bella, pure and simple. "She was crying and saying stuff like, 'How you just gon let me and your kids be homeless?' and I told her, 'Whatever', and she moved in. Everything is in my name, though and she ain't getting nothing." I kept thinking, 'big dick, no brains.'

"But y'all sleep in the same bed?" I asked. I can't believe it but I actually asked.

"Huh?!" He choked.

"You heard me. Was she there when I called all those mornings? Is this why you told me to not call you until you called me? It is, isn't it?" It all made sense. I know I said that I didn't care but I had to really make this look like I was really pissed at him and the more I talked about this to him, the more I sincerely got upset. Just know that his lies didn't set well with me.

"Was that her? Okay. Okay." It was like if he had kept saying 'okay' enough times, it would magically change the object of the preposition or something. "Yeah! It was her and we were in the same bed."

"You know what? I don't need this." I said. It was now or never. "How dare you talk to me this way. I've done NOTHING to you." He kept saying calmly, "I'm sorry. You're right. I'm sorry. I do love you I just need to leave at a time when she thinks everything is okay so she won't be suspicious."

"I mean, seriously. I have been there for you. Whenever you wanted me to meet you, I was there. I listened to all of your venting about Bella and everything. I ain't the one you need to be getting mad at." By then, I really was getting upset.

"You know," I said. "I can't deal with this right now. Just leave me alone."

"What do you mean, 'leave you alone?'" he barked.

"Just what I said." Maybe I have changed but you never will. You are such a liar." He was silent.

"Where is the key, Chaz? You said you loved me. What about that?" I paused briefly, waiting for him to redeem himself but he was silent. "Just leave me alone."

"FINE, I'll leave you alone." He barked. He never mentioned anything about the key which could only mean one thing: He never meant to give me one to begin with. I hung up and within minutes, he called me back. I didn't answer it. I only let it go to voice mail. I texted him and said that:

CNT WAIT 4 U 4EVR

He tried calling me a couple of more times but I wouldn't answer the call. I let it go to voicemail but he never left a message so I never knew what he literally wanted. It's over. I did it. Part of me felt relieved and the other part was scared that I was going to get stalked. I have to keep saying this because it will never make sense to me: This man choose to stay with a woman who shot him while he was caught in the very act of sleeping with her sister. He moves but let her move in with him. Somebody is lying but it's his sack of potatoes now and he's gotta peel them. I wanted out and it took some time but I got out and I'm so glad I am.

The next day, I changed my cell phone number.

Chapter 19

𝒟'Kyra was recovering quite nicely. Seven weeks and four days have passed since she woke up. She was able to feed herself, shower, comb her hair, brush her teeth, and she took a few steps with an aluminum walker. It was a very exciting day when we saw her walk.

One thing I wondered about was why she didn't ask anything about Isaiah. We were walking through her maze in her garden and I just had to ask.

"Why you never ask me about the baby, Dee."

"Because I knew you'd bring it up." she said. There was a bench in the maze that was labeled Fairy's Landing. It had carvings of fairies all over it. There were also little statues of fairies, elves, gnomes and even a unicorn in the garden. We sat on that bench and talked for a moment.

"You know, I didn't want that baby 'cause I knew it was Tony's. I got what I deserved and if I never fully recover, it'll serve me right. God knew what he was doing. I didn't even pray because I felt that I didn't even deserve for God to hear my voice. So, I figured that whatever happened, happens. Why pray when God is gon do what he wants anyway."

"But it was your baby. I mean, did Stan or anyone talk to you about it?"

"No. I guess they figured if I remembered that I was pregnant after I woke up then I may remember to ask about the baby."

"Did you see the photos?" I asked. She snatched her head towards me and asked,

"There were photos?! Hell, naw I ain't seen no photos." I thought, 'Ah oh.' and looked straight ahead.

"Khylee? Who got pictures?"

"I think Stan still does because he showed Deuce and Lizzi. You know, Stan was really hurt about the baby." She stared straight ahead and I wondered what she thought about or even if her mind was altered in some way because she never even asked what the baby's name.

"Dee, are you okay?" I asked.

"Khy, would I sound insensitive if I said that I'm glad that he didn't survive? I was baking bread in the oven that wasn't Stan's recipe and I tried to pass if off as his. Am I supposed to be worried about that baby?"

"DEE?" I yelled out, "How could you?" I guess the fact that I was never a mother means that I couldn't quite get the jest of what she was saying but she was very callus. "Don't you even want to know his name?"

"No."

"Why?"

"What for?" I took my right fist and knocked on her forehead lightly, saying, "HELLO! WHAT THE HELL IS WRONG WITH YOU?"

"Nothing." She said, "and stop touching me. I'm fine. I just choose not to dwell on things I can't do anything about. I just wish Stan hadn't shown the kids the pictures. I am thankful to be alive, Khylee."

"I know that and I was very worried about you. I can and . . . wait. So do you remember anything while you were sleeping?" D'Kyra looked at me with her face twisted and said,

"No, I don't think so."

"Well, I was at the hospital everyday. I would have combed your hair a lot but Zuae would come with Faye and she would put those barrette things in your hair. You looked pretty, too, *Mummy* Lady." She laughed. "Dee, do you remember anything? What's the last thing you remember?"

"Well," she started, "The last thing I do remember is being pregnant and going into labor and they said that I needed a caesarian because the baby was breached?" I nodded. "Is that right?"

"Yes, that's right. But do you remember *why* you had to have a caesarian other than being breached?" She shook her head. I took a deep breath and grabbed her hands and told her, "Your baby boy was born by C-Section because he was severely deformed." She frowned as though she was trying to wrap her brain around the words 'severely deformed' and she asked, "How severe?"

"Dee, he had an extra arm and an extra leg as well as . . ." Her face melted. I've never seen anyone's face melt before. Still hold hands, I could feel her palms sweat and her pulse race. " . . . . his head was . . . . well he was what looked like to be a twin but the two eggs didn't split."

"What . . . ah . . . . his head? What was wrong with his head?" She asked.

"Well, I forgot the actual name of it but his head was deformed. Would you like for me to see if Stan still has the pictures?" She shook her head and I could see that she was really trying hard not to cry.

"I want you to tell me and I know you not gon lie to me. So what was wrong with his head?"

"It was more like two heads fused into one. The one head had eyes, a nose, a mouth and ears but on his right side, just behind his ear, there was another head that was forming. They removed the extra arm and leg and he had trouble breathing because of all the weight from the head." By this time she was sobbing uncontrollably but I wasn't sure why. First she was acting as though she wasn't even pregnant before the coma and she didn't want to even hear about it much less talk about it. Afterwards, I was worried that she may need to see someone professionally. "Stan really stepped up and took responsibility.' I said. "He tried to wait as long as he could because he wanted both of you to make the vital decision on what should be done."

"Stan did that?" She asked.

"Yes and I never told him anything. It was our secret. I did, however, come to your bedside while you were in the hospital and begged you to wake up because Stan needed to know what to do. Danita came for a while. Before you had the baby, you told me to call her and said to make sure that I told her NOT to tell your mother until after the baby was born. I assumed your sister told your mom everything."

"What was his name?" she asked quietly.

"Isaiah. I don't know if there was a middle name or what but Stanley named him Isaiah."

"Was there a funeral?"

"No. The city took him."

"So, I can't visit my son's grave?" She sobbed. By this time, the sun was setting and the lights came on in the garden maze. There were solar lights that were hidden in the bushes but visible enough for the sun to absorb the light during the day. I never noticed them before as many times as I have been in this maze with the kids. I guess D'Kyra build up a resistance for fear and a tolerance for pain or something. Maybe this was her way of making sure that she stayed focus on walking. If she thought of Isaiah before hand, then maybe she would have recovered as well. I really don't know. I'm only make speculations but I really would like to know what she was thinking about while she was in a coma. Can they really hear you when you talk to them? Are they listening when you read to them? What about music? Does it really calm you or help you in some way? What was happening with her brain? Did she dream? Is the word coma code for the place where you go to talk to God face to face?

"I'm ready to go in now." she said as she stood up. I stood up and grabbed the walker to bring it over to her. She pulled up on it to stand. She was able to stand alone, that was surprising because soon, she will be able to walk without the walker. She adjusted her sweater and we walked toward the house.

Once inside, I made sure that she was settled. It was Nurse Amy's shift and I was wiped out: emotionally, physically and literally. I needed to make sure that she was okay before I left so I helped Nurse Amy with her. I sat with her for a few minutes while the nurse got her bath water ready. You could hear the water filling in the tub and the nurse humming like she was in the kitchen making biscuit.

"I'm gon leave now, okay. You know to call me if you need anything."

"Where are you going?" she asked.

"Well, I have a big day. You remember what happened to Harvey?" I asked her.

"Ah, huh. Yeah, he died." Then, as though she was shocked into attention, she blurted out. "Oh, it's the reading of the will or have you done that already?"

"Nope, I kept putting it off." I said softly.

"Why, Khy?"

"Because I have been with you. Do you know, I haven't been to the studio in months, either.

"Oh, I'm sorry."

"No, it's okay. I wanted to be here with you. I wouldn't feel right if I was anywhere else."

"So, you haven't had the reading of the will yet?"

"No. I'm not ready yet."

"What's wrong, Khy?" I guess I just couldn't take it anymore. I had tried so hard to be strong for D'Kyra and I couldn't afford for her to see me lose it but I couldn't help it. I felt the tears coming. I was angry. Angry that Harvey died and angry I couldn't do anything about him. Pissed that I will have to handle his drunk ass mama and angry that I felt that God forgot about me. I kept saying in my mind, "Don't cry. Please don't cry."

I went back over to the chair that was sitting by the bed. The same chair that I use to read and talk to her while she was in a coma and when I sat down, the chair felt different. It felt like my Dad's chair: The chair that was his special chair; just for the football games. It felt butt shaped and almost forbidden. It was like that chair started pumping and drawing tears from a well that had long gone dry. The chair needed a warning label ~~ **CAUTION: May cause weeping**. I didn't want to cry, not there, not now. What would the nurse think?

"Truth be told, Dee, me and Harvey wasn't even close. You know that we never even made love. I think I loved him. I know I did . . . once. But now, I don't know what to think. I almost feel guilt accepting everything that he left me. I feel like a fraud. Maybe he did love me. I wanted so much to be loved by my own husband and I almost told him just before he died that I had an affair but I couldn't." I looked up at D'Kyra and tears were rolling down her flawless face. "You know what the sad thing is?" I said. "The sad thing is that, I can't remember Harvey's face. I don't remember what he looked like." I closed my eyes tightly and sat silently for a moment. I felt someone put tissues in my hands. When I opened my eyes, I saw the nurse walk away quietly closing the door behind her.

"Khy, you've been through so much. It's amazing how you've handle everything thus far." Dee said. Right at that very moment, I missed Chaz. I know I can't go backward, after I tried so hard to get this man out of my system; I missed him so much that it hurt. (My bipolar ass.)

"Well, call me if you need anything. I'll probably come by or call afterwards, okay."

Walking out, I realize something. I started feeling a little bit like I had relieved some pressure like the elephant wasn't sitting on my chest anymore. It is very easy to get consumed with things that we feel are so important but once you allow yourself to let it go, you realize that it was only menial. Chaz wasn't menial. He was a substitute for what I was missing at home. I can't believe I lost my virginity to this man. They say you never forget your first and I know I will never forget Chaz because of how it was. I have tried not to think about him, I really did but I can't get over the fact that he lied to me about everything. And what's more, if he lied to Bella about me, then he'll lie to me. Yet and still, he's the one I dream of, not Harvey. And as much as I hate to admit this, one scripture keeps coming to my mind. I don't know where it's located or even if I am quoting it correctly but it goes something like this: some things come through much fasting and praying.

So here I am; I've legally inherit everything my husband had. He only stayed married to me because of obligation. Man, you can't make this stuff up!

When I got home, I decided to take a hot bubble bath and listen to Jazz on my little box that's in the connecting room. It was very relaxing. I wanted to be anywhere other than were I was right then. I really don't like being alone with myself. As much as I think I like peace and quiet sometimes, I am afraid of me when I am alone. I have no children, no husband but this big ass house filled with servants that are more loyal than a mob family.

Chapter 20

I couldn't postpone the reading of the will any longer. I guess I kept trying to hide behind D'Kyra and her recovery but Trey got wise to that. It was costing Wilcox Pharmaceuticals money not to mention Ethel wanted to know what was going on with the will. If Trey and Zoë were being honest, then I had nothing to worry about.

The date was set for three weeks from today. I guess if I do this, it would mean that Harvey is really gone because all this time, I kept trying to pretend that he was away on business like always. Reality was about to rear its ugly head.

I got a call from Zoë early that Monday morning wanting to know if I was prepare to keep an appointment for the reading of Harvey's will. I really wasn't but I had to go ahead and do this. I felt warm air leave my mouth but don't remember a sound. Apparently I said yes but for the life of me, I don't remember. I wanted to just run away and leave. I didn't want to do this. The only reason people want to be present at the reading of anyone's will is because they are greedy and they want something. I thank God that Harvey left me everything but I still didn't want to go.

What's more, I didn't want to have to call Harvey's family, especially if his drunk ass mama gon answer the phone. Trey asked if I wanted him to call but I told him that I would do it because that is something that they needed to hear from me.

* * *

We decided on March 10th for the reading of the will. It will be here in the grand room. (I should have let Trey call them.) I decided to call my parents, too. Since the Wilcox' will be present, then I felt like the Patterson's should represent. *Wahoo Dee Whoa!*

I tried to mentally be conscience for the reading but I realized that if I paid attention, I would feel and I wanted to remain as numb as possible. I sat on the edge of the chair in the grand room. I really don't know what was so grand about it. It's a room that collects dust because no one uses it. It's all cherry wood and deep burgundy. It's a very dark room. It reminds me of the Ponderosa. There's even a fireplace that has never been used and we've been here for over 10 years.

Over the fireplace mantel was a huge brass framed mirror greenery with pine cones carefully placed in front of the mirror. On the mantel were beautiful carvings of angels. It reminded of a story I remember my Dad telling me. There was also a small portable bar right in the corner that looked like a small saloon, complete with bar stools and the alcohol. I thought that this room would be the perfect place for the reading of Harvey's will. Ava and Myra always made sure that every room was spotless; they even went to my favorite store for an electric oil burner. It matches the decor perfectly. I don't recognize the aroma but it's very tasteful.

I stood up and walked around the room. I forced my mind to go back as far as I could with my life with Harvey. I searched my heart as well and really questioned myself why I didn't grieve for Harvey as I should have. I actually mourned Chaz's absence more than Harvey's.

Ava and Myra set a small cart beside the bar filled with snacks. She even lit a log on the fire. At first I thought it was stupid but it was March and still sometimes quite crispy outside. There were three leather sections, one love seat and four high back chairs. I sat in the love seat that was beside the window that face the garden that I looked at every morning whenever I eat breakfast in my bedroom. The garden looked different. Everything looked so small from upstairs but in the downstairs view, it looked just the opposite. I never noticed that bird bath in the middle of those flowers before. So this is where Myra get fresh flowers every morning.

Suddenly, someone tapped me on the shoulder. It was Trey. I heard his muffled voice asking me if I was alright. My mind came back to actuality and I noticed that he was blocking the view of the guest. Everyone was there. When had they come in? I didn't hear anything. Zoe handed me a bottle of water with a smile. She is so nice.

For the life of me, I couldn't remember why I chose that gray skirt. It really didn't match anything I had on. Maybe it was a metaphor? Everyone else had on black, dark blue, navy even dark brown. I chose gray?

Harvey's parents were sitting at the sofa closest to the bar. Guess why? Mom and Dad are in the chairs that are on the other side of the sofa that's next to the Wilcox'. Zoë sat with her legs crossed dressed in all black as well on the sofa next to H.C. When Trey walked in, there was a male figure behind him. Everyone's voice was to a low murmur which made their conversations inaudible. One distinct sound I would know anywhere was a high pitched bell. I heard the sound of Powder's nails on the hard wood floor. I didn't care about anything at that moment but getting Powder because she sounded confused. She was running in the house and whining as well. I got up and quickly walked over to the door only to find that Ava had scooped up my baby and was speaking Spanish to her. When I turned, the male figure's back was to me. He looked familiar. He was tall and dressed in dark gray as well. Coincidence?

Trey walked over to me, "Mrs. Wilcox, this is Anson Boler. He took care of your husband's will. Mr. Boler, this is Mrs. Wilcox." Trey stepped back as Mr. Boler walked forward and offered to shake my hand. "Mrs. Wilcox," He said, "I am so sorry for your lost. I worked with your husband on many different legal matters and he was a great man who will surely be missed. Take your time and we can begin whenever you're ready, alright?" I nodded. When he smiled, only one side of his top lip curled up. A lawyer with a crooked smile?

The reading of the will was a blur. I do remember that later, however, Trey giving me Wilcox Pharm. Here's the thing: I have never been in Harvey's office except for that one time when I went there trying to seduce him and he turned me away. I've never been back since and I sure as hell don't wanna go now but I am the only one they will allow in his office.

I drove to the office after hours so that I didn't have to see anyone. You know, what was really strange is that the night shift (cleaning crew, security guards, parking garage people) all knew me but I had no idea who they were.

When I reached Harvey's office door, it never occurred to me that it may be locked but it was. One of the security guard came up from no where, "Here, let me get that for you, Mrs. Wilcox. I am really sorry about Mr. Wilcox. He was a fair and generous man." It's amazing how everyone else knew all these things about Harvey that I had no idea of knowing. As he tried the lock, he continued to talk. He wanted to tell me about the time his wife died in child birth over 6 years ago. He said that Harvey took care of everything. He said that he told him to take as much time as he needed and not to worry about his job. I never looked at his name badge. I didn't want to know his name. I only glanced at his face a few times. "There is an extra set of keys inside the middle drawer." That's when I heard the lock give. He opened the door and turned on the light for me. "Can I do anything else for you, Mrs. Wilcox?"

"No. You've been most helpful. Thank you very much." I walked in and closed the door behind me and locked it. His office spelled of oranges. There were empty boxes from drug reps in the corner on the floor. I closed my eyes as I stood there for a moment. I could hear Harvey's voice telling me to go home because he was late for a meeting. I could remember standing there wearing only a pair of pumps and his London Fog.

Okay, if I were a vault, where would I be? I walked over behind his desk and I noticed that my heel got caught on something. I sat down in his chair and slid my shoe off. When I tried to free my heel, the carpet gave way. BINGO! The vault was in the floor behind the desk. I pulled the carpet up and there was a copper colored safe like vault right there in the floor. I pushed the chair to the side and sat on the floor. I really couldn't picture Harvey sitting on the floor every time he needed to get in the safe.

The key looked more like a vending machine key. Since there wasn't a handle on the safe, the key double as a handle as well. The door squeaked as I opened it. Inside the shallow dimly lit safe was our marriage license, an unlabeled DVD in a plastic case, his wedding ring and some photographs. I stuffed all the contents of the safe inside my bag and closed the door to lock it. I tried to make sure that everything was left the exact way I found it.

When I got home, I inserted the DVD in the player and sat on the bed to look at the photos. My favorite photo was the one of me and Harvey standing on the balcony of the mansion and we released doves. I didn't look up to view the TV screen until I heard "Khylee?" It was Harvey's voice. I slowly looked up at the screen. The footage wasn't professional. It looked more like a B list movie. I heard Mom's voice saying, "Harvey, now you know it's bad luck for a bride and groom to see each other right before the ceremony. You need to leave." The camera was directly on Harvey. I had forgotten how silly Harvey could be. It's like our wedding took the life right out of us. He was singing and dancing. He looked so handsome. Then he stopped and talked in the camera as if he was making a documentary. He motions for all the guys to keep quiet and stands outside the lounge door where I was getting dressed and with this Middle Eastern accent he knocked on the door. "Excuse please. Need to give message to bride." As I watched, I realized that I remembered that it happened. I can't believe I blocked it out. I also remember running up to the door, opening it and gasped as Harvey grabbed me and planned the biggest, juiciest kiss on my lip. Mom, off camera, screamed and said, "Harvey Wilcox, you get outta here this instant. You are just asking for this wedding to be cursed." I guess it was true.

Chapter 21

It's been 4 months and I still think about Chaz every day. He's the first thing on my mind in the mornings and the last thing I think about before I fall asleep. I am torn about whether I wanted to sell my home or not. It's only a few of my house whole who actually moved. This house is too big for just me.

I just got back from Oahu. I needed some time alone to think and clear my head. I didn't take my laptop or cell phone. Ava and Myra came back from the Dominican Republic just a few days after I did and I still haven't made a decision about selling the house. The only people that knew I went away were D'Kyra, my house whole and Trey; Travis took care of the house while I was away.

I got many messages, voicemails, text messages and even emails from Chaz. I didn't bother to tell him that I was leaving. I really didn't think he'd care but I was wrong. It turns out that Bella died from complications of AIDS about 9 weeks after I left. From what I understand, she didn't have Zal 4 like Harvey did and her death was very painful. Her death actually hit Chaz pretty hard regardless to all those wolf cookies he sold, bought and baked, he loved her. He sold his home and moved into an apartment alone on the north end. All his baby's mommas panicked and wanted them to move back in with her.

* * *

Last night I couldn't sleep. I got up and walked over to the fridge and pulled out the container of fresh strawberries and go back into bed.

I reached for the remote and literally searched for cartoons. It was 9:47 p.m. My cell rang. It was Chaz. Wow! What a surprise.

"Hello?" I answered.

"Hey. Whatcha doing?"

"Watching TV and eating strawberries. What's up?"

"Nothing actually, I'm online playing around on the computer." I heard these sci fi noises.

"What's all those noises?" I asked.

"Oh, I'm playing a game online."

We laid in separate beds on opposites ends of towns and instant messaged each other until the wee hours of the morning. It was a little exciting as well as unique. I became intrigued. He seemed to be handling the empty house syndrome well so I pretty much let him vent. Whatever he wanted to talk about it, I listened to him. Like, he wanted to know why he hadn't heard from me in weeks and why I didn't return any of his calls. See, its remarks like that that makes me remember he's got baby mammas, with an "s" on the end of mamma.

"Well, I didn't tell too many people I was leaving."

"But you did tell someone, right?"

"Yelp. I sure did. I told someone and your point would be?"

"Whatever." He barked out and I'm thinking that I really wanna smack him sometime.

"No, Chaz. Tell me." There was silence.

"You changed." He said after a few minutes. That's the best he could come up with?

"Tell me what the hell you so mad about now? I thought we were having fun. Now you called me and don't start with me because I'm not feeling this. I don't understand you. You stay mad at me all the time. You are touchy, irritable and moody. Well all those words mean the same but you get the point, and boy, I swear to God if you tell me that I have changed ONE more time . . ."

"Okay, okay, okay. I'm sorry for saying that you changed but Bella died while you were gone and I really wanted to talk to you. I tried being strong for the kids but it got really hard. I loved Bella even thou we didn't get along. She confessed to me about a lot of things."

"Chaz, look, I'm sorry about all that you went through with Bella's death and all but I know how you feel. Remember Harvey? Did you tell her about us?"

"No. Did you ever tell Harvey?"

"No. I never told Harvey. I started to but I decided against it."

"When were you going to do this?"

"On his death bed." After a few minutes, I asked, "Chaz, why did you call me? Are you trying to make me crazy? Do you know that I nearly lost my mind trying to get you outta my system? You make me crazy."

"No. I'm not trying to make you crazy. I just wanted to let you know that I missed you so much when I couldn't hear your voice when Bella died. I just needed a familiar face and voice."

"Chaz, let me ask you this question. Why do you insist on starting an argument with me?"

"I don't know and I am sorry but I need you in my life right now." He sounded so sad.

"Let me tell you this, Chaz. I miss you very much but you not gon be talking to me like you got a tumor in your brain with a knot in it from that knot on your head Bella left, you got me?"

Chaz laughed a little and said, "I know. Keep me straight, baby. I glanced down at my laptop and saw that he was still online so I typed:

"We can't have a friendship if you keep getting mad at me. I'm hanging up the phone know."

"Why you hang up? There's nothing keeping us apart now. When can I see you?"

"I don't know. I really need to make sure that I don't become another link in your chain. What makes me different from Bella or Darlene or Juanita or Bonnie? We started out as friends just talking about our spouses and it turned into a very special friendship until you started getting mad at me all the time. Chaz, I don't regret what we did nor am I sorry for anything that made me smile and you made me smile but it really makes me wonder if this is why you can't keep no woman?"

It took a minute for him to answer me but he typed:

"I can't really say what the problem was with them but you are different. You are more focused on your life." It was at that moment I wondered if he was in this for the money or what. Maybe he knew that I had inherited everything from Harvey but that really wasn't a mystery, it was a given. "I have been in love with you for a long time. I know we don't talk everyday because of my job and that doesn't seem to bother you but I wanna hear your voice everyday. I want to see your face as often as I can. Is that wrong?"

"No, it's not wrong. I just know that if you lied to Bella you are going to lie to me. I never lied to Harvey about anything and I never lied to you. Things between us just moved faster than I could keep up with. I guess by you being my secret romantic encounter really caused my heart strings to plunk to a different melody. You need to understand something about me." It was then that I decided to tell Chaz all about my wedding night. It was a lot of typing and since there was so much typing, I would stop every so often and asked "You still there?" Chaz would respond by typing, "That's right."

Typing was much easier than verbalizing. I didn't have to play on their emotions or let their emotions stray me from telling the story. The words would just seem to flow out through my fingers and after about two or three "are you still there" he asked for me to stop asking him that because he wasn't going anywhere. That's when I knew I had made the right decision in telling him. I guess I expected him to fall asleep or log off but he didn't. He was right there.

Suddenly my cell rang. It was Chaz.

"Hello" I said nervously.

"I want you to hear me say this and not read it on a screen. I love you and I ain't going nowhere. I am sorry that it happened and I wish that I could take your pain away. I wish I could hold you and literally absorb all you're hurting. I believe that Harvey and Bella brought us together unknowingly." I really did feel love from him. I felt like he was trying to make that proper connection with me in order for us to be together. Before I knew it, I was crying and as much as I tried to hide it, he picked up on it.

"Don't cry. I will always be here for you, okay?"

"Okay," I whispered. I looked at my laptop once more and I saw that he was still online and I typed:

"I have always been in love with you and I do believe that somehow Bella and Harvey made it possible for us to be together."

"Khylee, I'm turning my computer off. I'm twenty minutes away. Can I see you?"

The word 'yes' fell out of my mouth before I knew it. "Chaz, when you get to the gate, key in '1024' and the gate will open. Then, call me after you get through the gate and I will open the door for you, okay?"

"Gimme 10 minutes and I will be on my way." He hung up the phone and I sat there for a minute. I looked at the clock on the toolbar of the laptop. "12:38am," I whispered. "He'll be here around 1:30.) I quickly took the laptop and set it in the chair buy the desk. I went straight to the bathroom with my cell just in case he called, turned on the shower because

I knew I didn't have much time. I undressed, threw those clothes in the hamper and grabbed a scrungee for my hair.

After the shower, I reached for a pair of panties, a tank tee and pair of shorts. I looked at the clock. It was 12:51am. I quickly dressed and grabbed my brush and brushed my hair into a ponytail. I really didn't know what to expect. I looked at myself in the mirror. He did say that he wanted to see me. Sex wasn't in the equation, right? I mean, he could have said that he wanted to 'be with me' but that's not what he said. Okay, the best thing for me to do is to just assume that he wants to talk face to face, but at one something in the morning? I realized that I didn't have a bra on and I ran back to the bathroom to grab one from the lingerie drawer and quickly put it on.

I reached for the linen spray and to make the room inviting, I sprayed it on almost everything. I realized that the box of contents from Harvey's vault was sticking out from underneath the desk. I went to gather the book in hopes to find another storing place. I looked down at the contents and saw an unfamiliar envelope. "That's funny; I thought I went through all his stuff." I said. I sat on the bed with the box and attached to the envelope that had our wedding photo inside was another envelope stuck to it. "How did I miss this?" I asked myself. Inside was a picture of Chaz with a woman. She was sitting and he was standing with his arms around her shoulders. They looked so happy. They were dressed in jeans and green shirt with white athletic shoes. There was writing on the back of the photo that read: *This is what Chaz looks like. This is the only photo I could find.* Okay, this was weird. Why would Harvey have a picture of Chaz and Bella in his vault? "Harvey, there had better be something in this envelope that explains this. Don't make me hate you after I got peace." I said. I picked up the envelope and shook it. It was something else in there. I looked in there and saw another set of keys that looked like the first set and a note that read: vault behind the bar. Was this the bar in his office or the bar in this house? My cell rang! "Chaz!" I yelled out. I ran to cell and yelled out, "I'm on my way to the garage." I hung up and ran out of the room, down the hall, down the back stairs that led to the kitchen and when I got to the door that led to the garage, I unlocked and opened it. I reached my hand through the crack felt for the garage door opener on the wall. I heard the click and the jerk of the garage door. I waited for his truck to drive inside so that I could close the garage door.

Once he got inside, I jumped in his arms so fast, I accidently made him bump his head on the corner of door frame. I didn't realize how much I missed him. He smelled so good, he felt so good and he kissed my neck. I couldn't take it anymore, I broke down right then. I felt him pick me up and carry me toward the hall way from the kitchen. He's never been in my home so I guess he was looking for some place to take me. I could tell by the atmosphere and the echo that we were on our way to the media room. There was a humming in the south corner of the room which indicated we were in the media room. The humming came from the fish tank.

He sat me down in one of the theater seats. While wiping my eyes, I looked up at him and he asked what was wrong. I told him that I had some new information that I needed to share with him. He told me that he had something that he wanted to show me.

He followed me upstairs and as I turned the corner toward the landing, I heard that sweet little bell. It was Powder at the top of the stairs waging her tail. The closer I got to the top of the stairs, the more she barked. "Don't worry," I said, "She'll run as soon as you get to the top of the stairs," and sure enough, she did. I never looked back to see if he was following me but I knew he was behind me because I could hear the jingle of his keys from his pocket. I stopped short of the door, turned and said, "The house is asleep so if you need something to eat or drink, I do have a small fridge in the corner." I pointed toward the corner. "Come on in and have a seat." He sat on the chaise while I closed the door behind him. I walked over to the bed where I had placed the envelope. I picked it up and handed it to Chaz and asked, "What do you make of this?"

He was silent as he looked through the envelope. He was dressed in red and white. His K Swiss were spotless; his jogging pants were those breakaway pants. He wore a jersey on top of a t-shirt. I cleared my throat beside him. He took out the photo of him and Bella. "I wondered what happen to this picture. It was in a frame sitting on a table in the hallway." I pointed toward the back to the picture. "Where did you get this?" He asked.

"Ah, it was in that envelope along with these keys." I extended my hand showing him the keys. "Now, the note said that 'vault behind bar', Chaz. What vault, which bar? I got these from the vault in his office but that was the only thing in there."

"Was there another vault in there?" he asked.

"I don't know, I really don't."

"Well, is there a bar in his office?"

"I think so but there are a couple here, too." I said.

He stood and said, "Let's go. Show me." He reached his hand out for me and with the other hand; he reached for the door knob. *Wow! His muscles rippled. Okay, focus.*

"I remembered seeing one in the grand room. I noticed it at the reading of the will."

"Why are you always 'just noticing things' in your own home?"

"This mansion is too big for me to get lost in, so I only go to designated areas; kitchen, media room, pool, my bedroom and sometimes Harvey room."

"You and Harvey didn't share a room?" He asked surprisingly.

"No, nosey. Did you and Bella?" I looked him square in the eye.

"Sorry." He replied.

"Look, let's just get downstairs. The grand room is on the other side of the foyer just through those double doors."

I opened only one side of the doors and turned on the lamp that was sitting on the table next to the door. I closed the door behind us and locked it. "Now," I sighed, "The bar is over there." I whispered.

"You got the keys." He asked.

"Yeah." I answered.

"Khylee?" he asked

"Yeah?"

"Why are we whispering?" Realizing that we were, I let out this, "Boy, shut up and come on."

I walked over to where the bar was and looked around. I tried the floor and the walls by tapping on them looking for a false bottom but there was nothing.

"What are you doing?" Chaz asked as though he thought I was stupid.

"In Harvey's office at work, there was a small vault in the floor underneath his desk. I just thought that maybe the same was in here and don't talk to me like I'm stupid." He snickered for a minute while he looked around.

We must have looked around for a while until I stopped and sat in the love seat that faced the fireplace. I looked up at the mantle and looked at the carvings that reminded me of that story that Daddy use to tell me. For some reason I couldn't take my eyes off those carvings. Chaz was still looking around; walking back and forth in the room while talking. I really didn't pay any attention to what he was saying until he stopped and stood in front of the mantle.

"Hey?" he asked. "Are you listening to me?" he asked while waving his hands in front trying to get my attention. I stood up and walked slowly toward him but stood in front of the carvings. There were three different types of carvings on the mantle; they actually looked more like designs or hieroglyphics. I took my hands to feel them from left to write. I didn't know exactly what I was looking for but I knew it had to be something.

The two carvings on the outside were smooth like porcelain but the one in the middle was rough like drywall. He asked what I was doing and I asked him touch the carvings. He sighed but obeyed. "What am I looking for?" He asked.

"I'm not sure. Just tell me what you feel." He took both hands and rubbed both sides at the same time and worked his way to the middle. "Well, the two on the end are smooth and the one in the middle is rough like it needs to be sanded down or something." Then he stopped and said, "MMM. That's weird."

"What?" He took my hand and placed it on the crevice of the carving in the middle. I felt cool air coming from one of the breaks. Chaz followed the breaks with his hand just to see where it led. "Oh, my God," I said. "It's the vault! Where do I put the key?"

"Right here." Chaz pointed to a small crescent like design. I took the key from my pocket and tried the lock. As the small door opened, a puff of cool air escaped with a hiss. Inside were a mass of legal sized enveloped that were bound together by a rubber band. There was a somewhat unpleasant smell of mustiness. "Wow!" Chaz sighed. He reached inside the vault and pulled out a stack of notebook paper that had been stapled together. "This is Bella's handwriting." He took the papers and walked over to the chair and sat down. He started thumbing through them. He frowned while he shook his head. He bit his bottom lip and said, "They did this on purpose, man. They planned the whole thing." I walked over to him and kneeled beside him and asked, "What are you a talking about. They planned what?" He got up from the chair and let the papers fall from his hand. I caught them just before they fell to the floor.

The writing was mostly done in pencil with some black or blue ink. There were many things highlighted. The 'details' looked like notes or verbal plans mapping out a strategy. It looked like arrangements or preparations of a deal of some sort. I only read the highlighted parts first. There were thing like 'she's very beautiful and will be perfect for him', 'I agree with you in saying that she would make him a good wife because neither of them deserve this.' While I read silently, Chaz helped himself to a bottle of juice from the fridge.

"What does this mean?" I asked. "It looks like the deliberately got sick so we . . ." Without looking up, Chaz finished my sentence for me. "They wanted to make sure that we met. They wanted to make sure that we somehow got together." He walked over to me gulping down the rest of the juice and asked, "Did Harvey say anything to you? Did he leave you anything like a clue as to why he did all this?"

"Besides the fact that he left me completely loaded including all his businesses and a fat bank account in two different countries? No, but the only other thing he left me was a letter that I got just before I found out he was sick."

"Where is it?"

"Upstairs. Why? Did Bella say anything to you?" I walked over to the vault to shut the door and headed out the door back upstairs. I looked at the clock, it was almost 3am. Wow! Had we really been at this all night?

As we walked back upstairs to my bedroom, Chaz began to tell me bits and pieces of Bella's dying wish. She wanted to make sure that she was forgiven and she wanted to make sure that he wouldn't live his life alone. She wanted him to find someone but he said that he really didn't pay it any attention because he knew that I was the one who had his heart. "You know," he added, "The more I think about it, the more I think they wanted to get caught. Like those pictures of them from that restaurant. They are plenty of other restaurants around town and even more out of the city. Why would they go to Jackson's knowing that there's a possibility that they would get recognized? I don't know the whole thing sounded strange to me." I looked for the letter while he vented. I remember putting in the drawer beside the bed.

I sat on the bed and scanned the letter for any clues. The one thing that stuck out was when he said that he swore Trey to secrecy. It made me think that Trey was my best bet after all he knew everything else. By Trey being Harvey's best friend and all, why not get your BFF in on your scheme? After all, I kept D'Kyra's secret about Isaiah. I didn't want to tell Chaz anything about Trey until I talked to Trey first. I didn't want to jump to conclusions. I also needed to talk to Zoë as well. I needed to make sure that I had all my facts straight.

Chapter 22

I don't know how I feel about being an object of bartering. It's almost like a mail order bride or worse; one of those poor countries where people are promised into marriage. The whole think seems a bit Hillbilly. At least add a couple of goats and some chickens to sweeten the deal, like a dowry.

We talked about this for awhile; what we should do, how we should handle things and even if we loved them enough to carry on their wishes. We laid there in each other's arms weighing all the alternatives but when push came to shove, we welcomed the nudge and didn't retaliate. We both had a great deal in common; our life circumstances saw to that. Even though we tried to keep that ground rule by saying that we didn't want anything from each other and that there still were no strings attached, we failed miserably. The only thing that changed is that we needed each other and our strings attached themselves when we weren't looking. They not only attached, the fused together. I found out the hard way that love isn't over rated and it really does exist. It happened when you least expect it to, that's why it's called 'falling in love." When you fall, you don't plan it, it just happened. Whether it is falling down the steps or from 2 inch heels, it's an accident because the first thing you say is, whether you admit it or not, "Wow! I'm embarrassed. I didn't see that coming."

Chaz Boomerang made me smile when I needed to laugh. He made me cry when I need a release. He gave me love when I needed it most. He listened to me when I needed a male's point of view and he was the blue in my sky. I don't know what my future hold but I do know who's going to be holding my hand when I get there.

A little over two years have passed and as I finish the book for Khylee, she would like to let everyone know what happened to everyone:

Travis and Pierre went to San Francisco and got married. I mean, I often wondered but didn't want to cross this harassment barrier by asking.

Trey and Zoë got married. I must say that I didn't see it coming. They brought the vacant lot on the corner in the next sub over.

Stanley and D'Kyra are doing very well. Deuce is very active in sports; Lisette is still tutoring and has decided that she wanted to work in forensic science and Zuaenette just turned 4. She will be going to preschool this fall. She did, however, learn to stay dressed.

Powder died. I hung her collar with the bell on it from my rear view mirror.

Jackson and Jillian's ***Twist of Fate*** is blooming. As a matter of fact, Jillian won the lottery. They took a much needed vacation.

Momma and Daddy are doing great. They did a little renovation including repaving the parking lot, updating the sound system, putting in industrial toilets and sinks in all the bathrooms.

H C buried Ethel last summer. She died of cancer which she never told any of us that she had it. She tried to stay drunk so she wouldn't have to feel the pain. After a few days after the burial, H C came to live with me for a while. He moved into Harvey's suite and died in his sleep about 4 months later on Christmas Eve. I don't think he ever got over her death. He loved that woman; as mean as she was to him, he loved her.

Danita and Cookie are doing great. Danita moved to Quebec that January. She is now working in radio while Cookie moved into their parent's home and decided to ***come out*** of one of those closets.

JaVon still travels and tours. She still hasn't married yet but I'm not giving up on her. She needs to make me a godmother. She's so independent that I think it scares men away. She's determined to tour until she dies and I don't think any man could handle that. I convinced her to give up her apartment since she's never really there and to stay with me when she needs to.

Chaz's Blu Skye Repair has expanded; he's in three locations now and has people to work for him. Sadly, his grandfather developed early onset Alzheimer's and had to put him in a nursing home. Chaz sold his grandfather's repair shop and home. The money was put in an account to insure his residence, medications, etc. Chaz does, however, gets very sad after visitation because the first 30-45 minutes is spent trying to get his grandfather to remember him. Sometimes he knows who he is and sometimes he doesn't but when he does recognize him, it's usually during the time he got in trouble in school and Chaz has to hear a lecture.

Chaz's children are doing quite well. They are so successfully busy that it's hard to keep up with them.

Well, as for me? Well, Wilcox Pharmaceuticals is doing great. I even learned a few things about the business and travel little but not as much as Harvey. Some of that boring stuff turns out to be a little interesting; sometimes. I still work in cartoons once in a while but mostly commercials for radio and television.

I also went back to church; it was on Resurrection Sunday. Mom and Dad were really surprised because I didn't tell them I was coming and get this; Chaz went with me and he does clean up nice, very nice. He's never been to church that I know of. Maybe the pews burn his butt, I don't know.

When Daddy made the altar call, that's when he saw me. He was moved to tears. "Sister Patterson?" Daddy said, "Will you look at that beauty Easter lily that the Lord sent?" Of course, everyone turned around. Usually it would bother me that everyone looked at me but on this particular day, I didn't mind. I was ready to be delivered and I knew that my God was the only one who could do it but by using my Daddy.

I dressed in a lavender suit with a matching hat, purse and shoes. My hair was pulled back in a ponytail, gathered on left side with a braid draped down my left shoulder. I looked so retro.

Anyway, before I knew it, I was walking down the aisle toward the altar and fell into my dad's arms as he ran to meet me. Mom came up beside me and joined the embrace. My eyes were closed but I could feel other people around me, laying hands on me. Someone removed my hat and while Daddy anointed me with oil. Within minutes, I was filled with the Holy Ghost all over again. I wanted to run. I wanted to jump. I wanted to scream. Then I felt someone holding my hand. It was a familiar touch. It was Chaz. I slowly looked over at him and without looking at me, he addressed my Dad by saying, "I want what she got." I clinched my chest and closed my eyes as tight as I could to keep from screaming. I squeezed his hand so tight until my hand was numb.

During all this time, only the ones that were at the altar heard Chaz's request. Daddy quickly said, "Hold on, son." Daddy motioned for the cordless microphone and spoke, "Saints?" Now that he had the congregation's attention, he said, "Son, will you repeat that, please?" Daddy angled the microphone toward Chaz's full lips. Chaz took a deep breath, cleared his throat and said, "I want what she got." While Daddy snatched the microphone back toward his mouth and yelled out, "Let the church say 'AMEN'", the altar workers quickly whisked him away to the dressing room to be baptized. Our hands were stuck together. I tried to pry his grip but the more I tried, the tighter it got. His back was to me with his head down. I angled around to the side to tell him that it would be okay and that's when I noticed that he was balling like a baby. Tears gushed and landed hard on his beige suit. I whispered in his ear and said, "You can let go now. It'll be alright." Two men led him away but it still felt like I had a vice on my hand.

Mom returned my hat, the usher retrieved my purse and we walked over to where Mom always sat. I witnessed Chaz preparing to be baptized in the name of Jesus. There was a hush over the congregation as Chaz treaded holy water. I heard the deacon say, *"My dear brother, according to your faith and belief in the death, burial and resurrection of our Lord and Savior Jesus Christ, I indeed baptize you in the name of Jesus Christ for the remission of sin that ye shall receive the gift of the Holy Ghost."* I never really paid any attention to those words before. So, it has to be according to your faith, not no one else's that you belief. That's why Daddy always said that you have to know the Lord for yourself and you can't just live off someone else's salvation. You have to believe and have faith. Chaz followed me up because he loved me but when he heard me speak in tongues, he wanted that water that he may never thirst again.

When Chaz came up from the water, his hands immediately went up and Daddy went up with the cordless and aimed it toward Chaz. He was speaking in tongues. I had only seen one other person speak in tongues while they were still in the water. It took three men to lead him out of the pool.

Later, Mom and Daddy send me a card in the mail. It was one of those blank cards and the outside had a picture of a dog that looked just like Powder. Inside, he wrote:

"Ye have not chosen me, but I have chosen you, and ordained you, that ye should go and bring forth fruit, and that your fruit should remain that whatsoever ye shall ask of the Father in my name he may give it you." St. John 15:16

We were married in a very small but elegant ceremony at the mansion this past July 4; Independence Day. It represented more than just our country's independence but mine as well. I know that sounds rather stupid. Most people obtain their independence when they move out on their own, get potty trained or even divorced. My independence was electrifying because we both have the Holy Ghost now and active in the church.

Jackson was his best man and Zoe stood next to me. Chaz's daughters were the brides' maid.

I am no longer afraid to be alone. My 'me' time is not trying or a chore anymore with in itself. Whenever Harvey comes across my mind, I am no longer remorseful. I am grateful because he and Bella brought me and Chaz together. Sometimes things happen in your life and you have no idea why. At the time that you are going through it, 90% of the time, you are dwelling on the fact that you are hurting and you become angry and oft times in denial. I was one of those people. But now, I see that once you forgive, you not only heal, you can be used by God because he will take away all of the ugliness and their will be nothing missing, nothing lacking and nothing broken. God can fix anything. He restored my heart, my faith, my worship, my life and my womb. Yelp, that's right! I'm pregnant!

The End

Temporary Inconvenience
March, 2006
~~~ Note from the author ~~~

Most of the time, I feel pretty okay about myself. I mean, I have almost everything I need and most of the things that I want expect validation. Validation is very important to a woman who is over rapidly approaching 40 which is almost an oxymoron. Usually by 40 you stop caring what women say or think about you and start wondering what men thought of you. There is something to be said when you are about to turn the head of a man who is not your spouse and I am sure it's the other way around. Everyone wants to feel excepted, loved, and necessary. Hell, even Khylee's dog, Powder, wanted to be petted.

Forty is a whole different world. It's like you wake up one day and say, "Oh, okay. Now I get it." I don't really care about fashion that much. I wear what fits and what's comfortable and what matches. But it wasn't until a few months ago that I found out just what kind of power I had. (Sometimes things happen in life that make you really question everything you've always believe to that is truth.) When that good looking, great smelling, sexy man that you ain't married to tells you, "Dam! You got a sexy walk.' it really does something to your self esteem. I don't care if you got Holy Ghost oozing from every orifices, you'll get a little dew on your lily! Especially when he finds out how old you are and tell you that you are a liar because he feels that you don't look your age. I mean, seriously.

Now, when you have been married as long as I have, you get comfortable. You tend to take things for granted. You want spice and spontaneity while you are driving home from work but by the time you get home, get out of the car, check the mail box, unlock the door, pet the dog, check on the kids, walk upstairs and sit on the corner of the bed as you turn on TiVo, you say to yourself, "Whew! Maybe tomorrow." The husband is working doing his thing with his friends and you are at home doing the things that you normally do that you just don't realize that the fatigue you feel isn't fatigue at all, it's your body screaming," BITCH! Wake the hell up!" But you dismiss it as being tired by telling yourself,

"Ain't nothing that a hot shower/bath won't cure." You check on the kids, make sure that they are fed and watered and you retire for the night by catching up on your stories. Before you know it, it is morning again. What's sad is that when you awake in the morning, last night was all a blur. Hell, you don't even know what time your spouse came home or IF he came home at all. Then the whole thing starts all over again.

This goes on for a while until for once you realize you are in a rut. At least when you know that it has been raining and you park in the grass, you realize that there is a high possibility that you will get stuck in the mud, right? I thought that I would be the one that would catch the mishap before it fell. I always thought "No, not my marriage. We are never going to lose that 'magic' that makes us who we are." I always prized in the fact that we were the CUTE COUPLE. He got so involved in his job and I got so involved in mine that we were in passing. We were too busy to see each other or pay attention to each other except for church and by then it's too late. It was like packing a puncture wound with peanut butter in hopes that since the peanut butter matches your skin color, no one will know that you are wounded. Then from out of the rut came a temporary convenience for an inconvenient situation. When everything that makes you a woman screams so loud that you welcome deafening silence, you start making a list of those questions that you begin to inquire. That's just what I did, but not until I caught the attention of a man who at first was so gentle that I thought I was imagining the whole thing. I mean, seriously. I'm talking the whole package: really handsome, gorgeous skin, and that walk! WHEW! His voice was soothing like a great cup of hot chocolate and a warm blanket in front of the fire place.

He started telling me things about his wife and how she wasn't much of a mother or wife which should have been a red flag: 🚩 If he gon talk about her, he gon talk about you. It just started out as being conversation because we both needed someone to talk to and basically, just asked for a woman's point of view. But when things got really empty at home, I tend to be invisible. He gave all his attention to work I got that which was crusted if any leftovers at all.

For three months, there was nothing. We didn't talk; we didn't look at each other; we didn't even have sex. Of course the "I'm-old-and-ugly-and-my-body-looks-like-shit-cause-he-don't-love-me-no-more-cause-he-don't-pay-no-mo-attention-to-me" came across my mind.

Now, I believe that God allows two different people to come into your life: seasonal friends and permanent friends. This permanent friend turned out to be such a great help. It's good to know that you are not alone. Before I knew it, I was confiding in her about the things that were going on in my life and wouldn't you know it, she was in the similar situation. We bonded.

Whereas the seasonal friend was the one who fed you the "quick-fix" compliments and gave you what you needed. {*Sort of like a quick cup of caffeine and a donut in the mornings for energy: it helps but only for that moment by getting you where you need/want to be really fast but coming down is much worse than a crash and burn. It's a bitch with pointed shoes.*}

So, anyway, after having conversations with a man who was feeling pretty much the same way I was feeling sort of made things tolerable. It felt right. It felt safe. It felt like a rush.

The temporary handiness in this was that he WAS safe. He had just too much to lose as I did so there was no jeopardy. We protected each other because we respected the fact that we both were each other's muse. We gave each other what was lacking from our spouses. I can't speak for him but I stop longing for the attention of my spouse because I was getting it elsewhere. "It was only conversation." I kept telling myself. "It won't get outta hand because I can handle this. I've had many platonic friends before and I will always have male friends. This is safe." Oh, hell! Who was I kidding?

Pretty soon I started longing to see this man. I started wanting to call him all the time. We talked about many things until one day we REALLY started talking about everything:

We started playing a game called: 20 Questions. We texted each other a lot and the questions started getting pretty racy and then we started sending each other "pictures" of each other from our phones. It snow balled. I saw it getting out of control and I don't know if I couldn't stop it or even if I didn't want to. I was even mad at the fact that I saw *that* coming but didn't see the distance forming between me and my husband. I really got pissed when I realized that the things that we were doing were things that me and my spouse use to do. I got frustrated. I wanted the attention but only from my husband. Things started getting sloppy because he started calling and texting me all times of the day.

The opportunity came when he asked me to meet him. We talked about it. We joked about it. Hell, I even cried about it. It wasn't the first time that I was in this situation but as far as he was concerned it was. (Momma always told me to never tell a man everything about you.)

As I type this on my laptop, it's rather embarrassing admitting to myself or anyone that I actually did what I did but . . . okay, yeah! I did it and it was wrong but at the time it felt so right because of the situation. I lost myself in the things that he was saying.

I can now see how the women that I write about fall so hard from a two foot drop and from that drop, their spirit is broken. I understand now why Kitty and Khylee asked me to write for them you feel that you have to tell someone, maybe even as a confession but fear robs you of it. I feel honored and blessed that they choice me to speak for them. Now I understand my sisters: I lost myself in the way that a man made me feel and I knew that it was something about being with him that made me . . . well; I don't know exactly what to call it at that time. (See, at first I thought it was him but it wasn't him. It was what and who he represented. He really was a temporary inconvenience because I know who he reminded me of. When I was with him, I never said his name doing a climax. I closed my eyes and pretended I was with my husband.

He helped me get back what was missing in my life. He caressed ever inch of my body and looked into my eyes and told me how sexy I was just like the universal Chaz did when my husband and I were dating and he cuddle and laugh with me about silly stuff just like he use to. That little temporary inconvenience wasn't a waste of time and as godly wrong as it was, it helped me to put things back into perspective. That is why I will say that I am not sorry for what I did but I regret it because I spent two weeks being depressed because I decided not to talk to him again. I knew that the refusal was the right thing to do. I prayed about it, believe it or not, and every time he came to mind, I would say in faith, "Lord, I thank you for deliverance from this man." I use to see his face every time I closed my eyes. Now, I can't picture him at all. I could take a deep breath and hear his voice but now, nothing. I would catch a whiff of something and it reminded me of him but now, it doesn't bother me. What's more? I recently drove by one of the hotels that we spent one crimson sky rocketed night of passion and I swear to God, it made me wanna hurl. I really don't miss it because I am mad at myself for letting another man have that much control over me.

I kept calling and texting and emailing my best friend "Help! I know I am stupid but I really think I have lost my mind." She would pick up the pieces again and again as usual. I felt myself falling back into that state of depression again, that old too familiar pair of comfy depressing pajamas and I didn't want to do that. I tried to commit suicide once or twice because I always thought that "if I died, would I be missed?'

Temporary inconvenience means something that lasts for a limited time that brings unwanted extra work, effort and trouble. I would bug my BFF; just be downright pitiful, "What if I *67/ What if I text him or email him?"

The answer always came back the same, "Hell to the no." But I called him anyway and he sounded so pitiful and I thought that once I heard his voice I would crumble. I didn't. I stood strong. I stood my ground. I really didn't care to hear what he had to say. I don't miss him anymore. I don't even remember what he looked like, smell like or even his voice. These were all the things that made me crazy once upon a time.

Marie Walton

Get Published, Inc!
Thorofare, NJ 08086
26 January, 2010
BA2010026